SWEET T

"I want you," he said huskil... ...for you all of my life. Must I ...

Her heart pounding, her knees weak, Zoe knew what White Shadow was asking of her. She blotted everything out of her mind that had just been said, especially about her father, and lifted her lips to his.

"I have waited forever for *you*," she whispered against his lips. "It's been pure torture, White Shadow. Please make love to me. Please . . . You are all that is right in my world. You are my everything."

White Shadow covered her lips with his mouth and gave her a long, deep kiss, their tongues touching. He held her tightly against him as he gently guided her down upon the blanket.

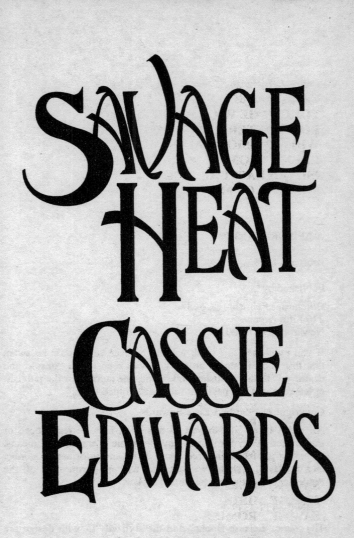

SAVAGE HEAT

CASSIE EDWARDS

LEISURE BOOKS NEW YORK CITY

A LEISURE BOOK®

February 1998

Published by

Dorchester Publishing Co., Inc.
276 Fifth Avenue
New York, NY 10001

ISBN 0-8439-4349-1

The name "Leisure Books" and the stylized "L" with design are trademarks of Dorchester Publishing Co., Inc.

Printed in the United States of America.

With love and affection I dedicate *Savage Heat*
to my very dear friends Lee and Bill Bell, and the cast and
crew of their wonderful daytime dramas *The Young and
the Restless* and *The Bold and the Beautiful*.

Love,
Cassie Edwards

You touch my body and I sigh my joy,
It feels to me like girl greeting boy.
I close my eyes, to hide my blush....
Kissing you makes my skin tingle and flush.
I touch your face and then your shoulder,
Your touches are suddenly sweeter and bolder,
Your eyes reach deep into my soul....
I can't hide...there is no place to go.
The years melt away, oh, so sweet,
We are warmed by our love's heat,
We strip away all our walls....
Answering all our natural calls.
Some say love is oft times blind,
Some call Heaven "a state of mind,"
Heaven, my love, is in your eyes....
In our love there will be no good-byes.

—Harri Lucas Garnett,
dear friend and poet.

Prologue

Oklahoma, 1863

The buckboard wagon was hot and oppressive as the sun poured down on Soft Bird. She lay at the back of the wagon, a thin blanket the only thing between herself and the hard, uncomfortable boards beneath her.

She had sat at the side of the road for many long hours waiting for some member of her tribe to come past, to give her a ride back to the Kiowa village.

She felt as though *Nuakalahe*, the creator, had led her rescuers to her when a family of four found her napping in the shade of a cottonwood tree on their way home from the trading post.

"Are you all right?" Her thoughts were interrupted by the voice of a child, the eight-year-old son of the generous Kiowa family who had offered her a ride in their wagon. He reached a hand over and placed it gently on Soft Bird's arm.

"You are so quiet," Lone Hawk said. "And you have not told me or my family why you were alone at the side of the road, sleeping. I know you. You are Soft Bird. You are the daughter of Chief Brave Charger. Your mother is Pale Rose. They thought you were dead, but you are alive! Where have you been?"

Soft Bird smiled weakly up at the child, and then glanced over at his younger sister, Blue Flower, who sat quietly beside him.

Soft Bird then looked past the two children and forced a broader smile when she found their mother gazing questioningly at her. Neither Tender Heart nor her husband Man Who Seeks had questioned her. Soft Bird was the chief's daughter and a Kiowa princess. She was to be treated with the utmost respect.

Tender Heart's gaze shifted to Lone Hawk. She frowned. "Son, do not pester Soft Bird," she scolded. She motioned with a hand toward both children. "Come and sit directly behind me and your father. Let Soft Bird lie down and rest. Soon she will be with her parents. *They* will question her."

Tender Heart's gaze shifted to Soft Bird again.

For a moment their eyes held, but then Soft Bird looked quickly away and moved over to lie on her side.

As Soft Bird slid a hand down to her abdomen and rested it there, she fought the tears that threatened to spill from her eyes. She still could not believe what had happened . . . that the *iapa-gya*, the precious babe she had given birth to only a few days earlier, was no longer hers!

Someone else was going to raise her beloved son!

As the wagon rattled onward, the wheels ambling in and out of potholes, she became lost in memories that tore at her very being.

Was it only a year ago that she had fallen in love with Timothy Livingston, an important colonel in the United States Cavalry? Was it only nine months since she had fled her Kiowa village to live with Timothy in his grand house inside the walls of Fort Cobb?

She had thought that he truly loved her. She had willingly given up everything of her Kiowa heritage to live with him, even her family. She had not even told them where she had gone!

It was best that her father and mother . . . that the tribe as a whole . . . thought her dead.

Feeling oh, so empty, so *barren*, Soft Bird was overwhelmed by heartwrenching thoughts. How bitter it was to know that Timothy Livingston had only kept her with him until she bore his child!

She closed her eyes and slowly shook her head. How foolish she had been when she allowed herself to get pregnant with this man's child.

As soon as she'd told Timothy that she was with child, *his* child, he had taken her into his home and kept her in grand style until the child was born. Only after she had given birth had she learned that he only wanted his son, not *her*.

After giving her just a few precious days with her son, Timothy had ordered Soft Bird from both their lives. No matter how hard she had begged, she had not been allowed to take her son with her.

She had left Timothy's home with empty arms, but not devoid of feelings. She now hated Timothy Livingston with a passion.

"We are almost home!" Lone Hawk cried. "Mother may I leave the wagon and run ahead and join in games with my friends?"

Tender Heart turned and gazed at him; then she looked past him at Soft Bird, who was now on her knees at the side of the wagon, her fingers clutching the side boards, her eyes on the approaching village.

Tender Heart patted Lone Hawk's head. "*Ho*, yes, go on," she murmured. As he started to scramble away from her, she grabbed him by an arm and stopped him. "But, son, do not tell anyone about Soft Bird. It is for Soft Bird to reveal to her parents and her people that she is alive. Not you, son. Not you."

Lone Hawk looked quickly over at Soft Bird, and then nodded at his mother. "I will tell no one, Mother," he said. He took his sister's hand. "Come, sister. Join in games with me and our friends."

Blue Flower gave her mother a questioning look. "May I, Mother?" she asked, moving to her knees. "I, too, will not tell anyone about Soft Bird."

"*Ho*, yes, go and play," Tender Heart said, smiling at her daughter. "You have been kept from your friends long enough today. Going to the trading post for supplies is so tiresome for children."

14

Soft Bird smiled at the children as they moved past her and jumped from the back of the wagon. She watched them run toward the village. She wished that she were as innocent and carefree as they, without the burden of lies that she was going to tell her parents as an excuse for her nine month's absence.

Lies would have to do, for the truth would hurt too much . . . could even cause a war between her people and the *yapahe*, the pony soldiers at Fort Cobb.

Ho, it was best left untold, how she had been treated so wrong, how her child was no longer her child!

But for Soft Bird, lies had never come easily. Until she had met Timothy Livingston, she had been an honest, forthright person, a woman whose courage and bravery matched any man's.

Now? She was nothing but a lying, deceitful coward. She was not even sure if she could learn to live with herself, now that she must play this new role in life: A woman betrayed; a woman whose womb and heart were empty; a woman who was oh, so alone in her grief!

When they entered the village and everyone recognized Soft Bird, silence ensued. As the wagon moved onward, past the long row of tepees, the people began following behind it, their eyes never leaving Soft Bird.

Self-conscious over being stared at, Soft Bird held her chin high and ignored everyone but her mother, who had just now stepped out of her lodge. Her father joined her, standing stately tall and dignified beside her.

When Soft Bird saw the utter shock on her parents' faces, which turned quickly to relief, she was not sure if she could lie to them. But she must, she kept reminding herself. There were too many dangers in telling the truth!

"Daughter!" Pale Rose cried as the wagon stopped only a few yards away from her. She ran to the wagon and reached out for Soft Bird as she slid down from the back of the wagon.

"Mother," Soft Bird cried, relishing the fleshy, warm arms of her mother as they wrapped around her in a fierce, tight hug.

She returned the hug.

Then when Soft Bird looked past her mother's shoulder and she saw the questioning in her father's eyes, she could no longer hold back her tears.

It was at this moment that Soft Bird felt she had betrayed her parents far more than Timothy Livingston had ever betrayed her. She had allowed her parents to believe that she was dead these past several months.

How could she have been so cruel? So heartless? If they knew the truth, they would be within their rights to banish her from the tribe.

Except that they would never know the real reason why she had left, or why she had come back home to them, so banishment would never enter their minds. She knew to expect, instead, a celebration of her return. Oh, how hard it would be to sit in the midst of such a celebration, knowing that she was not worthy of it.

Chief Brave Charger took Soft Bird into his arms and desperately hugged her. "Daughter, daughter," he said, holding her tightly against him.

Eaten away inside because of the lie that clamored to be spoken, Soft Bird felt tears flow from her eyes.

But for the moment she enjoyed her father's nearness, his strong arms, his warm breath against her cheek. She would never leave home again. She would never turn her eyes away from her people again. Especially her beloved mother and father!

Brave Charger kept an arm around Soft Bird's waist as he swept her inside the privacy of their lodge, away from the crowd of Kiowa who awaited answers.

Glad to be home, and vowing to forget that other life that she had known for too short a time, Soft Bird looked slowly around the inside of the *do-giagwa-guat*. The tepee was decorated on one side with battle pictures, fine drawings of fighting men and arms, and ornamented on the other with wide, horizontal bands of black and yellow.

She saw the beautiful rolled-up blankets, her mother's basket of sewing with its awls and strings of sinew and beads, and many other beloved objects that she had missed during her time away from her family.

Her father took her by an elbow and seated her on a pile of blankets at the back of the lodge, where the skins were rolled up to let in fresh air.

"Tell us how you are, where you have been, and what has kept you from us for so long," Brave Charger said, his eyes imploring Soft Bird.

Swallowing hard, Soft Bird waited for a moment. She looked from her mother to her father, and then began the lie she had devised on the day of her child's birth, when she had learned that she would have to give him up and return to her family.

"I have been living among Mexicans these past months," she blurted out. "I have been their captive."

She gazed from her mother to her father again, knowing that they had no cause not to believe her. Mexicans often stole Indian women and children to use as slaves.

She also knew that her father would not try to verify her story. The Kiowa were outnumbered by the Mexicans. They could not venture to war with them.

Again her parents hugged her. She vowed to herself that she would forget her son. She would start life anew!

She vowed to herself that she would carry her heritage proudly inside her heart.

Knowing that the people waited to hear about her disappearance, Soft Bird stepped outside the lodge with her parents and listened as her father explained it all to them. When everyone sympathized and took turns hugging Soft Bird, she tried not to feel despair at having lied not only to her parents, but to her people. She had much to make up to them. And she would!

But no matter how hard she tried, she could not help thinking of the child she had left behind. Her every heartbeat cried out to the son who was being denied his mother's arms . . . his mother's love!

Chapter One

Thy voice, slow rising like a Spirit, lingers
O'ershadowing me with soft and lulling wings.
                                    —Percy Bysshe Shelley

Thirty years later—1893

Soft Bird was now fifty. Her thin, white hair was held in place by a cap of black netting. She was dressed in the manner of a Kiowa matron . . . a dark, full-cut buckskin dress that reached nearly to the ankles, with full, flowing sleeves and a wide, apron-like sash.

At the Fort Cobb reservation Soft Bird sat in council in the large, domed council house with her son White Shadow and Thunder Stick, their village shaman. Soft Bird's father, Brave Charger, had been dead for only two moons. Her mother had died long before him.

Soft Bird had brought her son and the shaman together for a confession that she had held within herself for thirty years.

She had even succeeded at keeping the secret from her Kiowa husband, who had died long ago in a fight with Mexicans while raiding for horses.

White Shadow, her second-born, had felt closer to his grandfather Brave Charger than to his true father, who had died when White Shadow was only a baby.

When he became ill and was no longer able to lead his people as he wished, Brave Charger had handed over the title of chief to White Shadow, who was respected and revered among all Kiowa.

White Shadow was twenty-eight winters of age. With his jet black, penetrating eyes, square jaw, Roman nose, and rippling muscles, he was the epitome of manhood. He turned the eyes of all women, Kiowa and white, alike.

The Kiowa warriors were also in awe of him and followed his lead as though he were some sort of god. Even white men stepped aside and stared when White Shadow walked amidst them.

Soft Bird could not be more proud of a son than she was of White Shadow and she knew that he should be enough for any mother. He was a *nah-tan*, a brave man, and a great warrior.

But she had recently seen her first-born, grown now into a man, and she knew that she could not deny herself contact with him any longer.

"What is it, Mother, that brings us into council today?" White Shadow asked, shoving a small log onto the flames of the council fire.

It was summer, yet the morning had a strange chill to it. Dew had even spread its silvery wings across the grass as though it were autumn. The night noises the previous evening had seemed more pronounced, the moon's glow more intense.

Soft Bird drew a blanket across her legs and edged closer to the fire as she stared into the dancing flames.

She looked slowly at White Shadow, and then at Thunder Stick.

She had confided in the shaman earlier that morning, when the moon and stars were still sisters in the sky. She had asked Thunder Stick if he thought that she might lose the respect of her son White Shadow if she told him the truth that had been eating away at her heart through the years. She had not ever told her parents the truth. They had gone to their graves without knowing it.

Soft Bird had asked Thunder Stick if he thought White Shadow would understand the plan that she had conceived to bring her first-born to the village.

Thunder Stick had eased her concerns by saying that she must do as her heart told her . . . it was right to finally share the truth with White Shadow. Thunder Stick had reassured her that White Shadow loved her enough to understand.

And as for the Kiowa people, Thunder Stick had reminded Soft Bird that she was still a princess adored by everyone. No one would even consider condemning her for something she had done so long ago.

Thunder Stick had told her that the loss of her first-born had been punishment enough.

"Long ago, White Shadow," she began, "before you were born, there was a man who stole my heart and also . . . also . . . my first-born child." She kept her eyes directed at the flames to avoid seeing the questions . . . the shock in the eyes of her beloved son.

"This man was white," she continued. "He was a *yapahe*, a soldier, a colonel at Fort Cobb. My love for him was so intense . . . that . . . I left home and lived with him at the fort for nine months. That was long enough for me to give birth to our son, and long enough to realize that I had been made a fool of, for shortly after my son was born, his father sent me away without my baby. They took him to walk the white man's road of life."

"Mother," White Shadow said, his voice drawn. "What are you saying? When was this? You once told me that the only time you were away from your people was that time long ago when you were stolen by Mexicans. Could it be that you . . . that . . . you lied about the abduction? That you were, instead, with whites?"

"*Aalyi*, I cry," Soft Bird said as tears splashed from her eyes.

She looked slowly at White Shadow, who sat across the fire from her. She forced herself to continue with the tale of deceit. She wiped the tears from her eyes with the backs of her hands.

"*Ho*, my son, lies came quickly to this woman

23

when she had been made a fool of and did not want to admit it," she murmured. "I was never held captive by Mexicans. My heart was held captive by Colonel Timothy Livingston. I went with him to his grand home inside the walls of Fort Cobb. Expecting to marry Timothy, I lived with him while his child grew within my womb."

White Shadow was stunned into silence for a moment. He was trying to grasp what his mother had said, but he was finding it hard to believe her. The woman he knew had always been so truthful . . . so forthright. She was respected by everyone! How could she have lived a deceit for so long? And how could her story be true? Timothy Livingston. He knew his age. He was much younger than White Shadow's mother.

"The name Timothy Livingston is the name of the colonel who is now in charge at Fort Cobb," White Shadow said, his voice drawn. "That cannot be the man whose child you carried. He is close to my age."

"He is two winters older than you, White Shadow," Soft Bird said, still avoiding White Shadow's eyes. "He was the child who grew inside my womb before you."

When she heard White Shadow gasp, she turned slow eyes up at him. "He is your brother, White Shadow, your . . . *brother*," she said, her voice breaking when she saw anger leap into his eyes.

She knew his anger was not only that she had lied to him, but also that such a man as Timothy Livingston could be his brother, for Timothy was a bigoted man who was prejudiced against all Indians. Since his arrival at the fort, he had not worked for the betterment of the Kiowa. He had treated them as non-persons.

The silence was heavy in the council house.

The uncovered secret lay like a dark shroud over mother and son.

Thunder Stick reached a hand over to Soft Bird and patted her softly on the arm. "You have done well by telling the truth today," he said, nodding. "Now let me speak the rest to your second-born son."

"You act as though you already knew what my mother had to say before she said it," White Shadow said, frowning at Thunder Stick. He was still stunned by the secret that his mother had kept locked within her heart all these years.

The fact that she had told Thunder Stick before she'd told him made the hurt twofold. White Shadow had lost trust and faith in Thunder Stick long ago. The shaman was ill with *seni satop hodal*, peyote pipe sickness; his mind was lost often in the pleasure of smoking his peyote pipe.

And it was known that the shaman, who was now in his sixty-fifth year, had shady dealings with whites when it benefited himself financially. He was known to do almost anything, no matter how ruthless, for money.

White Shadow had often suspected that the shaman might be hoarding coins to use for his survival should he ever be banished from his tribe because of his cunning ways.

This saddened White Shadow, for if Thunder

Stick did have hidden riches, the Shaman ought to use them for the betterment of his tribe. But White Shadow had never confronted Thunder Stick about this. The Shaman was driven by demons White Shadow would never understand.

White Shadow only tolerated such a man being his people's Shaman because he had held the position for so long, and because White Shadow's mother still trusted him.

The old man wore a long robe with a necklace of beads and an eagle-bone whistle around his neck. He always carried a fan made from the feathers of a water bird. He now nervously patted it on his knee as he waited a moment longer before answering White Shadow's question.

"White Shadow, your mother came to me and confided in me because she knew that I would guide her well in her decision about whether or not she should finally reveal the secret kept locked inside her heart for so many years. She has a plan. I have offered to carry it out for her."

"Plan?" White Shadow asked warily. He crossed his legs and placed his hands on his knees. "What plan?"

"Your mother wishes to know her first-born," Thunder Stick said, looking slowly from White Shadow to Soft Bird. "I will see that it happens."

White Shadow jumped to his feet. He went around the fire and knelt down before his mother. "Mother, how could you want anything to do with this man Timothy Livingston? You already know the sort of man he is."

He took her hands and held them. "If you go to

him with the truth, that he is your son, he will only laugh, for it is apparent that he does not know that he is in part Kiowa. Although he does have dark hair and eyes, and pronounced cheekbones, his skin is not copper like that of his people. He has been raised as a white man and no one has disputed it. He will not welcome the truth."

"White Shadow," Soft Bird said, her voice breaking. "I know that all you say is true. Yes, he *is* a bigoted person, a man I would normally turn my back on. But I *do* have a plan. Thunder Stick has already agreed to carry it out for me."

"Again I ask you . . . what plan, Mother?" White Shadow asked dryly, finding her revelations hard to take.

"Thunder Stick is going to help abduct Timothy," Soft Bird said, yanking her hands away from White Shadow when he gasped and his eyes widened in horror. "Son, please . . . listen."

"I listen," White Shadow said thickly, feeling as though he were living in a nightmare. He wished that he could blink his eyes and discover that he was in bed, dreaming.

"I want my son abducted," Soft Bird said stiffly. "I will make sure that he is kept well hidden, so that the soldiers from Fort Cobb, should they come here to search for him, cannot find him. At first, he will not be told that he was abducted because of his mother. He will be forced to live in our village. He will learn everything Kiowa. Our way of life will be practiced by him."

She swallowed hard. "But most of all I wish to be near him, to watch him, to know him," Soft

Bird said. "He is my son. He has my blood . . . *your* blood, White Shadow, running through his veins."

She sighed. "He will eventually learn that it was his mother who caused him to be abducted. I want him to feel shame for showing such prejudice against the Kiowa. I hope that shame will change to something else . . . to understanding and loving."

"That is impossible," White Shadow said, frowning down at his mother. "Timothy Livingston was taught the ways of the white man. In his home, where he was raised by whites, he listened to people speaking against all Indians. He has known nothing but prejudice since he was old enough to reason about things and people. How do you think you, or anyone, can change him? He is what he is. That is the way he will be until he takes his last, dying breath on this earth."

"You are wrong, son," Soft Bird said. "My first-born will be broken like an Indian breaks a horse. In the end he will know that he is a half-breed, the sort of man most whites abhor and look down upon with disgust. This will keep him from wanting to mix with whites again. My deepest desire is that he will want to stay and be as one with his *true* people."

"Never," White Shadow ground out. "If you think he will ever confess to having wronged us, you are wrong."

He paused and then said, "Mother, what you are planning is wrong. This man should be allowed to stay where he is. He does not belong with the Kiowa. He *is* a bigoted man, but otherwise, in the eyes of the whites, he is an honorable man. He has given his life to the white man's army. He has served his country well in the capacity of a soldier. If you truly want what is best for your first-born, you will leave him be. He will never adapt to our ways. And if you tell him that he is a breed, you risk taking away all of his dignity . . . and his reason for living."

"I will chance everything to have him with me," Soft Bird said, her voice drawn. "I have been denied him long enough!"

With her eyes she pleaded with White Shadow. "You must agree to the plan," she said. "Not only for a mother whose heart cries out to a son she has held but a few times since he was born. But this will also be for the betterment of our people, for to them this man has been less than honorable. Once changed, he will work both for the sake of the whites and his true people! He will see the wrong in his prejudices."

"You wish for so much, I fear your disappointment when it does not happen," White Shadow said. He shoved another piece of wood into the fire and watched the flames lap at the dried bark.

Thunder Stick laughed. "I will delight in seeing the white man put in his place," he said; then he gave Soft Bird an apologetic look. "But of course, Soft Bird, I also will delight in seeing him change into someone who will appreciate his true people."

"White Shadow, please say that you approve of your brother's abduction," Soft Bird pleaded. "Do you want your mother to be happy, White

Shadow? Do you? You are our people's chief. I will not act without your approval."

"Mother, you know that I would do anything for your happiness, for you are all that is good on this earth," White Shadow said tightly. "But please give me time to think this over. I am chief now. I must do what is right, not only for you, my beloved mother, but for our people."

He could feel the heat of Thunder Stick's eyes on him, but he ignored his steady stare. Above all else, White Shadow wished that he could deny his mother this request, if only to spite the shaman! White Shadow knew that the shaman's eagerness to abduct Timothy had nothing to do with love and respect for Soft Bird. He wished to do it solely for himself, for the freedom to do something underhanded and mischievous.

White Shadow knew now that he would not be able to tolerate Thunder Stick much longer. He was just waiting for Thunder Stick to do something that would justify his banishment.

"I understand," Soft Bird murmured, yet unable to hide the disappointment in her voice. "But, son, do not wait long for your decision. I have heard rumors that Timothy is planning to return to a place called Boston, where he was raised after he was wrenched from my arms."

White Shadow tried not to envision the sad scene of his mother being denied her child those long years ago. That would only soften his feelings toward Timothy Livingston.

And White Shadow wanted to feel no sympathy for such a man.

"I will think and meditate over the decision, Mother," White Shadow said. "I will not wait long to tell you the answers my prayers bring me."

When she hung her head to keep him from seeing into her eyes, he almost agreed to her plan even then. His love for her was so deep, how could he deny her anything? Especially when such denial brought tears into her lovely, sad brown eyes.

Needing to get away from his mother's despair, White Shadow left the lodge and stepped out into a day of gloomy shadows and dark clouds.

Dispirited, he ran from the village and did not stop until he reached a high knoll that overlooked his village.

As he knelt down and raised his eyes heavenward to pray, he found it hard, for he knew, in the depths of his heart, what he must do. He must do what would make his mother happy, even though it went against everything White Shadow believed in.

How could he bring this man into his people's lives? Too much tragedy had come to the Kiowa because of whites like Timothy Livingston. When settlers had come to the land of the Kiowa, they had not only brought diseases which killed many of his people, but they had also decimated the vast herds of buffalo.

The great animal was representative of the sun to the Kiowa. Horned and shaggy-headed, it was the symbol and image of long life, abundance, and power. For many Kiowa, now that the buffalo were gone, the months were meaningless. Their days were now without design.

He, too, had been filled with despair until he met a woman whose heart seemed as pure and good as his mother's, a white woman named Zoe Hawkins. White Shadow had thought that things would change for him when he had gained her love. He'd begun to hope a union between them might join whites and Kiowa in a meaningful peace.

Because of his beautiful Zoe, White Shadow's heart had become filled with hope again. His days were no longer without design.

But now? To know that Timothy was his brother? That his mother wanted him in her life as her *son*?

Ho, White Shadow had much to think about . . . decisions to make . . . decisions that might change his entire future . . . his life.

For now, he would concentrate only on one thing. On his Zoe. Tomorrow he was to see her again. He would hold her. While he was with her, life was so good . . . so perfect!

Even his mother finally approved of Zoe, but it was easy now to understand why it had taken his mother so long to accept that he had fallen in love with a white woman. *She* had loved a white *man*, and he had broken her heart.

He now knew that his mother had been afraid that White Shadow's heart might be broken, also, by someone whose skin was white.

"Never," he whispered. He knew that Zoe's love for him was real. It was true.

"Tomorrow Zoe will prove again to me just how

much she loves me," he whispered. He smiled when, in his mind's eye, he saw Zoe smiling at him, her mysterious green eyes filled with laughter and love.

Chapter Two

Away, away from men and towns,
To the wild wood and the downs,
To the silent wilderness.
    —Percy Bysshe Shelley

Tall and willowy, her eyes as green as summer grass, Zoe Hawkins was filled with anticipation as she rode into the clearing and saw the man she adored waiting for her beneath a cottonwood tree.

Her waist-length brown hair blew in the breeze, and the hem of her green travel skirt hiked up past her knees as she pressed her roan into a harder gallop.

She had been meeting with White Shadow for several weeks, and as the time of each rendezvous approached, she felt an impatience that was new to her.

She had never loved a man before.

She never would have guessed that she would love an Indian, for long ago, an Indian had almost murdered her father.

That was when her father rode with the cavalry, a young lieutenant with a beautiful wife and an eight-year-old daughter waiting for him back in Boston. During a scrape with a band of Apache in Montana, her father had come close to dying.

The soldiers had all but annihilated an Apache village, and a brave whose wife and child had been killed attacked Zoe's father. He had already removed some of her father's scalp when her father's superior officer, Colonel Timothy Livingston, rode up to save him, losing his own life in the rescue.

When her father returned home to Boston to recuperate from his wounds and found that his wife had recently died from pneumonia, he sank into a dark world of despair.

For long years Zoe's father lived without joy, empty-eyed and broken-hearted. Then one day a soldier, the son of the very man who had saved her father's life, had come. Colonel Livingston, Jr., persuaded her father to return to a life that had meaning. He had talked him into going to Oklahoma to take over the duties of sheriff near Fort Cobb, where he, Timothy, Jr., was stationed.

Finally emerging from the black hole that was worse than death itself, her father had accepted the position of sheriff at Gracemont, Oklahoma.

But he carried with him the hatred he would never get over . . . his hatred for all people whose skins were red. In a strange way he blamed Indians for the death of his precious wife, for had he not been forced to leave her to fight the Indians, he could have been there while she was ill. His presence might have given her the will, the strength, to live.

Whenever Zoe heard her father repeat the tale of how he was wounded, she always cringed when he bragged of having killed many Apache women and children that day; she had never felt anything but compassion for the Indians.

Her compassion had grown deeper after she arrived in Oklahoma. She had seen then, firsthand, what the white man had taken from the Indians. He had robbed them of their land, their buffalo, and also their spirit. The Kiowa had been forced to live on a reservation.

Even with the wrath of her father to deal with, Zoe began defending the rights of the Kiowa whenever anyone brought up the subject.

And now, she was in love with a revered Kiowa chief.

As she approached the cottonwood where he waited, she dismounted and led her roan the rest of the way on foot until she felt that her horse was hidden from anyone who might pass by on their way to Gracemont.

Although she felt that loving a Kiowa chief was the most wonderful thing that had ever happened to her, there were those who would disapprove. It was taboo for a white woman to love an Indian.

It was not that she cared so much about what anyone thought, it was what might happen that made her cautious and wary. She did not want to arrive at their meeting place one day to find her beloved White Shadow swinging from a rope in the cottonwoods.

She especially had her father to worry about. If he knew about her secret trysts with the Kiowa chief, she knew he would not stop until he saw the chief dead!

When White Shadow stepped out of the shadows, wearing a breech clout and moccasins, Zoe's insides melted. His handsomeness always took her breath away. She could never get enough of looking at his broad shoulders, his muscled chest, and his long, lithe, copper body.

She was especially taken by his sharply chiseled face with its wide jaw and high cheekbones and heavenly dark eyes.

As each day passed, she could hardly wait to see him, yet their trysts were few and far between. She was always afraid that her father might be suspicious of the time she spent away from home when he did not know where she was.

"You were delayed today," White Shadow said, coming to take her horse's reins and tying them with his own. His white stallion stood grazing in the thick, green grass beside the stream.

"Yes, I'm late, but I had no choice," Zoe said, easing into his arms as he held them out for her. "Carl Collins, the outlaw who is ravaging the country gunning down lawmen, was said to be in the vicinity. My father warned me about going far from home. Since I am the daughter of a sheriff,

Father thinks the gunman might as soon kill me as anyone else."

"Then perhaps you should not have come at all," White Shadow said, framing her face between his hands so that their eyes met in a sensual stare. "*Manyi*, my woman, never take risks." He slid his hands down and cupped her well-rounded breasts through her blouse. "I could not live without you."

Feeling lightheaded with passion, Zoe closed her eyes. She sighed when he lowered his mouth to hers and gave her a long, deep kiss.

Each time they were together, Zoe felt their passion building. She was not sure if she could go much longer before giving in to the needs of her body.

Being the honorable man he was, and a man who seemed practiced in patience, White Shadow had not urged her yet to make love with him. He respected her. He had believed her when she had said that she had never been with a man sexually before. Until White Shadow, she had never met a man she wished to make love with.

Deep inside her heart, she had always felt that lovemaking should come with marriage. And she knew that White Shadow would ask her to marry him.

She was not certain how she could deny him what they both wanted with every beat of their hearts. But she knew without a doubt that her father would forbid a marriage between her and White Shadow. Her father would gun down White Shadow to prevent it. She dreaded having to explain this to the man she loved.

White Shadow stepped away from Zoe and spread a blanket on the ground. He took her hand and led her down on the blanket beside him. He started to draw her into his embrace when something a few feet away drew their attention.

"A mole," Zoe whispered, watching the tiny creature as it came out of a hole in the ground.

Its cheeks were puffed out as if it were a squirrel packing nuts. It looked all around for a moment, ignoring White Shadow and Zoe, who sat stone still as they continued to watch him, and then it blew a spray of fine, dark earth out of its mouth.

The animal did this again and again until there was a ring of black, powdery earth on the ground.

"I feel as though I'm intruding on his privacy," Zoe whispered.

White Shadow took her hand. "Come then, we shall give the mole its privacy," he said. "I have brought something for you. Now is a good time to give it to you."

Zoe went with him to his horse. Wide-eyed, she watched him open his buckskin parfleche bag.

White Shadow gave Zoe a soft smile as he reached inside the bag. "I have brought something for you from my mother, Soft Bird," he said. "We talk often of you. At first she disapproved of my feelings for you . . . a white woman. But when she finally understood that I would not love anyone else but you, she made something for you. It is a gift from the heart. When you go to meet my mother and my people for the first time, my mother wishes for you to wear this."

He pulled out a snow white doeskin dress and

unrolled it so that Zoe could see its loveliness.

Touched to the core that White Shadow's mother had made it just for her, Zoe slowly ran her hand over the beautiful dress.

The doeskin was as soft as the petals of a rose against her fingertips. And it was embellished with an assortment of colorful beads in the design of forest flowers.

"Do you like it?" White Shadow asked, anxiously watching Zoe's reaction as she touched the beads and traced their designs with a forefinger.

"I adore it," Zoe said, sighing. She took the dress as White Shadow draped it over her outstretched arms.

"When will you wear it?" White Shadow asked, smiling proudly at her reaction to his mother's special gift.

"Do you mean . . . when will I come to your village?" Zoe asked. She had put off going there, because she was afraid that her father would find out.

"*Ho*, when will you come to my village and allow my people to meet my future wife?" White Shadow said, easing his arms around her waist, drawing her and the dress against him. "Zoe, marry me. You have brought much sunshine into my life. Bring it now into my lodge."

The question that she had feared hearing was now there, awaiting an answer. She felt suddenly trapped.

She wanted nothing else but to marry him. However, it was not meant to be! She now knew that she had been wrong to allow their relationship to go so far.

"I can't," she blurted out, flinching when she saw the sudden hurt in his eyes. "I can't accept this dress." She shoved it into his hands. "I can't go and meet your mother." She lowered her eyes and swallowed hard. "And I . . . I . . . can't marry you."

White Shadow stared down at the dress, and then took an unsteady step away from Zoe. His lips parted; he stared disbelievingly at her. His thoughts were suddenly flooded with his mother's warnings about the dangers of loving a white woman.

His mother's confession of how a white man had wronged *her* made White Shadow's insides tighten. Was history repeating itself?

Then he found composure enough to speak. "Why then have you met with me, kissed me, held me," he said, his hurt turning to anger. "Did you do it to make a fool of me, an *Indian*? In your heart do you laugh at me and call me the ugly word *savage*? Did you never love me at all?"

Tears fell from Zoe's eyes. She turned and lifted her gaze to White Shadow. "I'm sorry if I have hurt you. I do love you," she murmured. "I do love you so much . . . more than anything. But I just . . . can't . . . marry you."

She could not come right out and tell him why, for she might be putting her father in danger. She had always seen the soft, kind side of White Shadow, but she had not truly known him long enough to know whether he might have a dangerous side. If he had cause to hate someone, did he act on that hatred?

"Give me reasons why," White Shadow said, his voice drawn, his jaw tight. "I will tell you whether or not I believe them."

"I cannot tell you why," Zoe said, her eyes wavering when she saw that his hurt had returned to erase the anger from his eyes.

"When I first saw you, you wore the clothes of a man, yet I saw past them and saw the loveliness of the woman you are," White Shadow said. "When you knew of my distaste for the man's breeches and shirt, you changed into woman's clothes when you came here. Other times I saw you do things that you knew pleased me. Only women who love men go out of their way to please them. You love me, Zoe. I know that you love me."

He shoved the dress back inside the bag, then turned and yanked Zoe against him. He gave her a deep, passionate kiss, and then shoved her away from him.

He went to his horse and yanked his reins away from the tree limb, swung himself into his saddle, stared at Zoe for a moment longer, and then rode off.

"When you are ready to tell me the truth about things, you know where my village is!" he shouted at her over his shoulder. "If I am not there, my mother will listen to what you have to say! She will also need an apology for your refusal to accept the dress she made solely for you!"

Zoe stifled a sob behind her hand as she watched him ride away from her.

"I've lost him," she whispered, her heart aching.

Chapter Three

To her father white
Came the maiden bright.
All her tender limbs were terror shook.
                              —William Blake

As people crowded around her on the dusty street,
Zoe knelt beside her father in the shadows of the
false-fronted buildings of Gracemont. Although
she had known it might happen, Zoe couldn't believe that Carl Collins had gunned down her father.

But there her father lay!

Blood was seeping from the wound in his chest
where his shirt had been ripped open by the blast
of a bullet. Her father's eyes were glazed over with
pain as he stared up at her.

"Oh, Father, please don't die," Zoe cried, lifting

his head and cushioning it on her lap.

She had scarcely slept a wink all night. She kept seeing the hurt in White Shadow's eyes when she had told him that she couldn't marry him.

This morning she had hardly eaten a bite of breakfast. While her father had been eating his eggs, milk gravy and biscuits, she had tried to find the courage to tell him about White Shadow.

But even as he drank the last of his coffee and left the table, his gunbelt buckled around his waist, Zoe still had not found the words to tell him that she was going to marry White Shadow . . . for she *was*. She had decided, somewhere between midnight and sunrise, that she could not live without him.

But still she could not tell her father. She had watched him ride off on his horse.

Moments later she had followed on her roan, determined to tell him as soon as they reached her father's office.

One blast from the outlaw's rifle had changed everything.

Zoe leaned closer to her father as he slowly lifted a trembling hand to her face. As he had done countless times before, he brushed her brown hair back from her eyes.

"You'll do just fine without this ol' codger hangin' 'round," her father said. He turned his head away from her and coughed, spewing blood all over the dirt road beside him.

Zoe gasped.

She swallowed back a lump in her throat and fought back the tears she did not want her father to see. She had always been strong. He had admired that trait in her.

Now she found it hard to find the strength to get through these next moments.

Her heart pounding, she looked up at the crowd. "Where's Doc Rose?" she cried. "Someone go and get Doc Rose!"

"Sis," her father said, drawing her eyes back to him with the familiar nickname that he had given her when she was only five and he had told her how she looked so much like his sister Bess.

"Sis," he continued, now struggling for each breath. "Don't pester Doc Rose. He can't do anything for me. I'm slippin' fast."

He reached for her hand and gripped it.

Zoe saw a sudden, desperate look in his eyes that made the pain of seeing him dying even more unbearable. She knew, as well as her father, that Doc Rose couldn't patch him up this time. Many scars ago, when Doc Rose had first sewed her father up after removing a bullet from his arm, Zoe had understood the possibility that her father might come to a violent end at the hand of someone like Carl Collins.

The outlaw had shot her father today from a dark alley, and then ridden off before anyone could catch up with him. But Carl Collins had been seen as he rode off. There was no doubt that it was the outlaw. For a full year now everyone had seen Wanted posters of Carl Collins plastered all over town.

Knowing that her father's life was draining

away, Zoe listened as he spoke his last words to her.

"Sis, you've got to marry Timothy," Bradley said, half choking as blood streamed from between his lips. He squeezed her hand. "Tell . . . me . . . you'll marry Timothy. Think of it, Zoe! Think of what he can give you!"

His gaze swept over her, taking in her usual attire—jeans, shirt, boots and Stetson hat. She had been a tomboy for so many years now, it was hard to remember when she had been a little girl running around in dainty leather shoes and delicate, lacy dresses.

"Sis," he continued, "you've been a tomboy for long enough. Marry Timothy. You can throw away all of those damn breeches. You can . . . dress . . . in . . . the latest fashion. Silks . . . satins . . ."

Zoe's heart sank as her father's eyes closed.

Then she inhaled a deep breath of relief when once again he opened them and he gazed up at her.

"Zoe?" he said. "Tell me you'll marry Timothy. I . . . can . . . die in peace knowin' my precious daughter will be taken care of."

Zoe could no longer hold back the tears. With her free hand she wiped them from her eyes. How could she promise to marry such a man as Timothy Livingston, Jr.?

Thirty years old, and unquestionably handsome, Timothy could have any woman he wanted . . . except Zoe. She had turned down his proposal more than once, for she saw him as he truly was.

He was a bigoted, narrow-minded man.

"Zoe, tell me you'll marry Timothy," her father wheezed out. "We owe him. We owe his *father*. His father saved me from an Apache. His son saved me when . . . I . . . was drowning in self-pity."

Panic grabbed Zoe at the pit of her stomach when her father closed his eyes, for she feared those were her father's last words. He expected an answer. He expected her promise.

Should she lie to her father to make his last moments on this earth peaceful? Oh, but it was hard to say something that she would despise so.

Yes, she had gone horseback riding with Timothy many times. But only because her father encouraged it. With her mother dead for so many years now, Zoe had tried to do everything within her power to make her father happy.

Even if that meant spending a few hours a week with the likes of Colonel Timothy Livingston.

Any other lady in Gracemont might jump at the chance to marry Timothy. He was from a wealthy family in Boston. He had recently begun talking about retiring. He had told Zoe that he would take her back home to Boston where she could live with him a life of affluence.

Zoe sighed with relief when her father's eyes drifted open again. She had been afraid that she wouldn't be able to say her last words to him. She just wanted to tell her father how much she loved him. She wished to thank him for all that he had done for her, especially since her mother's death. He had been both mother and father to her for the last ten years.

"Father, how can I thank you for all that you've done for me?" she said softly. She placed a gentle hand on his clean-shaven face, seeing so much of herself in his features. The green eyes. The straight nose. The oval face.

"All I want to hear is that you will marry Timothy," her father gasped out.

Still fighting the need to make a promise she could never keep, she wanted instead to tell him how she truly felt . . . that she wanted someone else. Yet, feeling that the lie was necessary, she slowly nodded.

"Yes, Father, I shall marry Timothy," she said, the words like poison as they crossed her trembling lips.

"That'a girl," her father breathed out. "Mark my word, he'll make you a good husband."

Zoe forced a smile. She realized there was more than Timothy's wealth that made her father approve of him. They shared the same deep loathing of Indians.

But most of all, her father seemed driven to repay his debt to the Livingstons, father and son. Her marrying Timothy would accomplish that in his eyes.

When her father returned the smile and whispered that he loved her, everything but her father and how much she would miss him vanished from her thoughts.

"I love *you*," she whispered, bending over to brush a soft kiss across his darkly tanned brow. "I . . . shall . . . miss you."

"We'll never be apart," her father whispered

back. "I'll . . . always . . . be there, lookin' over your shoulder, tellin' you one thing or another. You know me, sis . . . I'm a meddlin', foolish father who'll always—"

The words died on his lips.

His eyes suddenly took on a lingering, glassy stare.

The pulse stopped in his throat.

His hand dropped down to his right side and lay in his life's blood.

"Clear the way!" Doc Rose said in a husky rasp behind Zoe. "Damn it, step aside! Let me get to the sheriff! Get outta the way!"

Full of despair, and already missing her father so much it tore at her very being, Zoe moved her trembling fingers to her father's eyes and slowly closed them.

As she bent low to give him a final kiss on his cheek, Doc Rose fell to his knees beside her, his left hand gripping his black satchel.

"He's gone?" Doc Rose said. He yanked a handkerchief from his front pants pocket and dabbed it along his furrowed, sweaty brow.

Zoe looked over at the doctor, who was aging, gray, and as fat as a butterball in his black fustian suit. She nodded. "Yes, he's gone," she murmured.

"I'm sorry, Zoe," Doc Rose said, stuffing his damp handkerchief back inside his pocket.

"There was nothing you could do for him this time, Doc," Zoe said, slowly rising from the ground. "The damn cowardly outlaw made sure of that."

She looked past the crowd and down the dusty

road. She doubled her hands into tight fists and placed them on her hips. "I'm going to hunt down that sonofabitch and kill him," she said in a low hiss. "I swear I'm going to kill him."

She shifted her gaze and stared down at her father. The badge on his shirt reflected the sun back up into her eyes as though it were speaking to her.

It took no time for her to respond.

She knelt and unpinned the badge from her father's shirt, then pinned it on her own. Yes, as her father had said, she was quite the tomboy, and proud of it. She would take over her father's duties as sheriff. She knew there was no one in this flea-bag of a town who was brave enough to do it.

Everyone, even Harold Hicks, her father's favorite deputy, had recently deserted him. Afraid of the gunman who specialized in killing lawmen, all of her father's deputies had fled their posts.

Zoe knew that by being sheriff, she would be in constant danger. But only by taking the job could she draw the killer to her . . . so that she could kill *him*.

She would never rest until her father's death was avenged!

Even her plans to tell White Shadow that she would marry him must be postponed. Strange, even in death her father would keep her from the man she truly loved. He *would* be with her, in her every thought and deed until her father's killer was dead.

Chapter Four

When the silent sleep
Waves o'er heavens deep;
And the weary weep.
        —William Blake

Clouds hung low over the cemetery just outside of Gracemont, where Zoe's father had been laid to rest. The ceremony was over and all but Zoe and Timothy Livingston had departed for their homes.

Zoe bent to one knee and placed a bouquet of flowers on her father's fresh grave, then rose and stood beside Timothy.

"Zoe, it's time to go," Timothy said, placing a gentle hand on her elbow. "The breeze is brisk. Let's go to my home. We can sit by the fire and drink coffee. If you wish to remain quiet, lost in thoughts of your father, I will understand. But . . ."

He paused, and then said, "But, Zoe, I hope you will listen to me when I ask you to forget this foolish notion of being sheriff. Marry me. I will build you the finest house in the county until we move to Boston. Or you can go on to Boston. I will retire and follow shortly after."

Zoe stiffened as she listened to Timothy. She knew that he had heard of the promises she'd made to her father.

She gazed down at her stark black dress through the thin, black lacy veil that hung over her eyes, and hated everything this dress stood for: her father's death; her loneliness without him.

No, she could not give up her promise to herself to find her father's killer and make him pay for the hideous crime he had committed. When Carl Collins had chosen her father to shoot down in cold blood, he had not known what he had gotten himself into. Although Wanted posters hung everywhere in town, with the likeness of Carl's face on them, no one had tried to hunt him down.

Not until now.

Zoe would not stop until she saw him dead.

"Zoe, have you heard anything I've said?" Timothy asked, strengthening his hold on her elbow.

She felt his grip tighten and heard his voice take on a higher, frustrated pitch. She knew that she had him to deal with even before she could begin to search for Carl Collins.

She yanked her arm away from his hand and turned sharply toward him, lifting her veil to gaze at him. There was no denying how handsome he was. Today, in his blue uniform, with its braids and epaulets, and with his pants creases so sharp they could almost cut a finger, he proved just the sort of husband he would be.

He would be sure that she wore the best of clothes. He would give her a beautiful house filled with beautiful furniture. She would have maids at her beck and call. She would never want for anything.

Except . . . the man she truly loved.

"Zoe, *finally* I have your full attention," Timothy said, his dark eyes dancing as he smiled at her. He placed his hands at her waist, wincing when she stepped quickly away from him, forcing him to drop his hands to his sides.

"I've wired my sister. Even now she and her husband are on their way here from Boston for our wedding," he blurted out. "Zoe, darling, let us go to my home now and make plans. Can't you see how that could help you at such a time as this? Making plans for our wedding will help you forget the godawful way your father died. You have a future to consider. I offer you everything, Zoe. Everything!"

Zoe dropped the veil back over her face and placed her fists on her hips. She glared up at Timothy. "How dare you send for your sister in the presumption that I will marry you!" she said, her voice cold.

"But, Zoe, I was told that you promised your father you would," Timothy said, running his long, lean fingers through his thick black hair.

"Surely it . . . wasn't . . . a lie. Not to a dying man."

Those words "not to a dying man" cut through Zoe's heart as though Timothy had stabbed her with his fancy saber. Every time she thought of how she had lied to her father while he lay dying from an outlaw's bullet, she was overwhelmed with guilt.

And now she was having to pay for the lie. Surely Timothy would never allow her to forget what she had said. He had wanted her for a wife for so long, he was taking full advantage of her moment of weakness.

When Zoe turned her eyes away from Timothy and started walking away from the grave, toward her horse and buggy, Timothy followed quickly and fell into step beside her.

"Zoe, damn it, listen to reason," Timothy said thickly. "You're alone now. You need a man. You need *me*. You are a mere woman out here in Oklahoma, in a jungle of men. What will stop Carl Collins from shooting you down as quickly as he did your father? Or perhaps he might have other things in mind for you . . . like rape."

Her eyes flashed angrily. She was so tired of hearing Timothy rant on and on, and especially now that he had used a scare tactic like mentioning rape, Zoe stopped, turned and glared at him.

"Listen to *me*, Timothy Livingston," she said, glaring up into his face. "I need no one. At least not until I see Carl Collins swinging from the end of a rope, my father's death finally avenged."

She wanted to shout at him that as soon as she saw her father's murderer punished, she was going to marry White Shadow. But she didn't want Timothy to start preaching to her about Indians.

Her love for White Shadow would still be a secret for a while longer . . . until she felt free to go to him. She prayed that she wouldn't be too late to have him.

While Timothy stared at her, his jaw slack, his lips parted, Zoe stamped over to her horse and buggy and left him standing there.

When she heard him soon following her in his own horse and buggy, she snapped her horse's reins. She sighed heavily when Timothy's buggy came up beside hers, their horses trotting briskly, neck and neck.

Zoe refused to look over at Timothy. She continued onward until she came to her small cabin at the edge of town.

After she had tied her horse to a hitching post, she turned and gave Timothy an annoyed stare as he jumped from his buggy and tied his reins next to hers.

"Timothy, *please*," Zoe said, her voice sounding drained. "I'm tired. Please go on home." She removed her veil and held it at her side. "Out of respect for what I have been through today, leave me in peace."

"It wouldn't be healthy to allow you to be alone so soon after your father's burial," Timothy said. He took her gently by an elbow and led her toward the porch. "I was almost certain you wouldn't go to my home after the funeral. So . . . ."

"So what?" Zoe asked, looking quickly over at him when he didn't finish what he was saying.

"Just come inside with me and you shall see," Timothy said, his dark eyes filled with mischief as he smiled down at her.

"Oh, Timothy, what have you done?" Zoe asked, sighing.

Sometimes she could not help liking this lighter side of his character.

Yet she could never forget the ugly side that was filled with prejudice.

"It's not what *I* have done," Timothy said, leading her up the steps and opening the door for her. "Just go inside. You shall soon see."

Zoe gave him an annoyed stare, then went on inside and was taken aback by what she found. Pies, cakes, cookies, and all sorts of covered dishes filled with tantalizing food were sitting on her kitchen table.

"What is this?" she said, eyes wide.

"The women of Gracemont brought food for you," Timothy said.

He stepped away from her and dipped a finger into the frosting of one of the cakes. His eyes widened with approval as he licked the icing from his finger.

"But *when*?" Zoe said, laying her veil across the back of a chair. "The women were at the funeral."

"Did you notice that several came late?"

"Why, yes, now that you mention it."

"That's when they brought the food."

Zoe was touched deeply by their gestures of friendship. She smoothed tears from her eyes with the palms of her hands as she looked at the food, but she could not let herself forget the darker side of life.

She could not allow people's sympathies to soften her mood. She had much to do. And tomorrow would not be soon enough to begin. She must start making things right today.

Her jaw set, Zoe turned to Timothy. "I wish you'd leave," she said bluntly. She shivered as she stared down at her black dress. "I'm going to change out of this . . . this . . . damn black thing."

"I don't have to leave for you to do that," Timothy said smoothly.

He settled down on a wooden rocker beside the fireplace; the ashes were cold and gray beneath the grate.

"I'll wait, Zoe," he murmured. "Once your clothes are changed, then we can talk. I'm not about to let you forget that promise to your father. By damn, Zoe, I *will* have you for my wife."

Zoe sighed heavily. "Stay if you wish," she said, shrugging. "But you are wasting your time if you think staying is going to make me change my mind. I have things to do, Timothy. None of them include you."

"We'll see," Timothy said, slowly rocking back and forth, his eyes locked with hers. "We'll see. You should know me well enough by now to realize that I don't give up that easily."

"Yes, I know," Zoe said, sighing with annoyance. "Like making the Indians at the Fort Cobb Reservation miserable."

Timothy paled. He stopped the rocker. He

stared at Zoe as she went into her bedroom and closed the door between them.

Zoe couldn't get out of the dreadful clothes fast enough. She changed into her jeans and shirt and yanked on her boots, then slid her gunbelt of holstered pistols around her waist.

Standing before a mirror, she wove her fingers through her long, brown hair. "Except for your hair, Zoe Hawkins, you *do* look like a man," she whispered. She shrugged. "But who the hell cares? I've got things to do that require it."

She brushed aside sudden thoughts of White Shadow and how much he hated her wearing these clothes. She would not allow such thoughts to weaken her determination to make things right for her father.

Her fingers trembled as she reached for the badge on the bedside table. She put it in the palm of her right hand and stared at it. Oh, how many times had she seen her father pin this very badge on his shirt before he left for the sheriff's office?

She would never forget the pride in his eyes as he showed it off to her the first time he had worn it. It represented so much to him.

She didn't think it was the power that wearing the badge represented that pleased her father so much. It was pride he felt. As a lieutenant in the cavalry he had worked long, hard hours for his country. He deserved the honor of being sheriff and wearing the badge to prove his worth to the community.

"I shall wear it with the same pride and dedication," she whispered as she pinned the badge on her shirt.

She could not help reviewing in her mind what Timothy had promised her if she married him. She turned and looked slowly around her bedroom, at the drabness of her furniture. She frowned when she looked at the curtainless window, where a tattered and torn shade hung unevenly over it.

In the other three rooms of the cabin—the kitchen, the living room, and her father's bedroom—things were no better. A sheriff did not make good money.

It had been enough, though, to live comfortably with their less than plush furniture, and with enough money to put the food of their choice on the table each day.

Yes, she could have much more than this should she marry Timothy. But always, when she thought of being married, and the sort of home she would share with her husband, she could not help thinking of a large tepee with luscious pelts and blankets to embrace her and her husband while they made love before the fire.

She didn't need a home filled with riches to make her happy. All she needed was the man she loved. And that most certainly could never be Timothy Livingston.

Her hair thrown back across her shoulders, Zoe left her bedroom and heard Timothy's gasp of disbelief when he turned and saw her.

"Damn it, no," he said, scrambling from the rocker. "Zoe, why?" He raked his fingers through his hair. "Zoe, you didn't listen to one word I said. You're foolish. Why throw away your future . . . your *life*? You will be gunned down just like your father once the killer realizes that you have taken on the duties of sheriff and flaunt that badge like something to be proud of."

"Yes, maybe so," Zoe said, lifting her Stetson hat from a peg on the wall. "But, Timothy, before *I* die, I'll be sure that ruthless killer gets a bullet hole in his gut that matches the one he puts in mine."

She settled her hat on her head and turned on one heel, leaving him staring after her as she strode from the cabin.

She quickly unfastened her roan from the buggy, saddled it, then swung herself into the saddle and rode off.

She ignored Timothy's shouts pleading with her to stop. She hoped that he would soon understand that his words were wasted on her . . . that his hopes and dreams could never be the same as hers.

Her chin held high, her hair flying in the breeze as she rode at a hard gallop further into Gracemont, she noticed something at the far end of the road on the other end of town.

Kiowa.

Many Kiowa had come into town.

She yanked on her reins and rode at a slower pace until she reached the sheriff's office. She dismounted and secured her reins, but did not go inside the office. She was absorbed in watching the Kiowa Indians being issued cattle.

She knew that the Kiowa received grass-lease

money from the government. And at nine dollars a head, the government issued cattle to every Indian. Each family was assigned a different brand for their cattle so that they could mark them in case they got mixed up with each other. Some of the cattle were used as food. Some for milk.

Times were no longer the same for the Kiowa as they had been years ago. It was said that many Kiowa hated the taste of beef. Cattle had never taken the place of the buffalo that the white man had wiped from the face of the plains.

Suddenly Zoe was aware of a horse approaching her from behind. Thinking it was Timothy who had followed her into town, she placed her hands on her hips and spun around on a heel.

She opened her mouth to give him a piece of her mind, then stopped and stared, her knees growing weak when she discovered that it wasn't Timothy.

It was White Shadow.

As he rode toward her, now only a few feet away, their eyes met and held for a moment. She wanted to reach out for him and tell him that she needed him, that she was filled with despair over her father's death.

She wanted to tell him that she would marry him, to beg him to give her time to avenge her father's death. But she said nothing to White Shadow. This was not the right time. It had to come later . . . *after* she had found peace inside her heart.

She stiffened when his gaze shifted, sliding downward to stare angrily at the badge shining on her shirt. Her heart skipped a beat when his eyes moved lower to her holstered pistols.

This morning, his friend Lightning Flash had come to him and told him what he had heard the day before as Zoe's father lay dying on the street. Lightning Flash had heard Zoe promise to marry Timothy Livingston. He had even seen her place her father's badge on her shirt and take over the role of sheriff.

White Shadow had been stunned to know that she would take over the duties of the man White Shadow had despised for so long.

Tension had been high between himself and her sheriff father. Her father had not been kind toward White Shadow's seventeen-year-old cousin, Black Beak, nor his friends, who were wont to sneak into town to gamble and drink. They had been involved in barroom brawls with the whites that got them thrown in jail more than once.

White Shadow had always been the one who went into town and got the young braves out of jail, but not before paying the crooked sheriff well in hides and blankets. The sheriff also accepted payment to let outlaws run free instead of arresting them.

White Shadow doubted that Zoe knew the worst about her father, about how he sided with criminals, putting himself on the wrong side of the law by such actions. But she did know how he treated the young Kiowa braves.

White Shadow could not help wondering how Zoe was going to treat Black Beak and the other braves now that she was sheriff, for it seemed impossible to keep them out of town and out of trouble. Surely she approved of her father's treatment of them if she was to take on the role of sheriff now, herself.

It was hard for him to understand . . . this dark side of the woman he loved.

Zoe felt numb inside when White Shadow stared into her eyes, then wheeled his horse around and rode away from her without saying one word. He hadn't even told her he was sorry that she had lost her father.

Stunned by his cold aloofness, wondering if her refusal to marry him could have caused such a change in his behavior toward her, Zoe started to go after him, but then she held herself back. If she was to carry out her promise to hunt down Carl Collins, she must concentrate on that first.

She was afraid that if she went after White Shadow and explained things to him, telling him that she would marry him if he still wanted her, he would talk her out of going after her father's killer. She could not allow anything or anyone to stand in the way of justice. Not even the man she loved with every beat of her heart.

She watched the Kiowa people leave town, the cows trailing behind on ropes as the warriors rode ahead of them.

She strained her neck to single out White Shadow. She could not deny that the one regret, the only regret she felt over her decision to put on the badge, and to continue wearing her Colts, was White Shadow. He loathed such attire on her.

Feeling sad and disillusioned, Zoe went inside

her father's office and looked slowly around her.

It pained her so, for everywhere she looked she saw reminders of her father: the pipe stand on his desk; his handwriting on the wanted posters that were nailed to the wall; his locked cabinet of prized rifles and pistols; his ring of keys, which hung on a nail beside the door that led to the cells at the back of the jail.

She stared at her father's journals, which lay sprawled open on the desk with cigar ashes strewn across some of the entries, a half-smoked cigar resting in an ashtray close by.

Zoe sat down in the scuffed, worn leather chair behind the desk and reached for the cigar. She placed it beneath her nose and sniffed it. She held it out and gazed at the teeth marks that her father had left at the tip.

Thinking she might taste her father on the cigar, she slid it between her teeth, then yanked it quickly away when she suddenly realized the macabre thing she was doing.

Shuddering, she threw the cigar down on the desk, quickly rose from the chair, and ran from the building. Breathing hard, and holding her face in her hands, Zoe stood against the outside wall and tried to compose herself.

When she heard laughter and a shuffling of feet approaching her, she jerked her head up and found several girls and boys hurrying toward her.

"Zoe!" one of the girls shouted. "Zoe, are you going to be at the Fourth of July fireworks celebration?"

Zoe smiled at one and then another as the children circled around her. She was glad to have this sort of distraction from her sorrow. It was good to be surrounded by happy faces and eyes wide with excitement.

"Zoe, are you going to celebrate our town's first Fourth of July celebration, or is it too soon after your father's burial?" another girl asked.

"I'm not sure yet," Zoe said, gently patting the girl with the wide, blue eyes. "I hope *you* all have fun at the celebration."

"Oh, we will!" another girl squealed. "I wish the fireworks were tonight. I can hardly wait to see them. I've heard about how pretty they look against the dark sky. I can hardly wait to see them, myself! My first time, Zoe! My first fireworks!"

They all waved at her and ran away, meeting with another group of children in the middle of the street. Zoe listened to them laughing and talking and making plans for the celebration.

She hoped they wouldn't be disappointed. Too often she had heard about other towns trying to have such a celebration with disastrous results. Drunks had shot their guns at the fireworks, spoiling everything for everyone, especially the children.

She gazed into the distance and again watched the procession of Kiowa as they went on toward their reservation.

She wondered if White Shadow might be at the Fourth of July celebration. Would she be there to see if he came, or would she be too deeply involved in her search for the damnable outlaw?

Feeling tired and drained, Zoe went to her

horse, slowly untied the reins, and eased into her saddle.

She took a forlorn look over her shoulder to see if White Shadow might have had a change of heart and was coming back to talk to her. When she didn't see him, she sighed deeply and headed for home. Sleep. That was what she needed. Sleep would make her forget all of her troubles, at least for a few hours.

Chapter Five

My heart is quivering like a flame;
As morning dew, that in the sunbeam dies,
I am dissolved in these consuming ecstasies.
—Percy Bysshe Shelley

Glad to have the sorrowful, exhausting day behind her, Zoe sat down on the edge of her bed and yanked off one boot. When she had her hand on the other one, she stopped as she heard gunfire erupting in town.

"No, please, not tonight," she grumbled, dispiritedly yanking the discarded boot back on.

Realizing this would be her first duty to perform as sheriff, she slapped her gunbelt around her waist, checked each pistol to make sure they were loaded, then jerked on her hat and rushed from her house.

As her father had always done, Zoe had left her horse saddled. It was tied, ready, at her hitching post.

She grabbed the reins and swung herself into the saddle and rode off at a hard gallop. She rode past the stores that were closed for the night. Only the gambling parlors, whorehouses, and saloons were lit up.

Again gunfire split the night air and loud shouts could be heard coming from the outside of one of the gambling houses. She was now close enough to see a crowd gathering outside of *Jake's Gambling Emporium*.

When she got close enough to see the cause of the commotion, her heart sank. Frank Johnston, the manager of *Jake's*, was standing over three young Kiowa braves who were sprawled on the ground, staring up at him and his smoking revolver.

"Get up and start marchin' toward the jail!" Frank shouted, pulling the trigger and shooting another round of bullets into the dark heavens. "If you think you're goin' to get off easy and go back to your damn reservation tonight, you've got another think comin'. I'm sick and tired of you comin' into *Jake's*, causin' trouble. Now get walkin' toward that jail or, you damn savages, the next bullet I fire will be in the seat of your breeches!"

Zoe wheeled her horse to a halt just beyond the gawking crowd.

She quickly dismounted and elbowed her way through the crowd.

One of the workers from the gambling hall had brought a lamp outside and was holding it up, lighting the area.

The light from the lamp gleamed on the faces of the young braves, one in particular as he slowly pushed himself up from the ground.

"Black Beak," Zoe whispered. It was Black Beak, White Shadow's cousin.

Zoe had seen her father toss the same brave in jail more than once for gambling and boozing.

Not wanting to cause any more tension between herself and White Shadow and his Kiowa people, especially not the same sort of hard feelings that had existed between her father and the Kiowa chief, Zoe was unsure of what to do.

One thing was certain, she felt that the young braves might be safer in her jail tonight than loose on the streets, for it was obvious that Frank Johnston was out for blood. If there had not been so many people standing there as witness, he probably would have shot Black Beak and his friends on the spot.

"Step aside," Zoe said, continuing to elbow her way through the crowd of men. "Come on, break it up. Get on home. Don't you think you've had enough excitement for one night? Go home to your wives and children."

Grumbling, frowning, the men began to disassemble as one by one they turned and walked away.

Zoe watched the other young Kiowa braves get up from the ground and then huddle with Black

Beak as they gazed questioningly from her to Frank Johnston.

Zoe placed herself between the braves and Frank and rested her hands on her holstered pistols as she glared at the manager of the gambling emporium. "What happened tonight?" she asked, in her mind's eye seeing her father dealing with the same sort of commotion in the streets.

But her father had never sided with the Kiowa as Zoe was ready to do. He had always taken Frank's part and was more than ready to throw *any* Indian in jail, Kiowa or otherwise. He knew that he could do so, safe from any trouble from the Indians. The government ruled on the reservation, and it was always on the side of the whites.

Zoe had admired everything but this about her father, and she intended to change things.

"Zoe, it's the same as usual," Frank said, sliding his pistol inside his holster. His thick black mustache hid his sneer beneath it. His thick eyebrows shadowed his cold gray eyes. "The damn Kiowa brats always cause trouble in my establishment. They get too many beers in their bellies and it causes them to go haywire. Tonight I took all I could take. I never want to see them inside my establishment again. Arrest them. Throw away the key!"

"Frank, you know better than to serve alcohol to the young braves," Zoe said, sighing with exasperation. "You know that their tolerance for alcohol isn't the same as a white man's. Why did you serve them tonight, Frank? You knew that in the end you'd regret it. Haven't I heard Father ask you time and again not to give alcohol to the Kiowa?"

"I have to admit that when it comes to money, I haven't been looking at the color of the skin of those who spend it," Frank muttered. "It pays my bills, don't it?"

"At whose expense?" Zoe asked, glancing over at Black Beak. She wished it had been anyone else but White Shadow's cousin standing there caught in the middle of the confrontation.

Hearing the sound of an approaching horse, she turned and looked down the long avenue. When she saw a white mustang she did not have to look further to know who sat tall and straight in the saddle.

White Shadow.

As he had done countless times before, White Shadow had come into town to rescue Black Beak. Zoe was sure White Shadow had warned Black Beak not to get into trouble. She wondered why Black Beak didn't listen. The young brave seemed intent on rebelling.

"Oh, no, not that Injun again," Frank said, staring at White Shadow as he rode closer. "It's not enough that I have to be saddled with three damn wild young savages, but I have to deal with their chief, too."

Zoe only half heard what Frank was grumbling about. Her eyes were on White Shadow. Oh, he was such a striking figure of a man in his fringed buckskins. He was so tall and lean, so powerfully built and lithe.

And she knew beyond any shadow of a doubt that White Shadow had great strength and vigor.

He drew his mount to a stop and slid out of the saddle. Zoe's heart sank when he maintained an absolute, cold silence.

She was remembering how angry and hurt he had been when she refused his proposal. And she remembered how cold he had been earlier today when they had met.

"Well? What're you waiting for, Zoe?" Frank said, breaking the strained silence. "Arrest the sonsofbitches. Don't let the chief take them. They've got to pay for causin' trouble."

Zoe gave Frank a questioning glance. "Will you just shut up?" she said, sighing deeply.

She then turned to White Shadow. Their eyes met and held. Her knees went so weak beneath his steady stare, she felt as though they might buckle.

White Shadow, please speak to me. Say something, she said to herself, wanting him to break the silence between them. But she didn't get her wish. He was still too angry . . . too cold.

"Damn it, Zoe, has the cat got your tongue or what?" Frank said, taking a step closer to her, peering intensely at her.

Having lost her chance to say anything to White Shadow, Zoe swallowed hard as she watched him spin around, his attention now on his cousin and his friends.

"Black Beak, there are dangerous fires burning in your heart," White Shadow said. "My cousin, do you not recall how often I have told you that sometimes tiny flames explode into a wild fire? Tonight you tempt the fires again? You go against your chieftain cousin in such a way? You go against all that was taught you?"

He placed a heavy hand on Black Beak's shoulder and gave him a shove toward his tethered horse. "Go to your steed and go home," he said.

He then placed his strong hands at the back of each of the other young braves' necks and pushed them toward their horses. "Go home," he commanded. "Go to your parents and apologize for having worried them again tonight."

Frank went almost crazy when he saw that Zoe was allowing the young braves to get away without being jailed. "Damn it, Zoe!" he shouted. "Are you going to allow this? The boys deserve to be jailed! Damn it, Zoe, do it. Order them to the jail. Lock them in!"

White Shadow turned abruptly. He gave Frank a shove that sent him sprawling to the ground.

Then White Shadow stood over Zoe and gazed solemnly into her eyes. "You now wear the badge," he said, his voice flat. "Is it your decision to jail my cousin and his friends?"

White Shadow's continued coldness toward her made Zoe's heart constrict.

She was so stricken by his coldness that she was rendered speechless. But down deep inside herself, where her love for him was sheltered, she wanted to say something that would prove that she still adored him.

The words just would not come. They seemed drowned out by the nervous, thunderous beats of her heart.

"Zoe, say something!" Frank said, jumping to

his feet. "You should even arrest White Shadow. Did you see how he shoved me to the ground? What the hell's wrong with you, Zoe? Say something! Do something! You wear the badge! You have the right to arrest whoever you wish to arrest! Don't let that savage scare you!"

The word "savage" made White Shadow's hatred flare up. He fought against hitting the man, knowing that he could be arrested under the white man's law for such an act.

Instead, he ignored the insults. He still waited for Zoe to speak, to say what he wished her to say, to prove that she was not like her father, a crooked lawman with enough prejudice to wipe all Indians from the face of the earth.

White Shadow wanted answers to many things, yet he was too proud to ask Zoe. She had already made it clear whom she truly wished to have for a husband.

He not only wanted to know how she could wear her father's badge, the symbol of his unjust power over the Kiowa, but also why she had promised herself to another man when White Shadow knew she did not love him.

But most of all, he wanted to get this confrontation over with and get out of Gracemont. He must leave Zoe to the life that she had chosen over what he had offered her.

"You did not answer my question about my cousin and his friends," he said. "Do they go to jail? Or do they return home with me, their chief?"

"I'm sorry," Zoe finally said. "I'm sorry I didn't answer you earlier. But, no, White Shadow, the young men don't have to go to jail. Take them home. But give them a long, hard talk. This has got to stop . . . before one of them gets killed by a white man who doesn't like sharing his drinking and gambling with redskins."

Feeling insulted that Zoe had chosen this way to speak to him when he sorely wanted her to be the same sweet woman he had given his heart to, White Shadow stared at her a moment longer, then spun around, mounted his horse, and rode away with the young braves.

Wondering why White Shadow seemed angry over what she had said, Zoe sighed deeply. It seemed that nothing she did now was right in his eyes. She wanted to go after him. But she didn't feel free to pursue him. He seemed changed. He seemed not to want her any longer!

Downhearted, feeling as though she had lost so much these past few days, she ignored Frank, who was ranting and raving over how she had handled the situation. She swung into her saddle and rode toward home.

Never had she felt so alone . . . so unloved.

Chapter Six

I love to rise in a summer morn,
When the birds sing on every tree;
O! what sweet company!
—William Blake

Angry that Zoe had put on her father's badge, and still hurt that she had promised to marry someone else—his *brother*—White Shadow had left his lodge before the sun rose in the sky.

As always when he was troubled, he had gone to his private place of meditation on a high butte to pray aloud to the rising sun. He stood where his voice could go out along the rolling grasses, and where the sun came up in its glory.

On the high butte, alone beneath the waning stars, White Shadow sought answers to many things. But the most important question of all was whether Zoe's feelings for Timothy were true.

Should he turn his back on Zoe now and never think of her again?

There was so much about her now that would have made him turn away from any other woman with feelings of disgust. But he knew that there was much more to Zoe than how she had behaved these past few days.

He had held her in his arms often enough to know her sweetness, her loveliness. He had felt her need when he kissed her. He had felt her softness.

He did not see how any of that could change only because she had *said* that she was going to marry another man. And her wearing the sheriff's badge would not change her . . . the person.

But should he still want her? White Shadow questioned despairingly. Had he been wrong to think that she felt something for him, when all along her heart belonged to someone else?

If so, how could he have misread what she had silently said to him with her eyes? How could he have thought that she cared, when all along she was gazing at him only because he was so different from other men she knew. His skin was different! His culture was different! His clothes were different! Even his language was different!

As far as she knew, Timothy Livingston's skin, language, and culture were the same as hers. Was that what she looked for in a husband? Not love?

He sighed heavily and sat down on the edge of the cliff, watching the night sky change to morning. For a moment he concentrated on the wonders of this vast, beautiful land.

It was summer and the grass was high. Meadowlarks were awakening and calling all around him. Except for the meadowlarks and White Shadow, there was nothing but the early morning, the sky, the trees and plants, and the land.

Although he could no longer watch the shaggy buffalo, or hear their bellowing calls during mating season, there was still much about this land that he loved.

He had learned how to hunt here with his father. He had learned how to ride through the tall, waving grass. He had learned to be as one with the land, sky, and wind.

No matter how hard he tried, he could not help thinking of Zoe again. In their short time together he had thought that he knew her better than he had ever known any woman.

And he knew at this moment that if he could not have Zoe, he would have no woman.

There would be no sons . . . no daughters . . . nothing!

There would be only an empty place where his heart was supposed to be.

He now allowed himself to consider what his mother wanted to do about her first-born. White Shadow knew that he could not deny her this opportunity to finally know her other son.

And although White Shadow was leery of her plan, he had no choice but to allow Timothy's abduction.

Torn by conflicting feelings, White Shadow

stood up and stretched his arms high above his head. With palms up, he cried to the heavens. "*Nuakolahe*, oh, great creator, give me a sign!" he said, his voice showing his despair. "Do I forget her? Do I ignore the badge she wears? Do I ignore her promise to another man? Do I allow my mother her time with her first-born? Do I chance it? Do I?"

A hawk appeared suddenly in the sky above him. Its wingspread was vast. Its eyes were like two heated stones as it swept low and peered directly into White Shadow's eyes.

And then it was gone again, so quickly that White Shadow wondered if it had been an apparition.

No matter what it was, he had made more than one decision. Answers had come to him as quickly as the hawk had come and gone in the sky.

He smiled as he was filled with the peace that he had sought when he came to this high place of prayers and meditations.

"Zoe *will* still be mine. She *will* marry me," he said.

He lifted a warm robe around his shoulders. He held it snugly around himself and made his way down the side of the butte toward home.

"But there are things to do before she will know this," he whispered. "I must first give permission for my brother's abduction."

His chin held high, confident now of what he must do, White Shadow walked through the dew-dampened grass in his intricately beaded moccasins. He gazed toward his village, which was a mixture of log cabins and tepees. He had stayed away long enough for everyone to awaken and start the new day. He could hear the pleasant sound of children squealing at play, horses nickering in their pole corrals, and dogs yapping. A bluish haze of smoke rose from the cookfires that were just being prepared by the women in their lodges.

He could envision his mother puttering around inside her large tepee. As food cooked over her lodge fire, she would be rolling up her sleep blankets and placing them around the sides of the tepee.

"She is a good mother," he whispered as he entered the outer perimeters of the village. "She deserves all that she asks of life . . . of *me*."

What White Shadow had decided was right, he thought to himself, his jaw tightening. Yes, for many reasons, what he had decided was right.

White Shadow walked on through the village. He nodded a silent hello to first one person and then another.

Although he was in a hurry to tell his mother his decision about Timothy Livingston, he took the time to stop and lift a young girl and playfully swing her around. Her gleeful laughter filled the morning air with pure delight.

When another girl asked for a turn, he could not say no. Then, his eyes on his mother's lodge, he walked onward.

When he stopped outside the entrance flap, he inhaled a quavering breath, raised the buckskin, and walked inside. He stood there for a moment watching his mother. She was obviously in deep thought, for she was not aware of his presence. She methodically braided her hair as she stared into the dancing flames of the lodge fire. He wondered what she was thinking. Could it be about him? Or his brother?

White Shadow did not want to feel jealous of her feelings for her other son, but he did. All those years when he had seen a strange sort of sadness in her eyes, surely she had been thinking about the son she had given up to her lover. All those years, White Shadow had not been her only son!

"Mother?" White Shadow blurted out, tired of trying to sort out his emotions.

Startled out of her reverie, Soft Bird looked quickly up, then smiled and reached a hand out for White Shadow. "Son, I went to your lodge only a moment ago," she said. "I wanted to ask you to come and join me for the morning meal." She gazed intently at him. "Where have you been? Usually you come to me before your morning meditation."

"Today I left earlier than usual," White Shadow said, sliding the blanket from around his shoulders. He spread it out beside his mother and sat down on it. "And, *ho*, I was at my private place. I was asking *Nuakolahe* for guidance."

Soft Bird reached a gentle hand to White Shadow's smooth, copper face. "My son, have I put too much burden on your heart by what I have revealed to you about a past love, and about a son who is your brother?" she asked, her voice drawn. "If so, I am sorry."

"It has given me much to think about, that is true," White Shadow said, nodding.

He took her hand, kissed it, and then released it as she resumed braiding her hair. "Mother, about the abduction of my . . . my . . ."

He found the word "brother" so hard to say!

But he knew that he must say it. And saying it as often as possible was the best way to accept the truth that Timothy Livingston was, indeed, his blood brother.

"Your brother?" Soft Bird said, tying a thin leather thong around the end of her braid to secure it. "You are here to talk about your brother?"

"*Ho*, my brother," White Shadow said. He sniffed the tantalizing aroma of the stew that was simmering in the large black pot hanging over the fire. His mother picked up a wooden bowl and ladled some of the stew into it.

He nodded a silent thank you to her as she gave him the bowl of stew, and then a wooden spoon.

"Eat first, talk later," Soft Bird said, making White Shadow realize that she was afraid to hear his answer about the abduction.

White Shadow nodded and ate the stew. He had never before agreed to white captives being taken. This would be the first time, ever, for his people to hide someone from the pony soldiers at the fort.

When he had finished the stew, White Shadow knew that he could delay no longer the conversation that might ultimately bring misfortune to his Kiowa people. He set his empty bowl aside and stared into the flames of the fire.

"He may be brought here," he said in a rush of

words that brought a soft gasp from his mother. He looked quickly over at her. "But I will not be a party to the actual abduction. If Thunder Stick still volunteers to capture him, he has my blessing."

"My son, you have made this mother happy," Soft Bird said, taking his hands and clutching them to her chest, over her heart.

She paused and slowly took her hands away from his. "My son, what made you decide that it would be permissible to bring my first-born here?" she asked softly.

White Shadow knew that his decision had been partly motivated by a desire to remove Timothy from Zoe's life for a while. With her fiancé gone, Zoe would have time to think about the mistake she'd made in choosing Timothy over White Shadow. Surely she had been beside herself over her father's death when she'd agreed to marry the colonel.

White Shadow did not think her decision came from her being afraid to live alone. She had proven herself to be stronger than that. She had the strength, the stamina, the courage of a man.

With a little time, Zoe would come to her senses and realize that it was not Timothy she wished to share her life with.

That man was White Shadow.

"Mother, I cannot deny you an opportunity to know the son you lost," he said, speaking only part of the truth.

When White Shadow saw his mother struggling to get up from the ground, he eased an arm

83

around her waist and helped her. "Mother, where are you going to keep Timothy once he is here in our village?" he asked. "If whites come looking for him, he must never be found here."

"I have thought it over very carefully," Soft Bird said. She took White Shadow's hand and led him to the entranceway of her lodge. "Come. We shall go and tell Thunder Stick your decision. I shall tell him, how and where I want Timothy kept."

White Shadow and his mother went to Thunder Stick's lodge. It was a large tepee with bright drawings of the sun and the stars on the outside buckskin cover. The largest, most prominent drawings were of lurid streaks of lightning.

Looking at the lightning drawings, one could almost hear the loud crashes of the thunder sticks as they came from the heavens during fierce storms, a true representation of the Shaman's name . . . Thunder Stick.

Without warning Thunder Stick of their arrival, White Shadow and Soft Bird went inside the tepee. The interior of the lodge was dim except for the fire in the central fire pit, which had burned down to low embers.

But there was enough light for White Shadow to see Thunder Stick sitting beside the fire sucking on his *seni satop*, his peyote pipe. The stench of the peyote was so thick in the air White Shadow felt stifled by it. He did not approve of the plant, for it too often robbed its users of their senses.

White Shadow glared down at Thunder Stick; then he turned his mother around to usher her back outside into the crisp, cool, clean air.

"Thunder Stick, come outside where we can talk," White Shadow said over his shoulder, walking on outside with his mother.

They stood together as Thunder Stick came from his lodge, his gait slow and lazy.

"One day you will not awaken after filling your body with too much peyote," White Shadow cautioned.

Thunder Stick folded his robe around himself, wrapping it more closely against his body. "You did not come to my lodge to condemn me for my habit of smoking," he said, gazing from White Shadow to his mother. "Soft Bird, do you have answers now that you did not have before?"

He gave White Shadow a wicked grin. "Have you given your mother the answer she wished to hear?" he said, not waiting for Soft Bird to answer him herself.

White Shadow took a step closer to Thunder Stick. He folded his arms across his chest as he stared down at the shorter man. "You will use clever ways when you abduct my . . . white . . . brother," he said stiffly.

"But there is something you must do before you bring him here, Thunder Stick," Soft Bird said. She nodded toward a cabin that had been left vacant recently. "You choose someone who is good with hammer and nails. Have him build a false wall at the back of the cabin. Have enough space left between the two walls for Timothy to be comfortable. We will hide him there when Kiowa sentries warn of the approach of cavalrymen, Indian agents, or the sheriff of Gracemont. You will cover

85

the wall by hanging several blankets and pelts in front of the entrance. Can you do this soon for me, Thunder Stick? I wish to have my son with me before another sun rises."

"It can be done," Thunder Stick said, his eyes gleaming.

"As soon as you bring him to our village tonight, take him into hiding and let him think about this thing that has happened to him; then bring him to me, his mother, to share the morning meal tomorrow," Soft Bird said.

Thunder Stick rubbed his hands together anxiously. "Everything you ask will be done as you say it is to be done," he said thickly.

"Thank you," Soft Bird said, and then took White Shadow's hand. "I am ready to return to my lodge. Son, accompany me there?"

White Shadow nodded. He was feeling strangely ill at ease and empty inside to know that this was his last day as his mother's only son.

He wasn't certain now whether or not he had made the right decision. He knew it was possible that once Timothy became a part of the Kiowa's lives, he would never want to leave. White Shadow did not wish to have Timothy in the village when he brought Zoe there as his wife.

One thing was certain—Timothy Livingston, no matter where he resided, would be a part of White Shadow's life from now on, for he *was* his brother, his mother's first-born.

Chapter Seven

Oh, cease! Must hate and death return?
—Percy Bysshe Shelley

To get things settled with Timothy so that he would never mention marriage to her again, Zoe had invited him to her cabin for supper. Later, over coffee and cake, she planned to have a serious talk with him.

She would feel much better after she got this behind her, once and for all. Timothy could pursue someone else . . . someone who would delight in being adorned with diamonds and dressed in silks and satins as she put on airs in Boston among Timothy's affluent friends.

Although Zoe enjoyed a pretty dress as much as the next woman, she did not enjoy them enough to marry a man she detested to have them.

In truth, when Zoe thought of putting aside trousers, she envisioned herself in the lovely white doeskin dress that White Shadow's mother had made for her. When Zoe wore her boots all day and her feet ached unmercifully, she would think how wonderful it would feel to have soft buckskin moccasins in which to comfortably curl her toes. Whenever she thought of her future, she thought of living the life of a Kiowa wife.

"I hope I haven't ruined everything," she mumbled as she lifted a poker and scattered glowing embers beneath the grate of her fireplace.

She shivered when she recalled the way White Shadow had stared angrily at the badge on her shirt. It seemed as though at that moment things had changed between them, forever.

It had not been Timothy who stayed on her mind while she prepared the evening meal. It had been White Shadow. She had thought of how easy it would be to forget her vow to find her father's killer and just go to White Shadow, to set things straight between them.

Yes, it would be so easy, yet she just couldn't do it. She *had* to find Carl Collins and avenge her father's death.

Even if it meant that she lost White Shadow, vengeance must be achieved, or she would never be able to live with herself. She knew that if she didn't stop Carl, no one else would. How many more families must be torn apart by this filthy, cowardly man?

Yes, she would find him. She would end his reign of terror!

But first things first. Before White Shadow got word of her false engagement, she must clear things up with Timothy.

She felt that White Shadow would get over her wearing the sheriff's badge. But if he thought that she had refused to marry him because of Timothy, he might never even allow her to explain things to him. He might never forgive her.

Time. She needed just a little more time and then she would go to White Shadow and explain everything to him.

Sighing, Zoe glanced up at the pendulum clock on her fireplace mantel. "Where is Timothy?" she whispered impatiently.

She glanced over at the window and saw that it was pitch black outside.

She looked toward the kitchen table and saw that steam no longer rose from her creamy mashed potatoes or milk gravy.

"The green beans are probably ruined," she whispered.

She groaned, and then began to pace, the hem of her cotton dress tangling around her ankles as she made brisk, abrupt turns.

She raked her fingers through her long and flowing hair, which was held back from her face by beautiful wooden combs. Her father had bought the combs for her one day at the nearby trading post. It didn't matter that Indians, the very people he abhorred, had made the combs. He had known that Zoe would love them so he had given fifty cents to the elderly Indian who wanted twice that amount for them.

Whenever Zoe was reminded of her father's prejudice against Indians, she quickly brushed the thoughts aside. She didn't like thinking about that side of his personality.

The clock chimed nine times. Zoe was now truly puzzled. Timothy was the sort of person who would send word if something delayed him from keeping an appointment. On the other hand, perhaps he had come to his senses and realized that she wouldn't marry him.

"That does it," she murmured, yanking her combs from her hair and placing them on the table. "I've got to go to the fort and see why Timothy didn't show up. The rat. If he did this purposely to annoy me, to put me in my place, I'm going to give him a piece of my mind he'll never forget."

She stopped and lifted the hem of her dress. She stared at the lovely leather slippers she had chosen to wear tonight. They would never do for her ride to the fort. Nor would the dress.

She hurried into her riding clothes. She slapped her gunbelt around her waist and fastened it. She then put on her Stetson hat and tucked her hair up beneath its crown.

Leaving the food untouched on the table, she stamped outside and swung herself into her saddle. She rode off at a hard gallop toward the fort.

When she arrived there, she reined her horse to a sudden stop just outside the gate where two armed guards stood on each side.

"Good evening, Sheriff, what brings you to the fort this time of night?" one of the guards asked.

The moon's glow revealed his youthful face and collar-length golden hair.

"I'm here to see Colonel Livingston," Zoe said, straining her neck to look past the two uniformed men to see inside the gate. She could just barely see Timothy's two-storied stone house at the far left side of the parade ground. She saw no lamplight at any of the windows.

"Ma'am, I haven't seen the colonel since morning. As far as I know, he's retired for the night," the other guard said. He turned and looked at Timothy's house. "Yep. He must be asleep. I see no lights at any of his windows."

"The bastard," Zoe whispered angrily beneath her breath. Timothy had probably had a delicious, hot meal inside his grand dining room, while she had stood waiting for him as her dinner grew cold.

So angry she could spit nails, she spun her horse around and rode off.

"Ma'am, is there any message you'd like to leave for the colonel?" one of the soldiers shouted after her. "I can see that he gets it first thing tomorrow morning."

She wanted to give them a message for Timothy, all right . . . to tell Colonel Timothy Livingston to go straight to hell.

But, instead, she kept her silence and held the burning anger inside her. The next time she saw Timothy she would tell him herself.

And she would never give him the chance to make a fool of her again!

"Tomorrow," she whispered to herself. Tomorrow, before she started her earnest search for her father's killer, she would go to the fort and give Timothy the dinner he had turned his nose up at tonight. She would take him a large platter full of cold mashed potatoes and throw it in his face!

That thought made her smile.

And then another thought came to her that made her smile fade. She was thinking back to what the one guard had said. Hadn't he said that he hadn't seen Timothy since morning, and as far as he *knew*, the colonel was asleep?

Could that mean that Timothy might not be at the fort? Perhaps he had met foul play while out taking his late afternoon ride. She had expected him to come directly from that ride to her home for supper.

"If the guard hasn't seen Timothy since morning, that has to mean he didn't see him leave the fort for his afternoon ride," Zoe said aloud, suddenly yanking on the reins to stop her horse.

She wheeled her horse around and stared in the direction of the fort. Should she go and see for sure if Timothy was home, safely in his bed?

She turned her horse back around in the direction of her home and rode onward, but this time in a slow lope as she continued to think about the mystery of why Timothy hadn't come to her home for supper.

If he had stood her up, she did not want to chase after him, inquiring about his welfare. She did not want it to look as though she cared one iota about him.

On the other hand, what if he had been riding

to her home when Carl Collins abducted him, or shot him and hid his body?

Zoe paled and stopped her horse again.

"Could that have happened?" she gasped out in a low whisper. "If Timothy isn't home, could he be a prisoner of Carl Collins?"

Her father had teased her often about her active imagination, and Zoe tried to convince herself that it was out of control now to think that Timothy had been abducted by anyone.

"Hogwash!" she whispered.

She sank her heels into the flanks of her horse and rode off. She was glad when her cabin came into sight beneath the silvery splash of the moon. Although she tried to convince herself that nothing had happened to Timothy, she was still worried.

And thinking such things made her realize just how dangerous it was for *her* to be out this time of night alone.

A cold shiver raced up and down Zoe's spine as she took a quick look over her shoulder. Suddenly she didn't feel alone. She felt as though eyes were following her every movement. She felt as though a gun was leveled at her back . . .

Leaning lower over her horse, snapping the reins, Zoe rode onward and was glad to be home at last. She dismounted in one fast leap and wrapped the reins around the hitching post; then she hurried inside her home and slammed the door behind her.

Feeling suddenly unsafe and vulnerable, Zoe made sure that her door was doubly bolted tonight. Then she went to the window and slowly lifted the tattered shade just high enough for her to see outside. By the light of the moon she could see far and wide.

To the right, she could see downhill to the pecan grove her father had planted shortly after their arrival in Oklahoma. It was a dark growth along the creek. Beyond was a long sweep of open ground.

A grape arbor, also planted by her father, was open on all sides to the light and the air and the sounds of the land. Then there were groves of cottonwood, and a meadow filled with wildflowers, their faces closed for the night.

To her left were twin buttes looming high overhead.

Zoe felt a keen relief when she saw that everything seemed normal. No one was lurking about. Surely she had been wrong to think that someone was there.

Another thought came to Zoe. "If Timothy is playing tricks on me, oh, how I will make him pay!" she whispered to herself, suddenly thinking that it might be Timothy putting a scare in her to convince her that she needed a man to protect her.

Still, she couldn't shake the feeling that perhaps he might be in trouble. She would return to the fort tomorrow and see if he was there. If not, instead of beginning her search for her father's killer, would she be searching for Timothy?

Afraid, she yanked the shade closed and hugged herself.

Chapter Eight

Mind from its object differs most in this:
Evil from good; misery from happiness.
　　　　　　　　—Percy Bysshe Shelley

It was early morning. White Shadow sat on blankets and pelts on the floor at his mother's side inside her tepee. He looked up as Timothy was brought into her lodge flanked by two warriors; Thunder Stick followed close behind them.

White Shadow had seen Timothy brought into the village around sunset the day before. He'd been taken to the cabin that had been prepared for him. White Shadow had gone and stood outside the cabin and listened to Timothy's demands to be set free. When things went quiet, White Shadow realized that Thunder Stick had grown tired of listening to Timothy and had gagged him.

White Shadow watched Timothy struggle with the bonds at his wrists as he was brought to stand close. White Shadow saw how his blood brother's eyes were filled with a mixture of confusion and resentment as he looked from White Shadow to Soft Bird, and then at Thunder Stick as the shaman removed the gag and then went and rested on his haunches at White Shadow's right side.

His blue breeches and white shirt disheveled, his hair in disarray, Timothy slid his eyes over to White Shadow again and locked them with the chief's. "White Shadow, I demand to know what this is all about," he said gruffly. "Don't you know the consequences of abducting me in such a way? God, White Shadow, you could be sent before a firing squad at the fort for this. Release me now and I will make sure you are spared such a death. I will speak in your behalf. Just . . . let . . . me go, White Shadow. This is wrong. What have I done to deserve being treated in such a way? I've tried to be fair to the Kiowa. How could you want more from me?"

Soft Bird sat quietly listening as she looked at Timothy, her first-born. She was thrown back in time, to the day her child was wrenched from her breast, her milk still wet on his lips after having suckled contentedly. She could still recall his tiny, sweet fingers kneading her breast as he drank the milk from it. She could still hear his contented mewing sounds.

And now he was a grown man. So much time had passed since she had been denied him!

She was overwhelmed with emotion, so badly

did she want to go to him and pull him into her arms. She wanted to apologize for the whites who had turned him away from his own true people. Although he was part white, he had been denied the most important side of his heritage . . . the Kiowa side.

She rose to her feet and stood before Timothy. She kept herself from reaching a hand out to his face to touch him as she studied his every feature. She wondered if he had ever stood before a mirror and puzzled over his high cheekbones, his midnight dark eyes, and his coal black, coarse hair? The only thing he had inherited from his father was his fair skin.

Ho, she could see so much of herself and her family in her first-born. It was hard not to cry out to him who he was.

But that was not the plan. She would silently watch and observe him as he was taught the ways of his ancestors. When she thought the time was right, he would be told everything.

White Shadow saw how his mother studied her first-born. Her silent perusal had drawn Timothy's attention. In turn, he gazed back at her with a strange questioning in his eyes.

White Shadow wondered if his brother recognized the resemblance between himself and this woman.

White Shadow himself, now that he knew that Timothy was his brother, could see many similarities between them.

Even so, he found it hard to think of this bigoted man as his brother. He doubted he ever could feel the closeness toward him that Kiowa brothers usually felt for one another.

But he would play his mother's game. He understood now the importance of her having her first-born with her. It was so wrong that she had ever been denied him.

To think of how she must have ached for her son through the years made White Shadow ache for her now. And this made it easier for White Shadow to go along with her plan to turn Timothy into the kind of son that he should have been.

"Why are you looking at me in such a way?" Timothy asked, his voice breaking as he watched Soft Bird walk slowly around him, still studying him.

He turned as she turned. He winced when she reached out as if he thought she was going to hit him.

Instead, she untied the ropes at his wrists and released them. He rubbed his raw wrists as he watched her hand the ropes to a warrior.

He then gazed at White Shadow as he rose and stood beside her.

"My mother, Soft Bird, is the one who wished your presence among our people," White Shadow said, his voice dignified, yet devoid of emotion. "You will do as she says when she says it, for she is the one who eventually chooses your fate."

Timothy's eyes widened. He glanced quickly over at Soft Bird again. "But why?" he stammered. "What am I to you that you would do this to me? I don't recall having treated you differently than the others on the reservation. In fact, I scarcely recall seeing you at all. Why . . . are . . . you doing this to me?"

Soft Bird wanted to cry out to him and say it was because he was her son!

But she knew that it was the wrong time to reveal such truth. In time, his feelings toward the Kiowa would soften.

Then, and only then, would she tell him that he belonged here among his people. What he would learn while mingling with them would make him want to stay!

"Take him outside," Soft Bird said, nodding toward one of the warriors. "Let everyone who wishes see him. Then strip him of his white *yapahe*, soldier's clothes, and give him the clothes of our people to wear."

Timothy paled and struggled with the warriors as they grabbed his arms and turned him toward the entrance flap. "No!" he cried. "This is insane!" He glanced over at White Shadow. "If you don't stop this now, by God, I personally will be the one to shoot the first bullet in you when you stand up before the firing squad!"

A man who had long ago learned not to pay attention to threats, White Shadow smiled slowly at Timothy and waited for Timothy to be taken outside.

White Shadow then swept a gentle arm around his mother's waist and walked her outside with the others. Thunder Stick joined them and stood at soft Bird's left side while White Shadow stood on her right.

Seemingly tired of trying to reason with the Kiowa, Timothy stood, slack-jawed and empty-eyed, as he was stripped of his clothes, even down to his boots. For a moment he was made to stand unclothed before the people as they all stood silently watching him. Everyone was quiet for a while, and then there was a ripple of laughter.

White Shadow understood why his people were finding his mother's game amusing, for none of them liked this military man who never had a kind word to say to them when they were at the fort getting their allotments.

But seeing his brother's humiliation, White Shadow nodded to the warrior who carried the breechclout that would from now on be Timothy's.

White Shadow's spine and jaw stiffened when he saw Timothy visibly shudder with disgust as he was given the breechclout. This attitude was proof of the man's total disgust for the Kiowa.

"Put it on," White Shadow said, frowning at Timothy as he held the breechclout in front of his private parts. "Wear it. While you are among my people, that will be your only attire."

Timothy glared at White Shadow as he yanked on the brief breechclout.

White Shadow took a dignified step away from Timothy and faced the crowd. "My people, you have been told why this man was brought to our village," he shouted. "You have been warned not to tell anyone that he is here, or why. You are all to cooperate with the wishes of my mother and help change this man from white to Kiowa!"

He heard Timothy gasp behind him. White

Shadow smiled to know that Timothy's humiliation was deepening.

It would delight White Shadow to know that this man would not understand why he'd been abducted until he had been taught many Kiowa customs.

Then and only then would he know that he, himself, was Kiowa.

Everyone began a slow chant as they drifted past Timothy. Some just walked past him. Others stopped and stared at length at him.

And after everyone had acquainted themselves in this way with him, White Shadow watched Thunder Stick go to Timothy and grab him by an arm.

"Now what?" Timothy said, sighing as Thunder Stick forced him to walk toward a cabin where arrows were being made. This was to be Timothy's first lesson. Before the lesson was over, Timothy should be able to make arrows as well as anyone.

White Shadow hugged his mother, and then followed Thunder Stick and Timothy to the cabin at the far side of the village.

He stepped just inside the door and watched for a moment, to see if Timothy was going to cooperate or rebel and make things hard on himself.

White Shadow smiled as several other Kiowa filed past him into the cabin and resumed the arrow making that had been stopped long enough to see the white man forced out of his clothes and into a breech clout.

He watched as one of the warriors took charge of Timothy's lessons while Thunder Stick sat down on pelts in the shadows and picked up a pipe that he had taken there earlier so that he could smoke his peyote as he watched Timothy learn arrow-making.

Soon the peyote smoke hung about the ceiling of the cabin, but no one seemed to notice. Timothy was showing a quick interest in the arrow-making. His fingers were agile as he joined in, listening to the instruction as though he truly cared.

White Shadow listened, himself, as the warrior spoke in a friendly tone to Timothy.

"If an arrow is well made, it will have tooth marks upon it," Long Nose said as he showed Timothy arrows that were already completed. "The Kiowa make fine arrows and we straighten them with our teeth. Then we draw them to the bow to see if they are straight."

Long Nose glanced over at another warrior who sat beside the light of a window, making an arrow. He was an elderly, gray-haired man, impressive in his age and bearing.

"Old men are the best arrow-makers," Long Nose said. "They bring time and patience to their craft. Fighters and hunters are willing to pay a high price for arrows that are made well."

Seeing that things were going well for the moment, White Shadow left the lodge and rode from the village. His thoughts were now on someone else. On Zoe!

He wondered how she would react when she discovered that her intended had disappeared as stars disappear from the heavens at morning's first light.

Would she mourn? Or would she be glad? No matter how hard White Shadow tried, he could not see how Zoe could have ever loved such a man as Timothy Livingston.

White Shadow rode on until he came to a butte that overlooked Zoe's cabin. He knew that she was there. Her horse was still reined to the hitching post.

He drew a tight rein and stared at Zoe's cabin. It seemed an eternity since he had last seen her.

Chapter Nine

Shadow of annoyance
Never came near thee;
Thou lovest—but ne'er knew
Love's sad satiety.
—Percy Bysshe Shelley

The glint of the sun reflecting on what seemed to be the barrel of a rifle on another butte overlooking Zoe's cabin drew White Shadow's quick attention. He grew cold inside to think that someone besides himself was observing her.

He wondered who would do this and why?

No matter how angry and disillusioned White Shadow was with Zoe, he could not help feeling protective of her. He started to go and investigate the hidden stranger, but stopped when his attention was drawn down below by the sound of thundering hoofbeats.

He stiffened when he saw several cavalrymen stop in front of Zoe's cabin along with a lawman White Shadow recognized. It was Harold Hicks, the man who had been Zoe's father's deputy sheriff.

When Zoe came from the cabin and began talking with the men, White Shadow stiffened. He wanted badly to hear what was being said. It was certain that Zoe was unhappy with the deputy. He saw her frown as she held Harold in a steady, angry stare.

His gaze shifted to Harold when he began talking to Zoe. It was frustrating to White Shadow that he could not hear what Harold was saying.

His stomach clenched when he realized that the pony soldiers and the deputy might be at Zoe's cabin because of Timothy. Everyone surely now knew that he was missing!

"I apologize, Zoe," Harold said, his eyes wavering. "I have no excuse for deserting you after your father's death. That . . . that . . . was when you needed me the most."

"Harold, I'll get along just fine without you," Zoe said. She placed her hands on her hips and flipped her hair back from her shoulders. "I'll eventually find someone who'll willingly work at my side as deputy sheriff."

Harold shuffled his feet nervously. "But, Zoe, you can't do that," he said. He took his wide-brimmed hat from his head, revealing curly red hair. He held his hat down in front of him and took a slow step toward Zoe. "Your father always depended on *me*. Zoe, I promise you that you can, also, for as long as you need me."

"You deserted me and my father in the face of danger," Zoe said tightly. "How can I be sure you won't do it again? I need dependable men, especially a dependable deputy. I no longer feel that you can be trusted, Harold."

Harold began nervously turning his hat around between his fingers. "Damn it, Zoe," he said, frowning. "Be reasonable. I made a mistake. I fessed up to it. Now I'm back to make restitution. I'm as eager to catch that lowdown sonofabitch coward of an assassin as you are. He . . . killed . . . your father. Bradley was my best pal. I'm not going to let the sonofabitch scare me from doin' my duty. Zoe, I've returned to help you. You've got to allow it. I couldn't live with myself if you didn't."

"I hope I'm not making a mistake by trusting you again, Harold," Zoe said softly. "But for my father's sake, I will give you another chance. I know how he admired you."

"Then let's get the hell out of here and gather up a posse and go and find the sonofabitch," Harold said, plopping his hat back on his head.

"We can't, Harold," Zoe said, looking slowly over at the soldiers, who were somberly sitting on their horses waiting for her.

She then looked at Harold again. "You heard what's happened," she said solemnly. "Colonel

Livingston is missing. No one has seen him since yesterday morning."

"I know all that," Harold said, giving the soldiers a glance over his shoulder, and then frowning at Zoe. "Hell, Zoe, they came to me first, didn't they?"

"It was only by sheer coincidence that you were at the sheriff's office when they went there looking for *me*," Zoe said stiffly. "If I hadn't overslept this morning, I would've been there doing my job instead of . . ."

She didn't finish what she was saying. She would not feel guilty for having taken longer to get to work today than usual. These past several days had finally taken their toll on her.

But, thanks to this one night of uninterrupted sleep, she was finally rested and ready to assume her duties as sheriff.

It seemed strange to her that one of her first tasks as sheriff would be to search for Timothy. Although she had worried that something might have happened to him, she hadn't truly believed it. He had always seemed invincible.

Now she wondered what could have happened? Who was to blame? It was certain that Timothy had made many enemies since he had arrived at Fort Cobb. There were the Kiowa who hated the very ground he walked on. There was Carl Collins. . . .

She looked up at the lieutenant who was in charge of the search. "I'll only be a moment," she said. "I'll get my things. Then I'll be happy to ride with you to search for Timothy."

"I came to ask your help, not only because you are the sheriff and should know the lay of the land," the lieutenant said, "but also because you have gone horseback riding many times with Colonel Livingston. Surely you know places to look where he might have . . . met misfortune. He might have taken a fall. I've seen him push horses far beyond their abilities. I always thought one might throw him if pushed too hard."

"Yes, perhaps that's what happened," Zoe said, nodding. She, too, had seen Timothy's cruelty to horses. He was a driven man with hidden demons. He had never seemed to be content with who he was.

Timothy had told Zoe more than once that something seemed to be missing in his life, and he wasn't speaking of needing a woman. He had said that it was something else . . . a tugging at his heart. It was as though someone were trying to reach out for him, he had said.

It had begun to torment him so much of late, she had been concerned about his mental stability.

She hurried inside her cabin and fastened her gunbelt around her waist, hoping that the lieutenant was right, that a riding accident accounted for Timothy's disappearance.

But the more she thought about it, the more she believed that Carl Collins was to blame. He had a reason to abduct Timothy, for her fiancé's disappearance would surely draw Zoe out to search for him. She would then be a much easier target for him to gun down.

She doubted that Carl Collins would be stupid enough to come into town again as he had done when he shot her father. He had to know that Zoe was gunning for him now.

She truly doubted that the Kiowa were responsible for Timothy's disappearance. As far as she knew, White Shadow had never taken white captives. It didn't seem logical that they would begin now.

Thinking of White Shadow made a deep sadness engulf her. She wanted him so badly it hurt. And now she wondered just how long it would be before she was free to go to him, to reveal her true feelings to him.

She must now search for Timothy even before searching for her father's killer.

There was only one ray of hope this morning as she thought of where the search for Timothy might take her. Perhaps looking for Timothy would lead her to the killer.

She could hardly wait to get the best of Carl Collins, to see him swinging at the end of a rope.

With determined steps, she went outside and mounted her horse. She looked over her shoulder at the soldiers. "Let's ride!" she cried.

She sank her heels into the flanks of her horse and took the lead. Harold rode up beside her and tipped his hat to her and smiled.

She returned Harold's smile. She was so glad that he had returned to be her deputy. With Harold at her side, Zoe somehow felt her father's presence, and she glanced heavenward. "I *will* avenge you, Father," she whispered to herself as she rode across a meadow bright with Indian paintbrush, lupine, and wild buckwheat.

Chapter Ten

Ring out the want, the care, the sin,
The faithless coldness of the times.
                        —Alfred, Lord Tennyson

White Shadow watched Zoe ride away with the
soldiers and her deputy. He wanted to follow
them, to make sure they didn't get past the sentries posted around his village.

Yet he remembered seeing the shine of a rifle
barrel on the butte overlooking Zoe's cabin.

Determined to keep Zoe safe, he wheeled his
horse around and rode down the steep incline of
the butte, and then rode to the foot of the other
one.

Not wanting to be seen investigating, White
Shadow dismounted. He tied his horse's reins to

the low limb of a tree and slid a knife from a sheath at his right side.

His moccasins making no sound on the grassy slope of the butte, White Shadow crept stealthily upward, in and around lodgepole pines that clung to the sides of the hill, and through brambles whose thorns occasionally snared his fringed buckskins.

White Shadow flinched and stopped when he heard a sound a short distance above him.

He crouched down behind a thick stand of bushes and looked cautiously upward. He smiled when he discovered that it was only a grosbeak high in the branches of a lodgepole pine. Alone, the grosbeak stared down at White Shadow, and then began preening his feathers.

As always before, White Shadow enjoyed the sight of the lovely bird. Round and rose-colored, with its dark, striped wings nearly invisible in the soft, mottled light, it was a sight to behold.

But when it suddenly flew off, as though startled by something besides White Shadow's presence, he stiffened and looked carefully around him.

When he saw and heard nothing, he proceeded up the hill until he came to where the land leveled out before him.

He fell down on his belly and stared in all directions, his gaze stopping when he found the edge of the butte. It was partially obscured, with pines and cottonwoods and brush growing up to the edge, a perfect hiding place.

Seeing nothing except for an eagle that was soaring majestically overhead, White Shadow moved slowly to his feet and went onward. He stopped when he found a scattering of cigarette butts beneath a tree, as well as crushed grass.

"Someone was here," White Shadow whispered.

He knelt down to look more closely at the cigarette butts and the crushed grass.

He ran a hand over the grass, and then picked up one of the butts. He studied it, then gazed down through the break in the trees at Zoe's house.

"Zoe was being watched," he whispered. "She is in danger!"

He recalled the way her father had died: at the hands of an outlaw, a killer who took pleasure in gunning down lawmen.

Zoe was now the sheriff. She was just as much a target for the killer as her father had been.

He stood at the edge of the cliff and looked far into the distance. He could just barely see Zoe now as she rode with the soldiers and her deputy. *Ho*, he did believe they were banding together today to look for his brother Timothy.

If not for that, White Shadow himself would join them. He wanted to be there for Zoe, to make sure she was safe.

He wished that she would put this foolishness of behaving like a man behind her, and leave the men's jobs to the men, for he knew just how much of her was an enticing woman.

Frustrated and feeling at loose ends, White Shadow tossed the cigarette butt over his shoulder and went back to his horse.

As he rode hard across a meadow, a thought

came to him that made him make a sharp turn left. He had an opportunity this morning to do something that he had always wanted to do.

He smiled as he rode to Zoe's cabin and left his horse tethered in a thick stand of grass for grazing. Then he went inside the cabin and gazed around him.

He was stunned to discover that Zoe lived far less comfortably than he did in his tepee. If she married him, he could offer her luxuries she was not accustomed to.

She would have rich pelts in which to wrap herself. In the winter, when the winds blew cold and the snow fell in white sheets from the sky, Zoe would have wonderfully warm blankets to ward off the chill.

She would have a central lodge fire where cooking was made easy on large pots hung over the flames. The Kiowa cooking utensils were more advanced than those he now saw in Zoe's kitchen.

He gazed down at the crude wooden floor. The floor in his lodge was cushioned with mats, which would be soft beneath Zoe's feet.

Wanting to see one more thing before he left, he went to her bedroom and gazed at her bed. His heart pounded like distant thunder as he envisioned her lying there, so lovely and delicate, her hair spread out beneath her head like the soft wings of a butterfly.

He went and pressed his hands into the mattress. Again he smiled. Although this feather mattress was soft, nothing compared to the blankets made of the pelts of many white rabbits on which she would sleep when she was his wife.

Ho, now that he had seen how she lived, he knew that he had much to offer her when he asked her to be his wife.

Feeling content about this, at least, White Shadow left the cabin. He had changed his mind about going straight home. He would, instead, catch up with Zoe and the soldiers and follow them.

He must be absolutely certain that the soldiers and Zoe did not enter the outer perimeters of his village without his sentries being forewarned.

No one must ever find Timothy among his people. Especially not Zoe.

White Shadow was afraid that she might think White Shadow was responsible for Timothy's abduction, whereas White Shadow had only approved of the abduction to please his beloved mother.

Chapter Eleven

Which masters Time indeed, and is
Eternal, separate from fears.
—Alfred, Lord Tennyson

Black Beak and his two best friends were on
horseback, riding toward Gracemont. A travois
was being dragged behind each of their horses.
The travois were heavy with blocks of wood that
the young braves planned to sell to the townspeo-
ple, who used the wood as foundations for their
houses.

"Black Beak, selling wood is child's play," Red
Thunder complained, frowning. "We are Kiowa.
Why do we not act as though we are? Do you not
feel the same humiliation that I feel when we
stand on a street in Gracemont, being humble to
whites, selling them wood?"

"I agree with Red Thunder," Eagle Claw said, also frowning at Black Beak. "Your chieftain cousin is wrong to keep us away from the excitement that our forefathers knew before us. Today, Black Beak, there are other things I would rather do than sell wood." His long black hair blew in the gentle breeze, his dark eyes danced mischievously. "There are many *manly* ways to make money. I would like to steal horses. Black Beak, would you not also enjoy the thrill of stealing horses?"

Red Thunder brushed back long strands of hair that blew around the front of his face. He shifted his headband so that it would keep his hair back better. "I know just the man who would buy stolen horses," he said, nervously running a hand across the buckskin fabric of his breeches. "Do you not see, Black Beak, how stealing and selling horses would make gambling money for us much faster than selling wood?"

Black Beak heard all they were saying, and was tempted by it, yet he could not forget his cousin's many warnings to stay out of trouble. And stealing horses would be the worst kind of trouble, for they would be horses stolen from whites.

"Black Beak, speak up, tell us your decision," Eagle Claw said. "Are you not tired of feeling inadequate? Do you not wish to have pride and steal horses as our ancestors were free to steal them before the white pony soldiers came? Humbling ourselves to white men by selling them wood blocks is shameful."

Black Beak could not deny that he felt the same

117

shame as his friends. He wanted more out of life than to follow every rule dictated to him by his cousin. He would one day be a mighty warrior. He wanted to act like one now!

He gazed over at Red Thunder, and then past him at Eagle Claw. "Today *only* shall I steal horses," he said thickly. "Only today. I do hunger for the excitement of our forefathers. It is in my blood to steal horses, to ride free in the breeze as we chase them. I do want to have more money than the selling of wood could bring us, for gambling is also in my blood. Tonight we shall gamble and drink and not worry about the consequences if my cousin discovers us. My friends, we shall live for the moment. Was that also not the way of our ancestors? As now, who knew of tomorrow then? Were not so many of our ancestors' tomorrows robbed from them by the whites? Let us go and rob from the whites today."

They rode onward until they came to a creek.

Chanting together, they went to the muddy embankment and sank their fingers into the mud.

As their chants turned into prayers, they smeared the mud across their brows and then down their cheeks.

After loosening their travois and leaving their wood behind, they rode off together. Their loud war cries rang through the morning air, scattering birds from the trees with the fierceness of their voices.

They rode and rode until they came to a wide, open pasture where horses were peacefully grazing. The location of the ranch house on the far side of the hill made it easy for them to steal the horses without being seen.

Quiet now, concentrating on roping the horses, they each chose a steed to chase. When they had each roped a horse and tied them together beneath a tree, they galloped after more of the animals, until they had ten horses, in all, to sell.

They washed their faces clean. Then, not having enough rope to keep all of the horses tied to their steeds, they appointed Red Thunder to keep the loose horses rounded up as he led them and his friends toward a hideout in a canyon.

"How do you know of this man who buys stolen horses?" Black Beak asked, sidling his horse up next to Red Thunder's.

"Comanche friends told me about him," Red Thunder said, smiling smugly at Black Beak.

"Comanche friends?" Black Beak said, raising an eyebrow. "You have not told me that you are so close to a Comanche that he would confide such information in you."

"That is because I did not believe you should know," Red Thunder said, his jaw tightening. "Your cousin is chief. Too often, you follow his rules, not those made up by your friends."

"*Ho*, that is so," Black Beak said. He reached up and combed his fingers through his thick black hair and drew it farther back from his copper, oval face. "I love my cousin. I do not enjoy causing him problems."

"If he had his way you would have *no* fun in life," Eagle Claw said, sidling his horse close to Black Beak's. "For today, Black Beak, forget him and his rules. Enjoy what we are doing. Is it not something that makes your spirits high? Does it not fill you with excitement?"

"My heart is thundering from it," Black Beak said, smiling at Eagle Claw. "And, Eagle Claw, I do this today not only for the excitement and the money we shall have to enjoy gambling, but also to have more money to spend while enjoying the Fourth of July celebration. I have heard that many vendors will set up along the streets of Gracemont, selling things no Kiowa has ever seen before."

"Like what, Black Beak?" Eagle Claw asked, his eyes wide and anxious.

"I do not know exactly what," Black Beak said, shrugging. "I have listened to rumors, that is all. We will only know for certain when we go there."

"We are not far now from the outlaw's hideout," Red Thunder said, squinting his eyes against the bright rays of the sun as he gazed intently ahead of him. "Just follow me." He glanced over at Eagle Claw. "While I lead the way into the canyon, help keep the loose horses from straying."

Eagle Claw nodded.

Black Beak was troubled by the word "outlaw." He knew that the sheriff of Gracemont had been recently gunned down by an outlaw. He knew that the woman his cousin courted was now sheriff because of this outlaw.

"What is the name of the outlaw who will buy the horses from us?" he blurted out, frowning at Red Thunder.

"What does it matter?" Eagle Claw said, staring

back at Black Beak. "He will pay us money. Is not that enough?"

"No," Black Beak said. "That is not enough. To-day I am going behind my cousin's back doing many things that will cause him anger. I want to know the name of the outlaw."

"All right then, you will have his name," Red Thunder said, shrugging indifferently. "Carl Collins. His name is Carl Collins."

The name came to Black Beak like a slap in the face. He drew a sudden tight rein and brought his horse to a halt. "I cannot go with you and deal with such a man as that," he said, his voice tight. "He is a heartless man. And he cannot be trusted."

"But we are almost there," Red Thunder said, his voice rising. "We cannot turn back. We have nowhere else to sell the horses." His eyes narrowed. "And I have not thrown my wood blocks away and gone to the trouble of rounding up these horses only to turn them loose and return home with empty pockets."

"Nor will I," Eagle Claw said, siding with Red Thunder. "It is not fair that you would ask this of us." He laughed throatily. "*Ho*, Carl Collins is a man whose heart is as cold as the winter's sky, and he did recently gun down Sheriff Hawkins. But are not the Kiowa better off because of the sheriff's death? He did not work for our best interests."

"*Ho*, it is his daughter, Zoe, who suffers most from his death," Black Beak mumbled. "But still I cannot deal with such a man as Carl Collins."

"You have no other choice," Red Thunder said, edging his horse closer to Black Beak's. "We have come this far. The canyon lies just ahead. You will come with us, Black Beak, or forever see us as your ardent enemies."

Red Thunder gazed around Black Beak at Eagle Claw. "Is not that so, Eagle Claw?" he said darkly.

"That is so," Eagle Claw said, then rode onward toward the canyon.

Black Beak held back for a moment when his friends rode away from him.

He looked over his shoulder at the three horses he led, and then gazed ahead at Red Thunder and Eagle Claw who were determinedly riding onward. His jaw tight, he rode forward and joined them again.

"Friends forever?" Eagle Claw said, reaching a hand out for Black Beak.

Black Beak hesitated, but then clasped his hand around Eagle Claw's. "*Ho*, friends forever," he said, yet without much conviction. He could not help worrying about the consequences of his actions should his cousin discover everything he'd done today. In the past, Black Beak had seen young men his age banished from the tribe for being so disobedient to their chief.

Feeling trapped, Black Beak rode into the deep shadows of the canyon. The high stone walls on either side of him seemed to close him in.

Finally they came to the far end of the canyon, which leveled out into a flat terrain of rock and scrub trees; a slow stream wound across the land beside a cabin. Black Beak strained his neck to see the outlaw, who was already outside inspecting the horses as Red Thunder and Eagle Claw sat on their horses, waiting.

When Black Beak rode up and reined in beside Red Thunder, he got his first full look at the notorious outlaw who was going from town to town taking the lives of lawmen. He was a tall, lanky man with shoulder-length golden hair that was tangled and greasy. His eyes were gray, beady, and filled with meanness. A narrow mustache covered his upper lip, a cigarette hanging limply from the corner of his mouth.

Pistols hung heavy in holsters at each of his hips. He held a rifle clutched tightly in his hand.

It was his clothes that made Black Beak's nose twitch. There was such a stench emanating from his wrinkled and soiled breeches and shirt, Black Beak doubted the man had bathed for weeks. The smell was a mixture of tobacco, perspiration, horse leather, and urine.

"And so you also want to part with these fine steeds, eh?" Carl said as he walked over to Black Beak and gazed at the horses tied behind him.

Black Beak nodded stiffly and watched the evil man go back and inspect each of the strong, muscled horses.

"Yep, I think we can make us a deal," he said, inspecting the brand on the rump of each of the horses. "I can change the brand easily enough to look like mine. That way, I can sell them without question whenever I decide to."

Red Thunder and Eagle Claw smiled triumphantly at Black Beak as Carl Collins went inside his cabin and came out again with a bag of coins.

"I know you," Carl said, staring up at Black Beak. "You're Chief White Shadow's cousin." He chuckled. "I didn't know he approved of thievery, or is it something you do behind your cousin's back?"

Black Beak's spine stiffened, for Carl had said exactly the thing that would make Black Beak regret what he was involved in today.

He refused to answer the man.

He even hesitated to hold out his hand for the bag of *adalhangya*.

"The money," Carl said, looking from one Kiowa brave to the other. "Which one is trusted enough to carry the money?"

Black Beak quickly held out his hand, after all, for today he had lost much of his friends' trust and respect. If anyone was going to be in charge of money earned by underhanded means, it would be he.

At least until they got to the gambling halls.

Then he would divide it equally between Red Thunder and Eagle Claw. The sooner it was gambled away, the better he would feel about it.

And never again would he be a part of anything like this. He would not chance ruining his relationship with his cousin.

Black Beak rode ahead of Red Thunder and Eagle Claw as they made their way out of the canyon. When they reached the open spaces again, Black Beak was flanked on each side by the two Kiowa braves.

"We should go to a different town today to gamble," Eagle Claw said, eying the bag of coins that

Black Beak had tied to the waist of his buckskin breeches. "Surely the gamblers or owners of the gambling houses in Muddy won't care whether or not our skins are red or white." He laughed. "Not as long as we have many coins to spend in their establishments."

He still stared at the bag of coins, and then glared up at Black Beak. "We *are* going to spend the money today on gambling, are we not?" he asked, his voice a low hiss.

Black Beak looked slowly over at him. His eyes were cold as he nodded. "*Ho*, we will gamble," he said. "But it is my last time to gamble or steal with you."

"Do you think that truly matters to me?" Eagle Claw said icily. "You are not my only friend." He looked over at Red Thunder. "Is that not so, Red Thunder? Would you not choose friendship with me over Black Beak's?"

Red Thunder said nothing in return. His eyes wavered as he found Black Beak staring at him, awaiting an answer.

Red Thunder then turned toward Eagle Claw. "I make no choices now between friends," he said. "Do we not have many coins to gamble with today? We should be merry. Not sad. It is not a time to turn away from each other. Did we not plan to enjoy more than gambling together? There is the Fourth of July celebration. We should look forward to seeing it together. Have we not vowed a lifetime of friendship between us? Do vows mean so little to you both? To me they are forever."

Black Beak did feel loyalty to his friend Red

Thunder, with whom he had learned how to hunt, to do everything that would eventually make them warriors.

Yet there was his cousin.

There was . . . always . . . his cousin.

Chapter Twelve

When dark thoughts my boding spirit shroud,
Sweet Hope, celestial influence round me shed,
Waving thy silver pinions o'er my head.
                              —John Keats

After an exhausting day of following Zoe, who had
not gone anywhere near the reservation, White
Shadow headed for home. He was going to put
Zoe from his mind, at least until tomorrow, when
he would go again and observe her actions.

He now wanted to see how Timothy Livingston
had fared during his first full day at White
Shadow's village, forced into the life of a Kiowa.
White Shadow had expected more rebellion from
the pony soldier . . . his *brother*.

The more White Shadow thought about how
quickly Timothy had accepted his fate, the more

White Shadow thought that Timothy might be lulling his captors, while all along making plans to escape his bondage.

White Shadow smiled as he thought of his brother trying to make his escape. He would not get near the outer perimeters of the village without being stopped. Everyone knew how dangerous it would be for the Kiowa if Timothy managed to get to the fort and explain what had happened to him at the hands of the Kiowa. The pony soldiers would delight in making the Kiowa pay in the worst way for having wronged one of their leaders, not knowing that this very leader had Kiowa blood running through his veins.

Just as White Shadow saw the smoke spiraling into the sky from his people's lodges, he noted several of his warriors approaching him on horseback. Their hasty exit from the village stirred up clouds of dust beneath the hooves of their steeds.

White Shadow hated to guess why his men would be riding so swiftly toward him. Had Timothy escaped, after all?

White Shadow cast his eyes heavenward and saw that the sky was darkening. If his brother had just escaped the village, and if he had escaped on foot, he would not get to the fort before nightfall.

That would mean that he would be out there somewhere, vulnerable without a weapon, and cold without the sort of clothes he was accustomed to wearing. Although it was summer, night came down upon this land like cold, clawing fingers.

Strange, White Shadow thought to himself, how he was suddenly concerned about the welfare of Timothy Livingston. He wondered if, deep down, it was because of the bond he now knew he had with the man.

Or was it because he knew that if anything happened to Timothy, his mother's heart would break?

White Shadow sank his heels into the flanks of his horse and rode toward the warriors. He pulled his horse to a halt as they drew a tight rein around him.

White Shadow edged his horse closer to Lightning Flash's. "My friend, what is the cause of your haste?" he asked, waiting with a tight jaw to hear Timothy's name spoken. His eyes widened when someone else's name was spoken instead. My cousin? Black Beak he has not returned home from selling his wood blocks in Gracemont," White Shadow said. "The others also have not returned."

"No, none of the young braves are home and they should have been, even as early as the noon hour," Lightning Flash said. His brow furrowed into a frown. "Mothers are upset. Fathers are angry. Most blame Black Beak. They say he is leading his friends down the road to destruction."

"I did not know that my cousin was looked upon as someone who leads friends where they would not go otherwise," White Shadow said, his eyes flashing angrily. "It is wrong that he is singled out and accused in such a way."

"Red Thunder and Eagle Claw's parents fear the

young braves have gambled their profits away today and have gotten into trouble again with the whites," Lightning Flash said. "This is why there are many warriors riding this evening with me. We are going to Gracemont to see if the young braves are behind bars. If so, we plan to order the white woman sheriff to release them. I do not see white gamblers jailed as often as our young braves."

"You are getting way ahead of yourselves," White Shadow said, glaring at Lightning Flash, and then looking past him and giving each of his warriors an angry stare.

White Shadow then gazed again at Lightning Flash. "We will not condemn our braves or the new sheriff unless we see proof that there is a reason to condemn," he said, knowing that if his cousin had been imprisoned, Zoe could not have done it. He had watched her the whole day through. She had not gone to the jail while he had observed her.

Then he thought of the short time when he was not watching her, when he had thought that she was being escorted home. What if she had gone into town instead? What if she was at the jail? What if one of the gambling hall owners had placed the young braves behind bars?

Would Zoe approve? Or would she let them go free as before?

Without saying anything else to his warriors, White Shadow wheeled his horse around and left for Gracemont, his warriors following.

When they arrived in the town, the sky was a

shroud of black. Pale lamp light shone from the windows along the main street.

White Shadow, alone, went into one gambling house and then another. But even after he had been told by the saloon owners that his cousin and his friends had not been there, he wondered if they were lying just to get rid of him.

White Shadow stepped outside on the wooden sidewalk and gazed at the jail. There was no light. Everything was quiet. If his cousin and his friends had been arrested and placed in the jail, they were there without light. He had heard of the hardships of the jail, and how rats scrambled around at night along the wooden floors.

His eyes narrowed angrily; his hand clasped his rifle as he yanked it from his gun boot. White Shadow stamped toward the jail, his friend Lightning Flash beside him.

As he and Lightning Flash entered the jail, silence greeted them.

White Shadow gave Lightning Flash a wary look; then they went together to the back of the jail where the cells stood in rows on each side of the long, narrow room.

Moonlight coming through the small barred windows at the top of each cell gave enough light to prove that no one was incarcerated there. White Shadow was aware of a strange odor, a mixture of mildew and stale cigar smoke.

The smell of cigars reminded him of Zoe's father. He recalled how often he had seen Zoe's father strutting down the center of the town's main street, a cigar clasped between his teeth. He remembered the times Zoe had been with her father, pride in her eyes, completely unaware of how corrupt her father was. The payoffs from criminals surely weren't recorded in any journal, so White Shadow doubted that Zoe would ever know about that side of her father.

"If they are not in Gracemont's gambling houses or saloons, and they are not in the jail, where might they be?" Lightning Flash said, wrenching White Shadow from his thoughts. "White Shadow, what could have happened to them?"

Perhaps, to avoid trouble, Zoe had ordered her deputy to take the young prisoners where the Kiowa warriors could not find them.

"Lightning Flash, come with me," White Shadow said, hurrying to his horse and mounting it. He gazed at his warriors. "Come! There is someone I need to question. We will find our young braves."

The horses' hooves sounded like thunder as they rode through Gracemont.

When White Shadow came to Zoe's cabin, he raised a hand in the air as a command for his warriors to stop. He then motioned with his hand, gesturing to his warriors to surround the cabin.

Zoe had just changed into fresh, clean clothes. She had planned to ride into town to see if things were all right.

The arrival of the horses outside her cabin startled her. Her heart pounding, she went to the front window and slowly lifted the shade.

When she saw that her cabin was surrounded

by many Kiowa warriors, fear leapt into her heart. She singled out White Shadow among the warriors, as he sat tall and straight-backed in his saddle. What had caused him to come to her at this time of night, she wondered, and why had he brought so many warriors with him?

Fighting back the fear that she did not want to feel in the presence of White Shadow, Zoe opened the door and stepped outside on her small porch. Immediately her eyes locked with White Shadow's.

When he did not budge, nor offer her a friendly smile, the look in her eyes became challenging. Zoe would not allow him to see that she felt threatened, and hurt, at his being there in such a way.

Surely something had happened to his young cousin, she thought. There was no other reason why he would come with so many companions.

She looked slowly past him and saw that each of the warriors was heavily armed. And there was danger in the way the warriors glared at her, as though she were their enemy.

She tried to understand why they would feel this way. Maybe it was because her father had been so prejudiced against the Kiowa.

Probably they thought that she was no less prejudiced.

"Why are you here?" she blurted out, her eyes again locked with White Shadow's.

"My cousin," White Shadow said grimly. "My cousin Black Beak. Where . . . is . . . he?"

Chapter Thirteen

It is, past escape,
Herself, now; the dream is done
And the shadow and she are one.
          —Robert Browning

"Zoe, my cousin Black Beak and his friends are missing," White Shadow persisted, trying to hide how deeply he was disturbed by her obvious sudden fear of him.

That was the last thing he wanted.

It was hard for him to understand how their relationship had altered so quickly. Had it been only a few days ago that they had been sharing secret meetings filled with love?

"They are missing?" Zoe asked.

She breathed much more easily when she saw

that White Shadow's attitude had softened. His voice was now not so accusing.

"And you thought that I might know where they are?" she asked. "Why?"

"You are sheriff," White Shadow said. "Does that not mean that you should know what happens in Gracemont?"

"I don't know everything that happens," Zoe said, taking a slow step toward him. "But I can tell you that I am certain your cousin and his friends didn't cause trouble in the saloons tonight."

She looked down at the ground and kneaded her chin as she thought for a moment. She tried to imagine where Black Beak and his friends might have gone.

"Muddy," she whispered, her eyes widening.

She looked quickly up at White Shadow. "I bet they have gone to Muddy! Only recently a new gambling house was opened there. I heard that it's drawing many people from Gracemont's establishments. The owners of the gambling houses in Gracemont are mad enough to bite nails about this."

"Bite nails?" White Shadow said, arching his eyebrows. "White men bite nails?"

"Well, perhaps some are biting their *finger*nails out of frustration, but not actual nails," Zoe said, smiling up at White Shadow. "It was just a way of saying how angry the men have become. That's all."

"You believe, then, that my cousin and the other

135

two braves might be at the small town called Muddy?" White Shadow asked.

"Yes, I truly believe that's where you might find them," Zoe said softly.

She gazed into White Shadow's eyes, for a moment feeling the bond that had formed between them before she'd damaged it by telling him she couldn't marry him.

She could still see much depth in his feelings for her. And soon she would prove hers for him once again. He would never again be given a reason to doubt her love for him.

Not after she told him that she wanted to marry him and live with him forever.

"Do you want me to go with you to Muddy to see if they are there?" Zoe asked. "If they are, and they have gotten into trouble with the law, it would be best if I accompanied you there to speak in their behalf."

"*Ho*, I would like for you to ride with me and my warriors," he said, his heart leaping with joy when he saw how this made Zoe's eyes brighten.

Yet her exuberance and her obvious happiness to ride with him confused him. If everything he had heard about her was true, if she didn't love him, why would she seem so happy to do this for him?

He was discovering that white women were much more complicated than Kiowa women. He wondered if he had ever known the true Zoe?

With her Colts holstered at her hips, her hair loose and flowing down her back, Zoe rode beside him toward Muddy.

Beneath the moonlight, Zoe could not help recalling those days not so long ago when she and White Shadow had laughed and kissed.

Her thoughts were jolted back to the present when she heard gunfire and loud voices from somewhere up ahead. She could just barely see the outskirts of Muddy, but that was enough to show that the gunfire and the shouts were coming from there.

And as she grew closer, she could see torches. Many torches. A keen fear gripped her heart, for she knew where those torches were being held.

She knew the town of Muddy well enough to know where the jail was located. And that was where an angry crowd had assembled with their torches.

A terrible apprehension swept through Zoe. It seemed that everywhere Black Beak and his Kiowa buddies went, trouble followed them.

Zoe gave White Shadow a wavering glance, then rode on into town with him and drew her horse to a quick stop near the crowd of men. Their foul curse words almost burned her ears, they were so profane and loud.

Dismounting along with White Shadow, Zoe stood beside him. She glanced at the warriors who were still sitting in their saddles, and then peered up at White Shadow.

"Let me go and see what's happened," she said, resting a hand on one of her holstered Colts. "Please keep your warriors away from the crowd until I see if I need their help."

Seeing the logic in what she suggested, White

137

Shadow nodded and stood his ground. He watched Zoe as she elbowed her way through the crowd, and then waited with a stiff jaw for her to return.

He was sure that his cousin was responsible for the anger in this small town tonight. Black Beak seemed born for trouble. It was certain that he met it head-on and seemed to enjoy it.

"This has to change," White Shadow whispered, his eyes angrily flashing. "Enough is enough."

Zoe finally found her way inside the jail. She didn't have to ask the sheriff what the problem was. She saw it. She saw *them*. Black Beak and his friends were standing behind the bars, their eyes filled with defiance.

"Zoe, those damn savages just don't know how to stay on their reservation," Sheriff Sam Tate said, nervously fidgeting with his thick black mustache; his eyes were troubled. "A fight broke out in the new gambling house tonight between the redskins and whites. The whites started it. I put the Kiowa braves behind bars to protect them from that mob out there. It seems that even though Jack Potter started the fight, he convinced everyone that the savages were responsible. Those men outside are out for blood."

"You should have more control over things than this," Zoe said, placing her hands on her hips. "Lord, Sam, those men out there are ready to burn your jail down to get at the Kiowa braves. Where are your deputies?"

"Out there," Sheriff Tate grumbled, motioning

toward the closed door. "They joined the crowd. I'm in this alone."

"Well, you aren't any longer," Zoe said, yanking the keys to the cells from a nail on the wall. "Come on. Give me some cover with your rifle as I leave the jail with the braves. I'm going to take them under my protective custody until they leave town; then they'll go on to their reservation with their chief."

"It's risky," Sheriff Tate said, yanking up his rifle. He checked to make sure it was loaded.

"I don't think so," Zoe said, opening the door to the cell and nodding to the young braves. "Those men out there will soon come to their senses when they shut up their yapping long enough to turn around and get an eyeful of how many Kiowa warriors are on their steeds behind them. I think most men still have a fear of being scalped by Indians, don't you?"

"Yeah," Sheriff Tate said, laughing awkwardly. "Seems so."

"Go out there and tell the men I'm coming through with the braves. Then tell them to look behind themselves and see the warriors," Zoe said, yanking a Colt from her holster. "I'll bring the braves out with me. Keep the crowd under control, Sam, or we'll all be dead before you can say scat."

She watched Sam walk outside. She listened to him shout at the crowd. Luckily, he soon got them to quiet down enough to listen to what he had to say.

She smiled when she could almost see them

turning to look at the Kiowa warriors behind them. She knew that they wouldn't dare start anything.

"Come on," Zoe said, turning to motion with her head toward Black Beak. "All of you. Step outside with me. Stay close. And please don't start any more trouble. Ignore anything that might be said to you. I want to get you out of this town in one piece."

The young warriors nodded. They followed her outside and walked with her through the crowd of men, which parted for them reluctantly.

White Shadow glared at Black Beak, and then the other two braves. He grabbed Black Beak by an arm and yanked him over to Black Beak's horse, which was tied up outside the jail.

"You disgrace your chief again?" White Shadow growled. "When . . . will . . . this stop?"

Black Beak hung his head, and then mounted his horse.

Zoe kept a nervous eye on the crowd as Eagle Claw and Red Thunder swung themselves into their saddles. She gave White Shadow a quick glance and a nod; then she mounted her horse as he hurried onto his.

Her Colt still in one hand, her reins in the other, Zoe led the way out of Muddy.

When they got to the edge of town, White Shadow turned and placed a hand in the air as a command for his warriors to stop. Zoe drew a tight rein beside him.

"Lightning Flash, make sure the braves get home," White Shadow said. He again gazed sternly at the young braves. "Make sure each of them apologizes to his parents before retiring for the night."

Lightning Flash nodded.

Zoe watched them all ride off, and then looked at White Shadow. "I guess I'll be going on home, myself," she murmured. "I'm glad I was able to help you tonight, White Shadow. I'm just sorry it was necessary."

"You are sorry because it threw us together again?" White Shadow asked his voice tight.

Hearing the hurt in his voice, Zoe edged her horse closer to his. "I have much to tell you," she murmured. "I think now is the time. Can we go somewhere and sit and talk?"

"Follow me," he said softly.

Zoe nodded and smiled. As she rode beside him, she soon recognized where he was taking her. It was familiar to them both. It was their trysting place, where they had known feelings so sweet and sincere, but also where she had broken his trust by making him believe that she didn't truly love him.

She was not going to wait any longer to tell him the truth about everything. She was going to open up to him and tell him everything.

She was so glad that he was ready to listen. That had to mean that she still had a chance with him. Just perhaps their futures *could* still be intertwined.

Chapter Fourteen

Today or this noon
She dwelt so close,
I almost touched her.
—Emily Dickinson

The place was so familiar, so filled with memories, Zoe had to fight back a strong urge to fling herself into White Shadow's arms as he knelt beside a circle of rocks, in which a fire was taking hold in the small twigs and dried tree branches.

She hated delaying for even one more moment telling him just how much she loved him. She was ready to beg for his forgiveness, if that was required to regain his total love and trust.

But instead, she sat on the blanket he had spread for her, and watched him build a fire to ward off the chill of night.

It seemed he planned to spend some time there, instead of just rushing through their explanations. No. He did not seem ready to rush through anything.

The stars, the moon, the soft, dark sky overhead, and the magic of a fire at night would help them get through the necessary explanations and apologies.

And then? Oh, what then, she wondered? Would he hold her? Would he kiss her? Would he tell her that he still wanted her?

Her thoughts were halted when White Shadow turned to her, his dark eyes intense, his jaw tight. The fire's glow lent a sheen to his copper skin. It intensified the dark gleam in his eyes. It played on the sculpted contours of his face, accentuating his handsomeness.

"You came with me tonight because you have things to say," White Shadow said, resting on his haunches before her. "Say them, Zoe. I am here to listen."

"We've never been here at night before," Zoe said, her heart pounding as she felt a magical spell being woven between them.

"No, we have never been here at night before," White Shadow said.

He fought the urge to place his arms around her and draw her against him. He sensed that she wanted to be held and caressed. And he knew that she still loved him!

Her engagement to Timothy made absolutely no sense to White Shadow.

"Why, Zoe?" he blurted out. "Why did you

promise to marry Timothy Livingston?"

Zoe was taken aback by the abruptness of the question. So he did know of her promise to marry Timothy. That explained so many things.

His anger toward her had not been solely because she had taken on her father's duties as sheriff. He had been angry because he thought she loved someone else.

"I never truly promised to marry Timothy," she said.

"To the Kiowa, a promise is a promise," White Shadow said, his eyes narrowing. He doubted if she would be truthful with him at all tonight, since she had started their moments alone beneath the stars already lying to him! "You either promised him, or you did not. Which . . . is . . . it, Zoe?"

Zoe sighed heavily and lowered her eyes. She inhaled another deep breath, and then gazed up at White Shadow again, their eyes locking and holding.

"The promise was never made to Timothy," she said softly.

White Shadow reached out and gently clasped his hands on Zoe's shoulders. He drew her closer. "What do you mean?" he said thickly. "Word was brought to me that you promised to marry the man. Are you saying now that you never promised him? That you never intended to marry him? You lied?"

"Yes, I lied," Zoe said, her eyes searching his, hoping to see his anger and confusion change into soft understanding. "But the lie was necessary,

White Shadow. I . . . I . . . did it because of my father."

"The more you say, the more confused I get," White Shadow said, dropping his hands to his sides.

He stood and stared into the fire. He still felt that she was playing games with him. Unsure whether or not he would stay another moment with her, he doubled his hands into tight fists at his sides.

Seeing that she was making things worse instead of better, Zoe rushed to her feet. She placed herself between White Shadow and the fire. Then she took his fists and slowly undid his fingers until she could hold his hands.

"Darling, oh, darling White Shadow, please listen to what I have to say," she murmured. "If you still love me, you will listen. Oh, White Shadow, there have been too many misunderstandings these recent days. Let me explain. Then you will see that I never stopped loving you. Not for even one second."

White Shadow nodded. He reveled in the touch of her hands. His anger was soothed by her nearness and the sweetness of her voice, and he knew that things had never truly changed between them. Even without her explanation, he knew that she still loved him.

"White Shadow, as my father lay dying, he begged me to marry Timothy Livingston," Zoe said.

"Father wanted me to have the life of ease that Timothy could give me. When I saw how important it was to my father, I felt I had to make the promise. White Shadow, I loved my father. I would have done anything so that he could die in peace. *Anything.* When my mother died, Father became both a mother and a father to me. I owed him everything, White Shadow."

She slid her hands free of his and framed his face between them. "Now, my love, I am making a promise to you," she murmured. "I will never marry anyone but you. I have never loved anyone but you. I . . . just . . . never had the chance to explain things to Timothy. The very night I was going to tell him . . . he disappeared."

White Shadow's spine stiffened as he thought of why Zoe had not been able to explain things to Timothy.

"And, White Shadow," Zoe continued softly, "because of Timothy's disappearance, I am not free to reveal my love for you to the world. Not until Timothy is found and I can first tell him. I want to be fair to the man."

White Shadow's eyes widened. He felt caught between two women now: his mother, who wanted to keep Timothy hidden from the world; and Zoe, who would not marry White Shadow until she could tell Timothy the truth about the promise she'd made to a dying man. As long as Timothy was held captive at his village, Zoe would never be free to marry White Shadow.

His eyes narrowed angrily, for Timothy Livingston was not worthy of her loyalty.

"Fair?" he finally said. "You say you want to be fair to Timothy Livingston by postponing our wedding? Is that fair to me, the man you say you love? Have I not been forced to endure your silence . . . your rejection . . . long enough?"

Then he took a step away from her. "And, Zoe, Timothy has nothing to do with the reason why you walked away from me that day, when you told me that you could never marry me," he said thickly. His jaw tightened. "No. I do not think you are being entirely truthful with me tonight, let alone being fair."

"I have told you everything," she said, paling at his words. "Why do you think I am lying?"

"Do you forget how you rejected my proposal of marriage?" White Shadow ground out, his hands doubled into fists again. "Do you forget that I waited for you to come and tell me why, and you never came?"

Zoe's eyes widened. "I'm sorry," she whispered. "I forgot to explain about that." She rushed to him and flung herself into his arms. "My darling, it was my father! I was afraid to marry you because of my father! I was afraid that if I went to him and told him that I wished to be your wife, he would come gunning for you. He never would have allowed me to marry you. I had no choice but to—"

White Shadow placed a hand beneath her chin and urged her eyes up to meet his. "You were afraid for White Shadow?" he said thickly. "That is why you turned your back on me? Because you did not trust that White Shadow could defend himself against the likes of your father? Do you think so little of my abilities to fend for myself?"

Zoe took a step away from him. "The likes of my father?" she gasped out. "Even in death you speak so unkindly of him?" She choked back a sob. "I know that he was unfair to your people, yet on the other hand, didn't you ever see the goodness in the man?"

"Goodness?" White Shadow said, laughing. His laugh was full of sarcasm. "Your father? A man who was so corrupt?"

His eyes narrowed as he glared at the badge pinned on Zoe's shirt.

Then he gazed into her eyes again. "Now that you wear your father's badge, do you intend to carry on his corrupt ways?" he asked in a low hiss. "Are you made in the same mold as your father?"

Zoe's spine stiffened. She lifted her chin. "I'll have you know that I would gladly walk in my father's shadow any day!" she cried. "And what do you mean by calling him corrupt? I tell you he was a good man!"

Seeing that this argument was driving them apart again, White Shadow decided not to say anything more against Zoe's father.

Zoe lowered her eyes. She sobbed. "How can you say such things about my father?" she said. "Have you no respect for the dead? Have you no respect for me . . . my father's daughter?"

Feeling her hurt, and feeling guilty for having caused it, White Shadow reached out for Zoe and drew her into his tender embrace.

He held her close and ran his fingers through her hair. "I say words that hurt you," he said softly. "I will say them no more."

He placed a hand beneath her chin and forced her to gaze up at him. "I want you," he said huskily. "Now, *Manyi*. I have waited for you all of my life. Must I wait another night?"

Her heart pounding, her knees weak, Zoe knew what he was asking of her. She blotted everything out of her mind that had just been said, especially about her father, and lifted her lips to his.

"I have waited forever for *you*," she whispered against his lips. "It's been pure torture, White Shadow. Please make love to me. Please? You are all that is right in my world. You are my everything."

White Shadow covered her lips with his mouth and gave her a long, deep kiss, their tongues touching. He held her tightly against him as he gently guided her down upon the blanket.

While they kissed in a frenzy, the heat of their breaths mingling, their hearts athunder, White Shadow managed to remove Zoe's blouse. His hands trembled as he filled them with her round, warm breasts, the nipples hard against his palms.

Zoe sucked in a wild, quick breath of pleasure when White Shadow bent low over her and flicked his tongue across one of her nipples. Then he devoured it with his mouth, his tongue licking, his teeth nipping.

Breathless, her very soul on fire with the heat of their passion, Zoe eased out of his arms and watched him as he stood up and hurriedly undressed. She bent over and yanked off her boots, and then stood before him and shoved her breeches down her shapely, slender legs.

Finally they were both nude, the moon's glow like silver as it washed across their bodies. Zoe's breath caught when White Shadow reached a hand out and began slowly moving it along her body. She closed her eyes and sighed when he filled his hands with her breasts. He moved his hands lower, and her belly quivered as his fingers swept over it.

She held her head back and shivered when his hand went lower and slowly parted the curly fronds of hair at the juncture of her thighs.

She gasped and pushed herself closer to his hand when his fingers wove through the patch of hair and found her woman's center. Slowly he began to caress her.

"Touch me as I touch you," White Shadow said, his request spoken so huskily it drew Zoe's eyes open.

She gazed into his eyes as his free hand sought one of hers. She scarcely breathed as he led her hand to his manhood. Her breath quickened when he urged her fingers around his thick shaft.

"Move your fingers on me," White Shadow said, his body stiffening with intense pleasure when she did as he asked.

He closed his eyes as tremors cascaded down his back. He swallowed hard when he felt the heat of pleasure rising within him.

Zoe knew that she was giving White Shadow much pleasure with her hand. She was in awe of this part of his body. It seemed alive as it throbbed against the flesh of her fingers.

"Enough," White Shadow soon whispered. He

took her hand away from his aching heat. He sighed. "Enough . . . enough."

He held her within his arms as he once again led her down to the blanket.

He spread her out beneath him and then pressed against her, his manhood now softly probing where his fingers had readied her for his entrance.

"There will be some pain, but soon it will pass," he whispered. He kissed her long and hard as he slowly inched himself inside her.

It was good to know that he was the first man with her. He would make certain that he was the last. She was his, forever and ever.

They would make many babies! They would have many grandchildren!

Zoe winced when White Shadow shoved himself fully into her. She tightened beneath him as he began his slow thrusts, pressing deeper into her softly yielding folds.

Zoe clung to him and moaned against his lips as she felt the pain turn to pleasure. Desire washed over her. What they were sharing, what he was awakening in her, was far more wonderful than she had ever imagined it could be. As the pleasure built within her, her body jolted and quivered.

"It is good for you?" White Shadow whispered into her ear. "You are feeling everything that I am feeling? You are realizing that our bodies are meant only for each other?"

"Yes, only for each other," Zoe whispered back, whimpering with pleasure as he slid his mouth down to one of her breasts and swept his tongue slowly around the nipple.

She wove her fingers through his long, thick hair and urged his mouth even closer. "It feels so wonderful," she whispered, sighing when his teeth nibbled on the nipple.

"Wonderful in the Kiowa tongue is said in this way . . . *zedalbe*," White Shadow said huskily. "Tell me in Kiowa, it is wonderful."

"*Zedalbe*," Zoe said softly. "Loving you is *zedalbe*."

He then kissed her lips again.

Her response was quick. Her kiss was sensuous, demanding, hot. His tongue probed between her open lips, and her tongue eagerly touched his.

His hands went beneath her buttocks and lifted her closer to his aching need. Waves of liquid heat pulsed through White Shadow's body as he felt her arching up against him to eagerly meet each of his thrusts. He stabbed into her, his mind splintering with sensations never known to him before.

He gasped, slowed his strokes, then plunged into her again as the ultimate of pleasure overwhelmed him. He clung to her as he thrust over and over into her. He placed his cheek against her breast, smiling when he realized that she, too, was in the throes of wild passion. She gripped his shoulders and whimpered and sobbed as the pleasure pumped through her in waves of rapture.

Afterwards, as they lay clinging to each other beside the fire, their breathing ragged, Zoe was amazed by what she had just experienced. It had been pure bliss, utter joy! And to know that she had a lifetime ahead of her of such pleasure with the man she loved filled her with wonder.

"There are too many things still standing in the way of our being together," Zoe said, turning on her side to gaze at White Shadow.

She slowly ran a hand up and down his flat belly. His manhood looked strangely small compared to what it had been only moments ago. That, too, surprised her.

"I *must* find my father's killer," she said. "I must! And then there is Timothy. Where could he be? I must tell him the truth before I tell anyone about *us*."

White Shadow looked away from her, for he knew that he could not do anything about Timothy. Not yet, anyhow. But surely, his mother would soon realize that Timothy was never going to accept his Kiowa heritage.

Ho, White Shadow would have to wait for a while longer before encouraging his mother to set Timothy free. But what would happen then? If Timothy was released and he went to the white pony soldiers at Fort Cobb with the news that he had been abducted by the Kiowa, the Kiowa would pay for the abduction!

"You are suddenly so quiet," Zoe murmured, scooting closer, shaping her body into the contours of White Shadow's. "Was it something I said?"

"*Ho*, I do not want you to place yourself in danger by going out hunting for the killer of your father," White Shadow said, only giving her half-truths about his deep concerns.

This thing with Timothy would have to work itself out. He could not wait long before taking Zoe home as his wife.

"I must find Carl Collins," Zoe said, resting her cheek against White Shadow's chest. "Please don't ask me not to. My father's death must be avenged." She leaned up on an elbow and gazed into his eyes. "Surely you understand. Surely you have felt the need for vengeance sometime in your life."

"Many times," White Shadow did not hesitate to say.

"Then please don't ask me not to do what I must for my father," Zoe said, sighing.

Again he was tempted to tell her that her father did not deserve such loyalty. If she only knew how corrupt her father had been, she would not waste another minute worrying about vengeance.

But he knew how she loved the man who had been both mother and father to her. It would be cruel to erase what good she knew about him. It might even make her hate White Shadow for revealing the truth to her.

Chapter Fifteen

What heart alike conceived and dared?
What act proved all its thought had been?
    —Robert Browning

White Shadow had slept soundly through the night for the first time since the day Zoe had told him that she could never marry him.

Now that things had reversed, and he knew that she would one day soon be his wife, he felt as though all was right in his world again . . . except for Timothy Livingston.

No longer seeing Timothy as competition for Zoe's love, White Shadow had ceased to feel resentment toward him.

But Timothy did still complicate his life. Zoe would not marry White Shadow until she had been given the chance to explain things to Timothy. Yet how could she while Timothy was a captive of the Kiowa?

White Shadow stood in the shadows behind the lodges as he watched Short Legs, Timothy's teacher today, teaching Timothy how to butcher a cow.

"You slice the meat thin and hang it up to dry in the sun," Short Legs said. "That way it will keep for the winter. It is put into a bag made of hide to keep it."

"But what do you do with all of these bones from the cow?" Timothy asked, wiping his hands on a buckskin cloth. "Do you throw them away? Or do you give them to the dogs?"

"The bones are never thrown away and they are not given to the dogs," Short Legs said, seeming mortified at the mere suggestion. "Like the buffalo of long ago, nothing of the cow is wasted. The bones are broken up and boiled to get the marrow out. The marrow is put into a bag made of the cow's udder."

"Is beef the most important staple of your people's diet?" Timothy asked, feeling guilty that he had sometimes cheated the Kiowa of their full allotment of cows.

"My people do not enjoy the taste of beef," Short Legs said solemnly. "They still prefer buffalo. They eat cow because it is the meat your people allot to my people. But know also that, like our ancestors, my people still live from the land, from foods gathered in the wild."

Short Legs began to methodically break the cow bones with sharp blows from a hammer. "Wild grapes are gathered in the fall," he said. "They are boiled up, mixed with flour, and made into balls. They are placed in skin bags to keep. Mesquite beans are ground up and put away. The ground beans are used for cooking like corn meal."

White Shadow smiled at how Short Legs seemed to be enjoying his job of teaching today. And it surprised White Shadow to see how quickly his brother was learning each thing that the Kiowa warriors were teaching him.

White Shadow was astonished how Timothy's attitude had changed. His demeanor was no longer brash and arrogant. He no longer cursed the Kiowa. He was not rude to anyone.

White Shadow could not help but wonder if the Kiowa in Timothy was the cause of the change in the man.

Did he feel a closeness, a bond, to the Kiowa he worked with each day?

For his mother's sake, and for Timothy's own, White Shadow hoped that his brother would soon realize . . . and accept . . . his transition.

Having called a council with his top warriors, White Shadow turned and walked toward his large council house in the center of the village.

When he saw Thunder Stick sitting outside his tepee smoking his peyote pipe, a feeling of uneasiness swept through him. Thunder Stick and his love of peyote could jeopardize everything for White Shadow's mother. If he did not keep his thoughts clear, and Timothy managed to escape, all of the Kiowa's lives would be endangered.

But White Shadow had to trust his mother's

judgment, and she had chosen Thunder Stick to be in charge of Timothy while he was at the Kiowa village.

Soon White Shadow would meet with Thunder Stick and see how Timothy's lessons were progressing. He hoped they would be completed soon. He hoped Timothy would accept the truth about his heritage.

If Timothy did anything to hurt his mother, White Shadow would quickly forget that he was any blood kin to him.

White Shadow would destroy him!

Chapter Sixteen

Nay, thou art worthy of hearing my whole mind.
—Robert Browning

Zoe was dismounting from her horse in front of the jail when a stagecoach stopped a few yards away. She watched the door of the stagecoach open as she wound her reins around the hitching rail. Her eyes widened when she saw who stepped down. It was Mary Ellen Strupp, Timothy's sister, and her husband Rob.

Zoe could hardly believe they had arrived already. Timothy had only recently told her he had wired them. The fact that they'd arrived so soon meant that he had wired his sister long before Zoe's father had died.

Timothy had probably wired them the first time he had asked Zoe to marry him. Even though she had turned him down, he must have been confident that he could eventually persuade her to become his wife. So confident that he had wired his sister to come to Gracemont for the wedding.

Zoe scarcely knew Mary Ellen and Rob. She had become briefly acquainted with them when they had attended the same church. She had known Mary Ellen to be a stuffy, snobby person who flaunted her wealth with the clothes and diamonds she wore. It was known that she and Timothy had been spoiled rotten when they were growing up.

But that had been before Zoe knew them.

When Timothy grew old enough to leave home to attend military school, he had left Boston. Zoe had only become acquainted with him when she and her father had arrived in Gracemont. From that point on his wooing of Zoe had been endless, and oh, so very annoying.

And now he was missing.

How was she going to tell Mary Ellen? Although she didn't like the woman, she dreaded having to tell her that her brother had disappeared.

Zoe watched Mary Ellen scold the stagecoach driver for tossing her luggage too roughly to the ground. She could see that the woman was worn ragged. It had been wrong of Timothy to wire his sister and inconvenience her and her husband with the lie that he and Zoe were going to be married.

The nerve of the man! The conceit!

Zoe now also had to tell Mary Ellen that she had

been brought clear out to Oklahoma for a wedding that would never happen.

Wanting to get the worst of things behind her, Zoe went to the other woman. "Mary Ellen?" she murmured, watching Mary Ellen's violet eyes narrow as she turned and found Zoe standing there.

Zoe was amazed at how little Mary Ellen had aged.

She must be nearly thirty, yet she looked no older than Zoe herself.

"Zoe," Mary Ellen said stiffly. Reaching up to readjust her hat, which was covered with lace and artificial flowers, Mary Ellen stepped back from Zoe and slowly raked her eyes over her.

Then Mary Ellen forced a smile. "Seems you are still a tomboy," she said, her voice revealing her distaste at the way Zoe was dressed. Mary Ellen had surely not seen many women in breeches and a ten-gallon hat!

"Yes, it seems that I am," Zoe said, trying not to take offense. She lifted her hat from her head and held it behind her as Rob turned and smiled her way.

A man of forty, he was tall and thin. His baldness was revealed as he took his hat off as a courtesy to Zoe.

"The journey was ghastly," Mary Ellen said, fidgeting with the lace collar on her lovely violet silk dress. "The stagecoach was so hot, so . . . so . . . smelly."

"Yes, I'm sure it was all of those things," Zoe said, trying to find the courage to tell Mary Ellen what had happened. She decided to wait until she got Mary Ellen out of the sun.

She knew that Mary Ellen wouldn't enjoy being taken to the jail for conversation. She glanced at the only hotel in town. It was dirty and dingy, and the beds were said to be infested with bugs.

But until Timothy returned, Zoe did not feel it was right to invade his privacy by taking people to his house and telling them to make themselves at home. Not even his sister.

"Come with me, Mary Ellen," Zoe said. "I'll see to it that you get the best room at the hotel."

"But I thought as soon as Timothy was aware of the stagecoach's arrival he would send some of his men to escort me and my husband to his home at the fort," Mary Ellen said.

Mary Ellen slid a lacy handkerchief from where she had hidden it inside the cuff of a sleeve of her dress. She patted it along her damp brow. "Zoe, can't you arrange to take me and Rob to Timothy's home at the fort now? I'm anxious to see Timothy. And . . . and . . . he has told me of the wonderful comforts of his home." She frowned as she stared at the grimy windows of the hotel as she stopped in front of it. "This place. Is it truly habitable?"

Zoe wasn't sure how to answer that.

She was glad when Rob spoke up as he took his wife by the elbow and escorted her toward the door. "Now, dear, stop being so fussy," he said. "I'm sure the hotel will be just fine until Timothy can make other arrangements for us."

After they were checked in and taken to their room on the second floor, Zoe stood back and watched as Mary Ellen inspected the room, sneezing as she brushed dust from the furniture.

"Horrid," Mary Ellen sighed. "Oh, this is just horrid."

"Mary Ellen, please stop complaining," Rob said as he hung his hat on a peg on the wall.

He went to Mary Ellen and slid several hat pins from her hat, then lifted it gently from her head, revealing swirls of soft red curls around the crown of her head, held in place by diamond-encrusted combs.

Zoe went to Mary Ellen. "Mary Ellen, I think you might want to sit down," she murmured, nodding toward the only chair in the room. "There's something I have to tell you."

Mary Ellen stared at the upholstered chair; its stuffing was hanging out on each side.

Then she sat down and sighed. "I am beginning to think that coming here was a ghastly mistake," she said, again blotting sweat from her brow with her handkerchief. She nodded toward the one window in the room. "Rob, *please* open the window. I . . . can . . . hardly breathe."

"I don't think you want to do that," Zoe said, wincing when Rob went ahead and opened it and dust blew in from the street below as several horsemen came into town at a fast gallop.

Mary Ellen sneezed and sneezed.

Zoe sat down on the edge of the bed. She placed her hat on the bed beside her, and then explained everything to Mary Ellen.

"My brother is missing?" Mary Ellen gasped, paling. "And my brother lied to me?"

Zoe thought she saw relief flood Mary Ellen's face, but she dismissed that thought when the woman hung her face in her hands and began crying.

"Oh, Lord, here I am feeling sorry for myself and . . . and . . . my dear brother is missing," Mary Ellen sobbed.

Rob stood over Zoe. His dark eyes were heavy with concern. "What do you think has happened to Timothy?" he asked thickly. "How can a man just . . . disappear?"

"Out here all things are possible," Zoe said, slowly rising from the bed. She quietly explained about her father's death and burial.

"But don't lose hope about Timothy," Zoe concluded. "I haven't. I'm going out today to search for him again. I won't give up until I have answers."

A knock on the door brought Mary Ellen's head up with a jerk. "Timothy?" she said, bolting from the bed. "Oh, Lord, it's Timothy. Word has reached him about the stagecoach arrival. He's come to take me out of this horrid place."

"But Timothy—"

Zoe didn't get the chance to finish what she was saying. Mary Ellen had already opened the door. She gasped and took a shaky step away from the short, squat, red-whiskered man who stood outside.

Zoe rose from the bed. She took Mary Ellen's place at the door as Rob whisked his wife to the far side of the room.

Zoe recognized the man. He was a gambler. At

one time, he had ridden with her father when posses were formed. But he'd stopped when he had been shot in one leg and was no longer able to ride a horse.

"What is it, Jed?" Zoe asked.

"I was told I could find you here, ma'am," Jed said, taking his hat off and holding it behind him. "Ma'am, the news ain't good. It's Harold. Harold Hicks was gunned down last night just as he arrived at his home. He's dead, Zoe."

"Lord, no," Zoe said, feeling weak in the knees.

"Who was Harold Hicks?" Rob asked, cradling his wife against him.

"My deputy," Zoe said as she threw her hat on. "You stay here in your room. You'll be safe enough. When I have any news about Timothy, you will be the first to hear."

"Where are you going?" Rob asked, jumping at the sound of more horsemen coming into town.

"I don't think you'd want to know," Zoe said, striding from the room.

No, she didn't think that Mary Ellen or Rob would want to know that she had just decided to go to the Kiowa reservation and seek White Shadow's help. Things were getting out of hand. She didn't feel confident any longer about finding Timothy, or her father's—and now Harold's— killer.

"Zoe, don't do anything foolish," Jed said, limping as he followed her down the stairs. "Round up a posse. Let them go and search for the damn killer."

"Go on about your own business and I'll take

care of mine," Zoe said, running from the hotel.

She mounted her steed and raced out of town, just taking the time to glance up at the hotel where Rob was closing the window to keep out the thick dust.

As Zoe rode onward, leaving the town behind her, she looked constantly around her. She could almost feel the killer's presence. She knew that she was a ready target, yet she had no choice but to ride onward. She must seek help from White Shadow and his warriors. They knew the lay of the land better than anyone.

And it would be wonderful to work with White Shadow on this manhunt.

"If he will go with me," she whispered to herself, knowing how much he disapproved of her doing such dangerous, unfeminine things.

"If he loves me as much as he says, he will help me," she whispered.

She sank her heels into the flanks of her horse and thundered onward. It was July. The heat was savage. Great green and yellow grasshoppers were everywhere in the tall grass, popping up like corn to sting the flesh. Tortoises crawled about on the red earth, going nowhere.

Zoe rode at a harder gallop, welcoming the breeze her speed created against her flushed, hot face. She didn't have far to go. And she could hardly wait to see White Shadow again. The only thing keeping her sane at this moment was the memory of their sweet moments together.

Chapter Seventeen

I reason, earth is short, and anguish absolute.
                                    —Emily Dickinson

"I'm absolutely starved," Timothy said as he ladled stew from a wooden bowl so quickly that he spilled half of it before he got it to his mouth.

He had never worked as hard as he had since his arrival at the Kiowa reservation. The Kiowa seemed to delight in finding him things to do.

He had not known the Kiowa's lives were so diversified. And as each day passed, he could not help feeling respect for these people.

As he ate ravenously, Timothy glanced over at Thunder Stick, who seemed more intent on smoking than eating. His bowl sat half empty as he sucked more peyote into his body.

From the very first, Timothy had hoped that

Thunder Stick's addiction might afford him a way to escape. He hoped that Thunder Stick's mind might be so addled that he would not notice Timothy sneaking out of the old man's tepee.

But that wasn't the way it had been. The old man's body seemed so accustomed to the drug that it didn't cripple his ability to think.

Timothy knew that if *he* smoked even the smallest amount of the drug he would surely be disabled. He didn't even smoke cigars.

Timothy noticed how slyly Thunder Stick was smiling at him. Suddenly he felt more threatened than he had when he'd first been abducted. Timothy didn't trust the old man one iota.

No longer hungry, Timothy shoved his bowl away. He ignored Thunder Stick when he growled at him for leaving some food in his bowl.

Instead, Timothy focused on something else . . . on the strange feelings that had begun to stir within him as he learned the ways of the Kiowa.

All his life he had experienced moments of emptiness that he had not understood. While he had been at the Kiowa village he had not felt that emptiness. Somehow he was beginning to feel whole . . . as though there was something about these people that made him feel as one with them.

Chapter Eighteen

I knew not but the next would be my final inch.
                                    —Emily Dickinson

The farther Zoe rode, the more she became aware of the danger she faced. She felt foolish now for not having rounded up several men to ride with her, yet she knew why she hadn't. This would be the first time she'd gone to White Shadow's reservation.

This was the first time she would be with him since they had made love. She didn't wish to share their reunion with men who, for the most part, hated the very sight of a Kiowa Indian.

A sudden sound startled Zoe. She flinched, her hand going quickly to one of her holstered Colts.

She dropped her hand away from the Colt when she realized that what she had heard had only been the piercing call of a bobwhite. But as she looked to the left, then to the right, she gasped when she saw the flash of a gun barrel in the sunlight.

Someone was there.

Someone had been following her.

She scratched her brow when she no longer saw the flashing light. She wondered if it had been her imagination or the effects of the heat on her mind. The Oklahoma summer sun could do that to a person.

Even as she looked down the dusty road, she thought she could see small pools of water gleaming on it.

"Whew!" she whispered, shoving her hat back from her brow with a forefinger. "I'd better get to the reservation soon. The heat is playing tricks on my eyes."

Yet still she could not get what she had seen off her mind.

It had looked like the barrel of a gun picking up the gleam of the sun.

Having heard her father often boast of how he eluded many an outlaw as he rode alone on the trail, Zoe smiled. She recalled at least some of his tactics, and she would put them into practice today.

She steered her horse away from the road and traveled for a while beneath thick cottonwoods that would hide her from anyone who might be traveling on higher ground. She rode into one narrow valley and then another, making it all but impossible for anyone to take aim at her.

As she rode out into open land again, she sighed with relief when she saw tepees and log cabins in the distance. She had only a short distance to go to White Shadow's village.

She rode onward at a fast gallop and found herself riding through clusters of cottonwoods.

Again she felt uneasy. In her relief at seeing White Shadow's village, she had forgotten to watch out for anyone who might be hiding among the trees, a final threat before she found safety among the Kiowa.

Zoe's eyes narrowed and her heart skipped a beat when she heard a sound beside her somewhere in the shadows of the trees.

She started to look over her shoulder, but gasped when four Kiowa warriors rode out into the open and surrounded her.

Recognizing one of the warriors whom she had often seen with White Shadow, Zoe gave him a questioning look.

"Why did you stop me?" she asked. "Lightning Flash, I thought people were allowed to come and go freely from the reservation."

She looked away from Lightning Flash and gazed at the other three warriors, whose hands were resting on rifles in their gunboots.

"It looks as though you and your friends are working together in the capacity of sentries," she said, her voice wary. "Why do you feel the need to have sentries guarding your village? I haven't heard of any threat against your people. Or has something happened that I don't know about?"

Cassie Edwards

Her spine stiffened when Lightning Flash glanced down at her badge.

"I'm your friend," Zoe said, her voice drawn as none of the Kiowa responded to her. "You know me. You have seen me often in Gracemont. You know that I am a friend to all Kiowa."

Her jaw went tight. "Lightning Flash, you, especially, know that I am your friend," she said, trying to keep her annoyance . . . her impatience . . . from sounding in her voice. "You were there when I helped get Black Beak and his friends out of the jail in Muddy. Didn't that prove to you that I can be trusted to come to your village?"

She swallowed hard. "Lightning Flash, I need White Shadow's help. Harold Hicks, my deputy, was gunned down last night. I . . . I . . . no longer feel that I can find the killer alone. And I no longer feel as though I can trust the men in Gracemont enough to deputize them. I'd like White Shadow to help me."

She looked at each of the warriors again, and then edged her horse closer to Lightning Flash's. "Also, I need help finding Timothy Livingston," she said, her eyebrows lifting when Timothy's name caused a marked reaction among the warriors.

She wondered why.

Why would the mention of Timothy mean more to the Kiowa warrior than the mention of her father or Harold Hicks?

Then she recalled how the Kiowa disliked Timothy. It might be too much to ask the Kiowa warriors to help find a man they detested.

When none of the men responded to her questions, Zoe decided to break away from them and ride on into the village.

But just as she snapped her reins and tried to ride between two of the warriors, one of them reached over and took her reins from her, stopping her horse.

"Now why on earth would you do that?" she demanded, her patience at an end.

She tried to yank her reins away from the warrior, and almost fell from her horse when he yanked them back again from her.

"Damn it, let me pass!" she cried. "Just wait until White Shadow hears how you've treated me. He'll . . . he'll . . ."

Her threat died on her lips as Lightning Flash wheeled his horse around and rode off toward the village, leaving her with the other three warriors.

Looking guardedly from one to the other, she was almost afraid to know what was going on. She did know that she had no choice but to sit still and wait.

Restless, annoyed, and nervous, Zoe watched Lightning Flash enter the village. She hoped and prayed that White Shadow was there and would soon clear up this misunderstanding.

A chill went up her spine as one of the warriors edged his horse closer and he reached out a hand to touch her badge.

"Bad!" he said in guttural tones. "White man's badge is bad!"

Zoe's heart sank.

Chapter Nineteen

O, let me once more rest
My soul upon that dazzling breast.
                    —John Keats

White Shadow stepped outside his tepee when he
heard a horse approaching. His eyebrows lifted
when he saw Lightning Flash riding toward him.

Lightning Flash had been one of those who had
volunteered to stand as sentries today on the outskirts of the reservation. White Shadow knew that
the warrior would not have left his post unless
there was some threat to the Kiowa village.

Yapahe, he thought quickly to himself. It must
be soldiers. If so, they could be searching for their
missing colonel.

He started to go to Thunder Stick's lodge, to ask
him where Timothy was this morning, for it was

necessary to hide White Shadow's brother. But he stopped and waited when Lightning Flash shouted his name.

Lightning Flash brought his horse to a quick stop beside White Shadow. "It is the white woman," he said tightly. "White Shadow, she has come to see you. She is going to ask your assistance in searching for her father's killer and the man we hold as captive in our village. Not knowing whether or not you wished for the woman to enter our village, I came to you for answers."

The fact that Zoe had come to his village sent a slow warmth through White Shadow. That she had come to ask for his help made him think she might be feeling less confident in herself as sheriff. The possibility made him glad, for he hoped that she soon would give up the job altogether.

And if helping her search for her father's killer would hasten that conclusion, he would bring many of his warriors into the search.

But Timothy Livingston? If he told her that he would help her search for him, it would be a lie. In time she would realize the lie, and then how would she feel? Yet, until things were resolved about Timothy's whereabouts he could never marry Zoe.

"Go and see that Timothy is well hidden," White Shadow said, sighing. He saw no other way than to continue a while longer with the deceit that his mother had begun. "I shall ride out and escort Zoe into the village."

"You are going to help her search for the outlaw?" Lightning Flash asked, dismounting. "You see, there was another death which she believes is an act of the outlaw. Harold Hicks, her deputy, was killed last night."

"That is not good. That means she might be the killer's next target," White Shadow said. "*Ho*, I will help my woman search for the outlaw. And you will be among our many warriors who will also go on the manhunt," White Shadow said, his long hair swinging over his bare shoulders as he swung himself onto Lightning Flash's horse. "Hide Timothy and then gather together our warriors for the manhunt."

"And what will you tell her about the captive?" Lightning Flash asked.

"Nothing," White Shadow said, his eyes momentarily locking with his friend's. "Nor will anyone." He paused and then added, "Not just yet, anyhow."

Lightning Flash reached a hand up and gently placed it on White Shadow's arm. "My friend, must I remind you that all of this could bring our people much trouble?" he said thickly. "The captive. The woman. The outlaw. Why must we be involved in things that have nothing to do with our people?"

"I understand your concern," White Shadow said. "But do not carry your concern too far, my friend. Do not question your chief's decisions."

Lightning Flash stared for a moment longer at White Shadow, removed his hand from his arm, then turned on a quick heel and ran toward Thunder Stick's lodge.

White Shadow wheeled his friend's horse

Join the Historical Romance Book Club
and GET 4 FREE* BOOKS NOW!

A $23.96 Value!

Yes! I want to subscribe to the Historical Romance Book Club.

Please send me my **4 FREE* BOOKS.** I have enclosed $2.00 for shipping/handling. Each month I'll receive the four newest Historical Romance selections to pre-view for 10 days. If I decide to keep them, I will pay the Special Members Only discounted price of just $4.24 each, a total of $16.96, plus $2.00 shipping/handling ($23.55 US in Canada). This is a **SAVINGS OF AT LEAST $5.00** off the bookstore price. There is no minimum number of books I must buy, and I may cancel the program at any time. In any case, the **4 FREE* BOOKS** are mine to keep.

*In Canada, add $5.00 shipping/handling per order for the first shipment. For all future shipments to Canada, the cost of membership is $23.55 US, which includes shipping and handling. (All payments must be made in US dollars.)

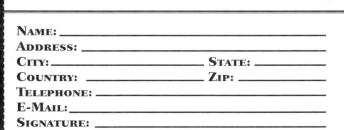

NAME: _____

ADDRESS: _____

CITY: _____ **STATE:** _____

COUNTRY: _____ **ZIP:** _____

TELEPHONE: _____

E-MAIL: _____

SIGNATURE: _____

If under 18, Parent or Guardian must sign. Terms, prices, and conditions subject to change. Subscription subject to acceptance. Dorchester Publishing reserves the right to reject any order or cancel any subscription.

around and rode through the village at a fast gallop. When he saw Zoe and his three warriors on their horses in the distance, he kicked the animal again, anxious to be with his woman.

Zoe watched White Shadow's approach, her pulse racing at the mere sight of him. Today, in the savage heat, he wore only a brief breechclout. She savored the sight of his muscled body, trembling inside with ecstasy at the memory of how his hard body had covered hers and had brought so much to her that she never knew existed.

She wished she had come to him today to tell him that they could be married. It would be wonderful to discard her dreadful jeans and shirt and slide the deliciously soft white doeskin dress over her head. And then they could make love over and over again in the privacy of his tepee . . . or at their trysting place . . . or anywhere.

It would be so easy to tell him that he was all that she wanted in life now. But she knew that she would never rest until her father's killer was caught and punished. She must never forget, also, that this very same killer could be gunning for her.

Yes, it was best that he was dealt with, and then her life could progress without the constant threat of Carl Collins out there waiting to destroy it.

And then there was Timothy. She had to find Timothy.

Just as White Shadow drew near, a sound on the ground close to her horse caught her attention.

It was at that moment that the rattler she had heard reared its ugly head and lunged its forked tongue toward the right front leg of her horse, spooking it.

Zoe tried to hang on when her horse reared, but it was impossible. She was quickly thrown from the saddle, and the horse rode off in a crazed gallop.

Screaming, Zoe hit the ground hard, but knowing that she had fallen near the rattler, she rolled quickly away just in time for one of the Kiowa warriors to shoot the snake.

Breathing hard, Zoe slowly sat up and stared at the snake, whose head had been shot off.

She gazed at her horse, which had been captured by one of the warriors and was being led back to her.

She looked up at White Shadow as he slid from his saddle and knelt down beside her, a hand gently touching her cheek.

"Are you all right?" he asked, watching her as she winced and grabbed at her right foot.

"I don't see how it could have happened, but I think I might have broken a toe," Zoe said, wincing when she tried to move her big toe in her right boot. "I always thought my boots were too tight. But apparently they aren't tight enough. They didn't protect my foot when I hit the ground!"

She smiled awkwardly up at White Shadow. "Lord, White Shadow, of all things, a *toe*," she said, embarrassed.

"I will take you to my lodge and see how badly it is broken," White Shadow said, gently lifting her from the ground.

He held her close as he carried her to her horse

and placed her on the saddle. Then he went to his horse and swung himself into the saddle and rode off with Zoe beside him.

Although the pain reached clean past her ankle, Zoe was hardly aware of it. She kept glancing over at White Shadow, at his handsomeness. She was thrilled knowing that soon she would be in his tepee with him. So often she had dreamed of such a moment as this, though under different circumstances.

In her thoughts she had always been there lying by the fire with him on a soft pallet of furs. He had been holding her and making love with her. They had been speaking soft words in one another's ears.

Her insides tightened as they entered the village and all eyes turned toward her. She wasn't sure if everyone was staring because she was wearing men's clothes, or because of the badge on her shirt. Or were their cold stares because their chief had invited her into the village?

She had to wonder how they would react when White Shadow brought her to their village in the capacity of his wife.

When dogs came yapping at her roan's hooves, causing the animal to whinny and shake its head nervously, Zoe kept her hands steady on the reins, silently praying that she wouldn't be thrown again from the saddle. It had been embarrassing enough to fall in the presence of three Kiowa warriors, much less the whole village!

She sighed with relief when several children ran out and dragged the dogs away from her horse.

She went onward with White Shadow and was glad when she was finally inside his tepee away from the scrutinizing stares.

"It will be cooler at the back of the lodge where my skins are rolled up for the breeze to enter," White Shadow said, carrying Zoe there and easing her down on a pallet of blankets.

Now alone, White Shadow framed Zoe's face between his hands and lowered his mouth to her lips. She quivered when he kissed her, and everything else was momentarily forgotten.

But when her toe began throbbing again, she winced and drew away from White Shadow.

White Shadow rested on his haunches beside her. "We must remove the boot," he said thickly. "Your toe will be swelling. It is best that it does not swell any larger inside the boot."

"Yes, I can tell that it's swelling," Zoe said, groaning when just moving her leg made sharp pains shoot through her toe.

She tried to pull the boot off, but it wouldn't budge.

She winced when White Shadow placed both of his hands on the boot and tried to remove it slowly, but also without success.

"I must cut it off," White Shadow said, sliding his knife from the sheath at his side.

"But my boot will be ruined," Zoe complained.

When she saw a soft smile flutter across White Shadow's lips, she frowned at him. "You've always hated my boots," she said. "You'll be glad to ruin one of them, won't you?"

"Moccasins are always better for the feet,"

White Shadow said, placing the tip of the knife just inside the top of the boot. "Sit still. I shall be careful."

Zoe stiffened. She watched, wide-eyed and scarcely breathing, as the knife slid through the leather boot until the entire side was cut open.

She sighed with relief when White Shadow laid his knife aside and slid the boot from her foot with ease.

After removing her sock, and seeing just how bruised and swollen the toe was, Zoe grimaced. "It looks awful, but I don't think it's broken," she said.

"I will go for our village shaman," White Shadow said, rising quickly to his feet.

"No, I don't want a shaman," Zoe said, reaching out for White Shadow as he left the tepee. She held her ankle and slowly rocked back and forth, moaning. "I . . . don't . . . want a damn shaman. I want Doc Rose."

Moments later she turned when she heard someone enter the tepee with White Shadow. She carefully watched the lean old man in braids as he came and knelt down beside her in his long robe. There was a necklace of beads and an eagle-bone whistle around his neck. He carried a fancy fan made from feathers in one hand, and a large buckskin bag hung from his left shoulder.

A strange odor arose from his clothes that was quite unpleasant to Zoe. She squirmed and covered her nose, but then dropped her hand away, afraid that she might offend him.

Zoe gave White Shadow a soft, pleading look as

he knelt on one side of her while the shaman knelt on the other. White Shadow gave her a slow nod, his quiet way of asking her to accept the old man's medicine.

She looked quickly again at the shaman as he took the buckskin bag from his shoulder and began searching inside it with one of his lean hands.

"Do not be afraid," Thunder Stick said, gazing up at her. "I see things that other men do not see. Trust me. I will make you well."

Eyes wide, she softly nodded. She was at least glad that he didn't begin chanting over her. Instead, he took a prickly pear cactus from his bag. She could tell that he had already burned off the stickers. She watched him cut the prickly pear in half and then put some sort of grease on it before he placed it over her aching toe.

"What sort of grease is that?" she asked. It was already giving her some relief from the pain.

"Many moons ago this shaman was smart enough to collect and save buffalo grease," Thunder Stick said, wiping his hands on a long, thin piece of buckskin. "For you see, white woman, the buffalo are long gone, but not Thunder Stick and his knowledge of medicine."

While he had been placing the medicine on her toe, Zoe had noticed how the shaman had kept staring into her eyes, as though he wanted to say more to her than what he had said.

His staring unnerved her. She wondered what he might have on his mind beside his medicine. It was obvious that he did not feel free to say whatever he wished to say in the presence of White

Shadow. She wondered if he made it a practice to hold things back from his own chief. Or was it all her imagination?

She started to question the shaman, but he stepped outside. She could still see the shaman as White Shadow held the entrance flap open for his return. She could see the shaman standing beside an outdoor fire. He had taken a white root from his bag and now threw the root into the fire, causing a great burst of smoke to rise.

Zoe watched as the shaman then held a piece of hide over the smoke, brought the hide back into the tepee, and spread it over her toe.

Thunder Stick lifted his eyes heavenward and began praying. "You are the power that gave this medicine long ago. Now it has come to me. I am using it to help this woman get well. Help me."

Thunder Stick then gazed into Zoe's eyes. "This medicine is not mine," he said. "It has come to me from a long time ago. My grandfather learned this medicine for curing injured bones. He taught it to me."

Zoe had no chance to question him further about it. He stood up and was quickly gone.

"He's a strange man," she murmured, hoping her truthful words didn't offend White Shadow. "And he smells so strange. It is a smell I'm not familiar with. Could it be from him mixing various herbs for his medicine?"

"What you smelled is also offensive to White Shadow," he said, slowly wrapping Zoe's toe with a thin strip of soft doeskin. "Our village shaman is ill with the peyote pipe sickness. He smokes much too often. In the past, peyote was used only for religious purposes. But now the shaman smokes it for the pure enjoyment he gets from it. It makes him into a strange person, yet his medicine is strong."

"Thank you so much for helping me," Zoe murmured.

She then told White Shadow why she had come today. She only mentioned that she needed help to find Timothy. Now that she was injured, she could do only one thing at a time. At this moment, finding Timothy was more important than finding the killer.

"It is best that you not go anywhere today to search for anyone," White Shadow said somberly. "You are injured. Do not injuries slow you down?"

"I'm afraid if I don't find Timothy soon, it will be too late," Zoe said. She tried to get up, but the pain shooting through her toe sent her back down on the blankets.

"Today you go nowhere," White Shadow said. "You rest. Tomorrow we will talk about whether or not you are well enough to go on your manhunt."

"Another whole day and Timothy may be dead!" Zoe cried, again trying to get up.

She fell back down on the blanket. "All right," she murmured. "I *can't* ride. But tomorrow I will! I must!"

"There is a Rabbit Dance tonight," White Shadow said, easing her down on the blankets close to the fresh air. "You will attend the Rabbit

Dance with me. You will observe my people in a new way."

Glad to be lying down, Zoe reached a hand up and took one of his. "What is a Rabbit Dance?"

"I will tell you during the dance," he said, gently releasing her hand. "Now rest. I have things to attend to while you rest."

"Thank you again for everything," Zoe said, smiling as he left.

She turned on her side and fell into a soft sleep.

Chapter Twenty

There the passions cramped no longer
shall have scope and breathing space.
—Alfred, Lord Tennyson

"I demand to know why I've been rushed to these cramped quarters again?" Timothy shouted, glaring at Thunder Stick as he came into the small space at the back of the cabin. "I heard horses arriving. Who came? Was it someone to check on me? You can't keep me hidden forever, you know."

"I thought you had begun to accept your new way of life," Thunder Stick said, glaring at Timothy. "It is best that you do, you know."

"I just find this all so damn confusing," Timothy said. He glanced down at his breechclout. "I want

186

my clothes back. Can't I even have my own clothes?"

"My people need buffalo," Thunder Stick replied sarcastically. "If I promise you your clothes, do you promise our people buffalo?"

"Don't be ridiculous," Timothy snapped back. "You know there are no buffalo."

"And why is that?" Thunder Stick said, his eyes narrowing. "Because of whites like you."

"I've never understood why the Indians put such importance on buffalo," Timothy said, sighing heavily. "It's an ugly animal. And I've eaten its meat. I think it's ghastly."

"The meat of the buffalo was good for the Kiowa," Thunder Stick said. "To the Kiowa the buffalo was an elder, a *teacher*. It taught all manner of men, but its innermost secrets were revealed only to medicine men. To our medicine men, like my father and grandfather before him, it explained where to find medicinal plants. From the animal's habits and movements came the shape and names of the months."

Thunder Stick paused, lifted his peyote pipe, filled it with ground peyote, and lit it. He drew from the pipe, inhaled, and then rested the bowl of the pipe on his knee as he again gazed at Timothy.

"The buffalo, horned and shag-headed, was the symbol of leadership," Thunder Stick said. "It was the image of long life, abundance, and power. Ceremonies were held in the buffalo's honor and myths have been made about its history."

"I never knew . . ." Timothy said.

"Just as you do not know so many things that you should, since you are. . . ." Thunder Stick stopped just short of disclosing the truth of Timothy's heritage to him.

"Since I am what?" Timothy asked, leaning toward Thunder Stick. "You were about to say . . . ?"

"No more talk," Thunder Stick growled. "Eat."

"I hate stew," Timothy said, staring into the bowl of vegetables and meat.

"If you are hungry enough, you will learn to look forward to stew," Thunder Stick said. "But when you learn to cooperate fully with the Kiowa, you will enjoy the varied diet of the Kiowa. When one is not a captive and eats normal meals, dried meat and dried fruit are eaten at every meal."

"That sounds no better than stew," Timothy replied.

Thunder Stick shrugged. "My people have meat soups a lot," he said. "We also eat eggs from wild turkeys and prairie chickens, boiled hard. When we eat fish, it is cooked right in the ashes of the fire. Rabbit meat is also roasted that way."

"I'm still hungry," Timothy said after he took the last of the stew from the bowl with his wooden spoon.

"There is more stew," Thunder Stick said, pushing the pot of stew toward Timothy. "It is all you deserve for now."

Chapter Twenty-one

Tho' rapt in matters dark and deep
He seems to slight her simple heart.
                    —Alfred, Lord Tennyson

A movement behind her awakened Zoe with a start. She turned over quickly and gasped when she found Thunder Stick resting on his haunches close to her, his feather fan clutched in his right hand as he fanned himself.

"What are you doing here?" Zoe asked, moving away from him. She looked past him and became even more frightened when she saw that White Shadow was nowhere about. She was alone with the shaman.

She looked guardedly at Thunder Stick again. The wickedness in his eyes caused a cold chill to race across her flesh. "Well?" she said, trying to look as though she weren't afraid, though her pulse was racing. "Aren't you going to answer me? Why are you here?"

She wanted to shout at him that she didn't like or trust him . . . that she didn't want him around her. But she felt that it might be dangerous to be truthful with him.

Thunder Stick moved his feather fan slowly back and forth. "*Hilugu*, wait. Do not be frightened. I have not come to give you medicine this time," he finally said, his voice a low, daring hiss. "I am here to bargain with you. I am a rich man because I have the power and knowledge of extortion." He leaned closer, the strong smell of peyote on his breath causing Zoe to flinch and cough. "If you promise to pay me well, I will tell you a valuable secret."

"What sort of secret?" Zoe asked, placing her hand over her nose and mouth to keep his scent from her.

Her eyes widened and her breath quickened when White Shadow entered the tepee and stopped when he saw Thunder Stick there.

White Shadow's jaw tightened. He could tell that Thunder Stick was up to no good, for he had come without his medicine. And he could see that Thunder Stick had frightened Zoe.

Thunder Stick saw Zoe's eyes focus past him. He turned his head with a quick jerk. When he saw White Shadow standing there, he hid his face behind his fan, rose to his feet, and hurried toward the entrance flap.

"Thunder Stick, stop," White Shadow said, reaching out for him.

But Thunder Stick was as slippery as an eel; he slithered past White Shadow and was quickly gone from sight outside the tepee.

Zoe was stunned by what had happened. She stared blankly at the entrance flap, which was still swaying from the shaman's quick exit.

Then she gazed up at White Shadow as he came and knelt beside her.

"Thunder Stick should not have been here without my permission," White Shadow grumbled. "Although he is our village shaman, my word is law among our people."

Zoe was thinking about what the shaman had said to her, about a secret. She was puzzled over what he might have meant. Probably he was trying to trick her into promising to give him some money. She scoffed at how she had thought that he might truly have something of importance to tell her.

How could he? she thought to herself. Today was the first day he had ever met her. How could he know anything that might be of importance to her?

"Before, when I called Thunder Stick strange, I thought I might have offended you," Zoe said, welcoming White Shadow's arms as he swept them around her and drew her into his embrace. "But I can't help it. I still feel that way about him, even more so."

"I do not like having to warn you about our village shaman, but I feel that you, a white woman, should know never to trust anything he says," White Shadow said. "Thunder Stick has practiced extortion among whites by use of his powers. It is known among our people that Thunder Stick has amassed considerable wealth by such means. He is feared by many. Some have even hired Thunder Stick to diagnose witching brought on them by an enemy. They, in turn, hire him to witch their enemy."

He frowned. "I recall times as a child when my mother would place a cross of ashes from her fire pit on my forehead and on my chest to protect me from witching," he said. "That was just after Thunder Stick had been appointed our village shaman. I grew up afraid of him. When I reached adulthood, my fright changed to distrust."

"And you keep this man among you as your shaman?" Zoe gulped out. "He's dangerous, White Shadow. How could you trust him for one minute?"

"Because my mother and Thunder Stick were friends long before he became shaman, and Thunder Stick knows the limits of my tolerance for his witching," White Shadow said.

He shrugged. "It matters not to me how much he uses it against whites," he said. He swept his hand up and twined it through Zoe's hair and brought her lips close to his. "Except you. You are white, and he had better never use his powers on you."

Just as their lips touched, Zoe leaned away from White Shadow. "Perhaps he was trying to use it today," she said guardedly.

"What do you mean?" he asked, his jaw tight, his eyes filled with fire.

"He said the strangest thing to me," Zoe said, raising an eyebrow as she remembered exactly what Thunder Stick had said, and the way he had said it . . . in a low hiss.

"What did he say?" White Shadow asked, his voice tight.

"He told me that he has the power and knowledge of extortion and that if I promised to pay him well, he would tell me a valuable secret," Zoe blurted out. "I wonder what he could have meant?"

White Shadow frowned. His pulse raced to think that Thunder Stick might have come to Zoe to tell her about Timothy, disregarding everything but his greed for more money.

"I will go to him and warn him against such behavior again," he said, getting to his feet. He stood over Zoe and gazed down at her. "I will forbid him to come near you again."

He turned and strode toward the entrance flap.

Zoe reached a hand out for him. "But what could he have meant?" she asked, stopping him. She gazed into his dark eyes as he looked down at her.

"His reason to be here was money," White Shadow said. "It seems that his greed blinds him to what is right not only for his chief, but for his people as a whole. I must replace him soon with someone more reliable."

"But your mother . . . ?"

"She will be made to understand."

Zoe watched him leave, but she still couldn't get what Thunder Stick had said off her mind. If he had come to her for money, he had to have a way to convince her to part with her money.

"A secret?" she whispered. She sat up and smoothed her hair back from her face. "I wonder what he was going to tell me."

But recalling White Shadow's warnings, Zoe ignored her curiosity. She reached down and pressed her fingers around her sore toe. She winced when she found that her toe was hurting again, as much as it had before the shaman had treated it with his peculiar way of healing.

"Where is Doc Rose when I need him most?" she groaned, slowly lying back down on the soft cushion of pelts and blankets.

She closed her eyes and enjoyed the breeze as it wafted beneath the rolled-up skins. Then she opened her eyes and gazed outside. She peered through the darkness in the direction of the twin buttes that were near her home and felt an ache in her heart as she thought of her father.

"I've been momentarily stopped from searching for Carl Collins," she whispered. "But, Father, I promise you, I won't give up. I will still avenge your death!"

Then she thought of Timothy. "Where are you?" she whispered. She could not help thinking that he was dead. He had been gone for too long now.

Chapter Twenty-two

O, let the solid ground not fail beneath my feet
Before my life has found what some have found
so sweet.

—Alfred, Lord Tennyson

White Shadow stormed into the cabin where Timothy was being held hostage. Moonlight was the only illumination in the lodge as it came through the window in a soft glow. That was enough light for White Shadow to see Thunder Stick. He was sitting on the floor leaning against the far wall filling his pipe with freshly ground peyote.

"What were you doing in my lodge?" White Shadow asked bitterly. He placed his fists on his hips and glared down at Thunder Stick, then gazed over at the door that led back to where Timothy was being kept.

"I find your woman beautiful, that is all," Thunder Stick said. He looked slyly up at White Shadow as he rested the bowl of his pipe on his knee. "Does it offend you that an old man my age finds your woman beautiful? Surely you do not feel threatened by Thunder Stick's attentiveness toward her."

"Attentiveness goes just so far," White Shadow said. He bent down and rested on his haunches directly before Thunder Stick. He looked into his eyes. "Does it include telling my woman secrets? Asking for pay in exchange for the secret?"

Again White Shadow looked toward the door behind which sat his brother, Timothy.

"What secret?" White Shadow demanded, glaring into the shaman's eyes again. He placed a firm hand on Thunder Stick's narrow, frail shoulder. "What were you about to tell my woman when I came into my lodge? Did it have anything to do with my mother's captive?"

"And if it did?" Thunder Stick said, smiling cunningly.

"If you break not only my trust, but especially my beloved mother's, your banishment from our tribe will come quickly and without mercy," White Shadow growled.

He leaned lower so that his eyes were level with the Shaman's. "You have been warned, Thunder Stick," he said in a low hiss. "I am sorely tired of your antics. When you turn against my mother, that is when my patience runs out. Hear me well when I say that no matter how much my mother complains, you . . . will . . . be gone . . . from our village."

White Shadow rose quickly to his feet. He went to the door at the back of the lodge and stepped inside, where a lone kerosene lamp lit the small space. Timothy was huddled on the floor, asleep. Gently, White Shadow placed a hand on Timothy's shoulder and awakened him.

"How much longer am I going to be made to stay in this crawl space?" Timothy growled out. "There's hardly room to breathe."

"You are only confined here in this smaller area while Thunder Stick leaves the cabin," White Shadow said, placing a gentle hand on his brother's shoulder. "Come. Thunder Stick has returned. Come out and sit in the larger room."

"Why am I being kept hidden at all?" Timothy asked, pushing himself up from the floor, his breechclout damp with perspiration. "Who came into the village that you are keeping me from seeing? Surely it's someone who came looking for me. I can't imagine the soldiers under my command not searching here for me."

"But why would they?" White Shadow asked, walking to the outer room with his brother. "The Kiowa are at peace with the pony soldiers at Fort Cobb."

"Until now, you mean," Timothy grumbled. "When they discover you have taken me captive, the word 'peace' will be wiped from their vocabulary as far as you and your people are concerned."

Although White Shadow was listening to what

Timothy was saying, he was not paying much heed to it. There was something odd about Timothy today. There was a sluggishness in the way he walked and talked. His eyelids drooped, as though he might be drugged, or sleepy.

He watched as Timothy sat back down on the floor across the room from Thunder Stick and held his face in his hands.

White Shadow went to him and knelt down before him. "You are ill?" he asked, placing a gentle hand on his shoulder.

Timothy raised his head and glared at White Shadow. "As if you care," he growled out. Again he hung his head. "I'm not sure what's wrong. I just suddenly seem drained of energy."

White Shadow looked slowly over at Thunder Stick, wondering why the shaman looked quickly away from him when their eyes met for an instant.

Then he looked at Timothy again. "Your sluggishness is probably only because you have not been able to get out and ride on your horse, or get proper exercise while you are being held captive," he said, his words soft and full of apology.

Timothy looked quickly up at White Shadow. He questioned him with his eyes, then again hung his head and drifted off into a drugged sleep.

White Shadow was taken aback by how quickly his brother fell asleep. He could not help being concerned, for White Shadow had begun to see more good than bad in his brother's character. He had silently observed Timothy as he moved among the Kiowa people, learning their ways with an eagerness that surprised White Shadow.

Ho, White Shadow was beginning to like this man who was his blood brother.

He went to Thunder Stick and yanked his peyote pipe from his mouth. "From now on, while you are sitting with Timothy you will not smoke the pipe," he said, breaking the stem and handing the pipe back to Thunder Stick. "Can you not see that the peyote is affecting him? Do you think my mother had this man captured so that you could make him ill with peyote smoke? Just because you are burdened with the *seni satop hodal* does not mean that those around you should be."

Thunder Stick's eyes narrowed as he glared at the broken pipe; then he smiled crookedly up at White Shadow. "You should not have done that," he snarled.

"You are now voicing threats to your chief?" White Shadow said, leaning closer to Thunder Stick.

Thunder Stick said nothing more. He looked away from White Shadow. "I have other pipes," he mumbled.

White Shadow rose to leave, and then took another look at Timothy. Even knowing that Zoe might see him, White Shadow had no choice but to take Timothy outside to walk off the effects of the peyote smoke, for White Shadow was almost certain that was what was wrong with him.

He knelt down before Timothy and placed his hands on his upper arms. "Come with me," he said, awakening Timothy. "We will go outside and walk awhile."

Timothy nodded sluggishly.

White Shadow placed an arm around Timothy's waist and led him outside. After walking with him back and forth before the cabin, White Shadow decided to take him somewhere else for a while.

He took him to his mother's lodge.

Soft Bird gazed up at Timothy, and then looked questioningly at White Shadow. "Why do you bring him here?" she asked softly. "Is it safe?"

"He needs a reprieve from Thunder Stick," White Shadow explained, helping Timothy down onto a blanket across from Soft Bird. "Peyote smoke has overwhelmed Timothy. The sleepiness will soon pass. Then I will take him back to the cabin."

Timothy gazed over at Soft Bird, and then looked up at White Shadow. "Don't you think it's time to explain why I am here?" he said, his words slurred. "If you will let me go, I promise I won't tell anyone where I've been."

"You have seemed to enjoy being with my people," Soft Bird murmured. "I have watched you. You work with the ease and gracefulness of a man who enjoys his labors. How can I be wrong about that?"

"I have found many of your ways interesting," Timothy said, nodding. "But they are not *my* ways. I am white, Soft Bird. Not Kiowa. Why would you wish for it to be any other way?"

Soft Bird and White Shadow exchanged quick glances; then Soft Bird's eyes lowered.

White Shadow placed a hand on Timothy's arm. "This was not the best thing to do, at least not tonight," he said thickly. "Come. I shall return you to the cabin. Surely the peyote smoke has thinned enough so that you will no longer be affected by it."

"But I thought—"

"As I said, I was wrong."

After White Shadow took Timothy back to the cabin and warned Thunder Stick to do what was right by him, White Shadow went back to his own lodge and knelt beside Zoe, who was dozing. He lifted a hand to her face and slowly smoothed away some fallen locks of her brown hair.

"Secrets?" he whispered. "*Ho*, there is a secret being kept from you. If you only knew."

Chapter Twenty-three

Best and brightest, come away—
Which like thee to those in sorrow
Comes to bid a sweet good-morrow.
—Percy Bysshe Shelley

Attired in buckskin, White Shadow sat tall and straight on a thick layer of soft pelts spread over the ground. "Are you comfortable enough?" he asked as he leaned closer to Zoe.

Her toe throbbing, Zoe squirmed on the pelts she was sharing with White Shadow. She gave him a nervous smile. "As comfortable as I can be under the circumstances," she said.

Her aching toe was not Zoe's only problem. She was apprehensive about being among the Kiowa. White Shadow's people were sitting on the ground on all sides of her outside a large domed house made of bark and buckskin. He had already explained to her that the large lodge was the village council house, and that it was where the rabbit ceremony was to be performed tonight.

Large torches made of bundles of grass were stuck in the ground all around the council house. They burned brightly, shedding their light inside the lodge, where the buckskin sides were rolled halfway up from the ground so that the people could see the activity inside.

Earlier Zoe had watched several young boys file into the council house, followed by someone a few years older. Black Beak. White Shadow had told Zoe that his cousin was going to be a figure of authority tonight during the ceremony.

"Black Beak plays the role of the bull tonight during the Rabbit Dance," White Shadow said as the children inside the lodge began to sing and dance. "As you see, Zoe, Black Beak carries a whip and a knife. He has the power tonight to strike a child or cut his hair if any do not cooperate with the rules of the dance."

"That seems a bit harsh," Zoe said, hoping Black Beak wouldn't take advantage of his powers tonight.

"Rarely does a child have to be punished, for they enjoy the ceremony too much," White Shadow said, his head slightly nodding as he kept time with the children's singing. "Every child belongs to the *Kasowe* or Rabbit Society. As soon as the child is old enough to take part in the dancing, he joins this group. This society provides an opportunity for Kiowa youngsters to become acquainted from an early age and to form bonds of friendship that often endure throughout their lives."

He smiled. "My friendship with my best friend Lightning Flash began during my very first Rabbit Society meeting," he said proudly.

"What are the children doing now?" Zoe asked, her eyebrows lifting when she saw Black Beak take one of the children from the group. "Why is Black Beak urging that child to place his hands up by the sides of his head?"

"Look carefully." White Shadow said, leaning closer to Zoe. "Do you not see rabbit ears when you look at the other children and the way they hold their hands up by the sides of their heads? That is what Black Beak is teaching the young brave. And watch the other children closely. They are hopping up and down in imitation of rabbits."

Zoe nodded and laughed softly. "Yes, I see it now," she murmured. "Oh, but the children are so cute."

"Cute?" White Shadow said, raising his eyebrows. "What is that word cute?"

Zoe looked quickly at him. She smiled. It was so refreshing to see a grown man who was not afraid to ask questions. It made her love this man even more when she saw this side of his nature. None of the white men she had known would have allowed such vulnerability to show, especially not to a woman.

"Cute?" she murmured. "It is a word used to describe something sweet . . . something pretty."

"Then the word 'cute' describes *you*," White

Shadow said huskily. "When we are alone again I shall tell you just how cute you are."

In Zoe's mind's eye she was remembering how wonderful it had been to make love with White Shadow. It was like nothing she'd ever imagined.

And the way he looked at her now told her that tonight, when they were once again in the privacy of his lodge, they would once again make love.

For a while at least she would forget the killer and Timothy's disappearance. She would even forget her throbbing toe.

Her thoughts were brought back to the present when she heard a lone voice take up the tune that all the children had been singing.

She looked quickly back inside the large council house and saw Black Beak standing amidst the children, who were now sitting in a wide circle around him. As he sang, his voice deep and filled with emotion, Zoe saw Black Beak no longer as the rebellious teenager, but instead as someone who had deep feelings for his people, especially the children.

"At this moment Black Beak is how he should be and how I wish he would be all of the time," White Shadow whispered to Zoe, his eyes on his cousin. "So often he troubles me with his restless ways."

His gaze shifted to a group of young braves who stood back away from the seated Kiowa. His eyes narrowed on Red Thunder and Eagle Claw, who seemed to be poking fun at Black Beak's performance.

"My cousin is as restless as those who urge him

into rebellion," he said thickly. "I hope that soon he will put that sort of life behind him and learn the ways of being a great Kiowa warrior."

Zoe's gaze followed White Shadow's and she saw the two young braves who were trouble-makers.

She knew that White Shadow realized that Black Beak was as rebellious as those who White Shadow's eyes accused tonight. It was just hard for him to accept that his own blood kin could be at the heart of so much trouble.

"Since Black Beak is your cousin, will he one day be chief?" Zoe asked, her eyes shifting quickly to White Shadow when he turned and gazed at her.

"The one who will be chief after White Shadow will be White Shadow's son," he said thickly. He placed a gentle hand on her cheek. "*Our* son, Zoe. Our son will be chief when this chief grows weary of the task."

Zoe was swept away on clouds of rapture at the thought of being free to marry White Shadow and have his children. If only she could marry him to-night. If only she would soon be carrying his child within her womb.

She wished that she could just blink her eyes and make her wish come true. But that wasn't possible. She would have to take it a day at a time and hope that her troubles would all be over soon.

She was drawn from her reverie when White Shadow's hand left her face and he became ab-sorbed in what was happening inside the council house.

She turned and watched, also. Black Beak knelt in the circle of children and lifted his hands and eyes heavenward and prayed. His prayers asked for the salvation of the young braves.

Once the prayer was finished, several women took large containers of food and eating utensils and set them just outside the lodge. After they left, Zoe watched Black Beak pick out two boys, who dished out the food and carried the bowls back inside, until everyone had been served.

Zoe's eyes widened as the children took their bowls of food and positioned themselves on two sides of the lodge, sitting opposite each other.

She could hardly believe how quickly the children gulped the food down; their bowls were refilled over and over again.

Zoe turned to White Shadow. "They act as though they are starved," she said. "Look at them eat! How can such small children eat so much?"

"It is a part of the Rabbit Society ceremony to see which group can consume the most food," White Shadow said.

"I imagine there will be many bellies aching long after the ceremony is over," Zoe said, laughing softly.

White Shadow took Zoe by the hand and gently drew her to her feet. "Come," he said, leading her away from the crowd. "For the most part the ceremony is over. My presence as chief is no longer required."

Limping, her toe aching, Zoe leaned against White Shadow.

White Shadow was aware of her discomfort. He

stopped and gazed down at her. He knew they were far enough from the crowd that he could lift Zoe up into his arms.

As he did so, their eyes were locked in silent understanding. They knew that only moments from now they would both fulfill the longing that ate away at their hearts. While making love they would float together to paradise again. There would be only the two of them; for the moment the whole world would be blotted from their hearts and minds.

Breathless, her heart thundering inside her chest with excitement at what was soon to happen, Zoe laid her head against White Shadow's chest.

When she felt the thumping of his heart against her cheek she smiled, for she knew that he was as excited as she. He loved her as much as she loved him.

As he nudged the entrance flap of his lodge aside with his elbow and he carried her inside, Zoe drew a ragged breath.

When he took her over to the pelts upon which she had slept earlier, Zoe trembled as White Shadow laid her upon them and then knelt over her, his hands slowly undressing her.

"I want you so much," Zoe murmured.

She sucked in a wild breath when he pulled her shirt open. He bent low over her and flicked his tongue over the nipple of one of her breasts. He nibbled on the other nipple, and then licked it until it was a tight nub against his tongue.

Zoe leaned up on an elbow as he continued undressing her until she lay nude beneath him, his own clothes also finally removed.

White Shadow swept a hand beneath her head and brought her lips up to meet the fierce, possessive heat of his as he kissed her. She clung to him as she felt the velvet tip of his manhood gently probing her softly yielding folds.

When he gave a deep shove and was quickly inside her, she gave herself up to rapture. She lifted her hips to meet his eager, rhythmic thrusts.

He plunged into her, withdrew, and plunged again, his lean, sinewy body tightening with each entrance. White Shadow slipped his lips away from Zoe's mouth and moved them again to one high, full breast, his tongue rolling the nipple beneath it.

Pleasure was hot and piercing through him, his body growing feverish from the heat. He leaned up away from her and smiled down at her.

"You are a vision," he whispered, and then once again kissed her long, hard, and deep. His thrusts became faster as he moved powerfully within her.

When White Shadow's hands cupped her aching breasts, kneading their soft fullness, Zoe groaned against his lips. Waves of ecstasy washed over her as she found that place where joy and bliss were as one inside her.

As her body trembled with release, she felt White Shadow's body tightening. When his body made one last, deeper thrust into her, Zoe knew that he was lost in the same throes of passion as she.

Afterward, as they lay side by side, the night

breeze cool on their heated flesh as it blew in through the open space at the bottom of the tepee, Zoe was once again aware of something besides pleasure. Her toe. It ached unmercifully.

"It hurts so," she murmured.

White Shadow leaned on an elbow and gazed down at her with concern. "Did I hurt you while making love?" he asked thickly. He swept her hair back from her face. "I was not gentle enough?"

"Darling White Shadow, my pain has nothing to do with you," she said, laughing softly. "It's my toe. It's so sore."

"Thunder Stick's medicine did not help all that much?" White Shadow asked. He sat up and reached down to cradle her foot in his hand. He studied how purple the toe was, and how swollen.

"No, your shaman didn't help me," she said. "What I need is a true doctor. Doc Rose. I wish he were here."

"I have heard of a Doc Rose and how his magic is not always useful to the ill," White Shadow said, defending his people's use of the shaman over white doctors.

"Well, no, not always," Zoe allowed. In her mind's eye she was seeing her father and how his life had so easily ebbed away. "He couldn't do anything for my father."

She swallowed hard. She gazed at the entrance flap, and then turned over and looked outside, where the moon's glow was whitewashing the land. "No matter how much my toe hurts tomorrow I must get back to my duties as sheriff," she said, looking quickly up at White Shadow when he placed his hands at her waist and turned her toward him.

"The duties you speak of put you in danger," he said hoarsely. "Forget them. Your father is dead. Nothing will bring him back."

"I know, but his death must be avenged," she murmured. "And if I don't do it, no one will. Deputy Hicks is dead. His death has surely scared off those who were willing to help me."

She gazed at the entrance flap and sighed. "And it's only Father," she murmured. "I still must find Timothy." She looked up at White Shadow. "Where can he be? Where?"

White Shadow's jaw tightened.

Chapter Twenty-four

I regret little,
I would chance still less.
        —Robert Browning

Too restless to sleep after the excitement of the celebration, Black Beak had sneaked from his parents' lodge and was now riding with Red Thunder and Eagle Claw beneath the bright moonlight.

Black Beak planned to ride for just a little while until his restlessness wore off, and then return home and go to bed without getting into trouble. He had not only promised himself that he would stay out of trouble, he had also promised his cousin and his parents.

Tonight Black Beak had been honored by having been chosen to portray the bull during the rabbit ceremony. He would not forget how his cousin had trusted him enough to give him such an honor.

Black Beak didn't want to disappoint White Shadow again.

"I know where there are some horses that can be easily stolen," Eagle Claw said, breaking into Black Beak's thoughts. "Black Beak, come with me and Red Thunder to steal horses again. Carl Collins pays well. Do you not crave a taste of whiskey tonight? Do you not hunger for the gambling tables in Muddy? Until whites caused us trouble, the owners of the establishments in Muddy looked past the color of our skin. They welcomed our money there as much as they welcomed the white man's."

Black Beak frowned at Eagle Claw. "Eagle Claw, we got into bad trouble at Muddy. And you heard my promise to White Shadow that I would not disappoint him again," he growled. "And did you not see tonight how I was honored? I was chosen to portray the bull. I will receive many more honors from our people . . . from our chief . . . if my behavior does not turn reckless again."

"You are a fool to think that you were chosen tonight for any other reason than because you are blood kin to the chief," Eagle Claw scoffed. "And did you not feel foolish standing there amidst the children, as though you are a boy yourself? No, Black Beak, I saw nothing tonight that was in the least bit honorable."

"You are wrong," Black Beak said angrily. "I was wrong to come with you tonight. I vowed to myself that I would not mix with you again, for I see that you especially, Eagle Claw, are anything but a friend." He drew a tight rein and stopped his horse, wheeled it around, and rode back in the direction of his village.

Eagle Claw and Red Thunder turned their horses around and caught up with Black Beak.

Red Thunder reached over and grabbed Black Beak's reins from him. "Eagle Claw did not mean what he said," he cajoled, holding the reins away from Black Beak as he angrily tried to yank them from him. "He only knows how to speak in angry, jealous tones. He means you no harm. He says things that hurt you only because he is hurt that you refuse to help steal the horses. Come on, Black Beak. What can one more night of stealing hurt? It takes three of us, not two, to make a successful raid."

Black Beak's jaw tightened. "Give my reins back to me," he said.

"Only if you say that you will ride this last time with us to steal horses," Red Thunder said. "Also, Black Beak, come this one last time with us to receive pay from Carl Collins. Come this one last time and enjoy what the coins can buy us. Let us gamble and drink together this one last time. Then if you wish to separate yourself from us, your very best friends, we will not ask anything of you again, ever."

"Just this one last time?" Black Beak said, his heart pounding at the thought of accompanying them on this mission. "You will not tell anyone that I went with you this one last time? The secret stays among the three of us?"

"*Ho*, it will go no further than the three of us," Red Thunder said, giving Eagle Claw a guarded look and smiling when he nodded his approval of the plan.

"Then, Eagle Claw, show us where you found the horses," Black Beak said, casting all promises and vows aside for the sheer pleasure of adventure.

The temptation was too great. But this would be the last time! Black Beak couldn't chance being banished from the tribe by his very own chieftain cousin!

They rode off in a mad gallop across the moon-splashed land until they came to a fenced-in area where they saw a herd of browsing horses. Past the fence, a short distance away, was a dark cabin. Those who lived there were fast asleep.

"The cabin is too close to chance stealing several horses," Black Beak whispered as he sidled his horse closer to Eagle Claw's. "We will take one apiece tonight. That should get us enough coins to enjoy a short time in Muddy. A short time is all that I should allow myself. Should my mother or father awaken and find me gone, all is lost to me . . . my future, my pride."

"We will stay for only a little while at Muddy," Eagle Claw said, glancing over at Red Thunder and again receiving a nod of approval.

They leapt from their horses, tied them to a post, and then stealthily climbed over the fence. Each threw a lariat around the neck of a horse, and then led it through the gate to their tethered horses.

After mounting their steeds, they clung to the ropes and rode off in a gentle lope in an effort to make as little noise as possible.

As soon as they were some distance from the cabin, they rode off in a hard gallop and stayed at that pace until they reached Carl Collins' hideout.

Again Carl was pleased with what they brought him. He paid them in coins, led the horses into the corral with the rest of those he now claimed as his, and then turned to the young braves, his hands on his hips, a cigarette hanging from the corner of his mouth.

"Lads, the night is young," he said, glancing from one to the other. "I have lots of whiskey. I have a deck of cards. Why bother going into town when you can get all you need right here under my roof?" He chuckled. "At my establishment the whiskey is free. But as for gambling? It ain't free, not if you lose. Are you game? Want to spend some time here and keep this lonely outlaw company?"

The braves questioned each other with their eyes; finally Black Beak smiled and nodded. "We will drink and gamble with you," he said, finding this much safer than chancing going into Muddy. "But only for a little while."

"I've had trouble sleepin' so *any* time spent gamblin' and drinkin' will be welcomed," Carl said. He took the cigarette from his mouth and flicked it over his shoulder. "Come on inside, gents. Let's see just who is the best card player among you." He chuckled. "Let's see who can hold the most whiskey in his gut."

Not having consumed that much of the white man's poison, Black Beak hesitated before going into the outlaw's cabin. Then he shrugged and went on inside with the rest.

As he entered, he stopped and gazed slowly around. A fire burned in the grate of a large stone fireplace. Two kerosene lanterns flashed their golden light on grimy wood floors covered with mud and debris, and a few sticks of furniture. The only pleasant thing was the aroma of coffee brewing in a pot on the coals of the fire.

"Come and sit yourselves down at my kitchen table," Carl said, motioning toward a crude, hand-hewn table and chairs.

He grabbed a bottle of whiskey from a shelf on the wall and slammed it down on the table. He then placed tin cups before each of the Kiowa braves, grabbed one for himself, and tossed a deck of cards in the center of the table.

"Ready to lose your socks tonight, gents?" Carl said, roaring with laughter as he sat down on the chair and scooted close to the table. He nodded toward Black Beak. "Shuffle 'em and deal 'em, sonny boy."

As Black Beak shuffled and dealt the cards, Carl lit another cigarette, his eyes squinting as the smoke swirled up into them.

He poured whiskey in each of the cups and watched as the boys began drinking, choking on the first swallows, then consuming the liquor as quickly as one might a glass of water on a hot summer day.

Game after game was played, and the coins began stacking up in front of Carl. He glanced over at the whiskey bottle and noticed that it was almost gone. He dealt another hand of cards as he watched Eagle Claw pour the last of the whiskey into Black Beak's cup.

"Drink up," Carl said, his eyes gleaming as he watched Black Beak lift the cup to his lips and swallow every last drop.

Black Beak felt giddy. He laughed throatily as he stared down at his latest hand of cards. "Queens and kings," he said, chuckling. "All black queens and kings."

"Do not tell what you have in your hand," Red Thunder scolded. "Black Beak, just *play*, not talk."

Black Beak spread his cards out on the table before him, face down. He looked over at Carl and saw two of him instead of one. "Did you know that my people take captives?" he suddenly blurted out.

"Black Beak, stop!" Red Thunder gasped. "You do not know what you are doing. The firewater has loosened your tongue too much." He rose quickly from his chair and went to Black Beak. "Come. I am taking you home."

"Leave me alone," Black Beak said, wrenching himself free of Red Thunder's grip when Eagle Claw tried to take him by an arm.

"You say that your people take captives," Carl said, leaning closer over the table, his eyes on Black Beak. "When? Who?"

Eagle Claw scrambled from his chair. He went and stood on the other side of Black Beak's chair. "Say no more, Black Beak," he said, placing a firm hand on his shoulder. "Come. It is time to go home. We have stayed much too long. This man has robbed us tonight. Do not give him anything else, especially information that is secret to the Kiowa."

Black Beak looked over his shoulder at Eagle Claw. "You do not tell me what to do," he said, his words even more slurred. "I am the cousin of our chief. Do you not know that makes me more powerful than you? I can say what I please, when I please."

Red Thunder and Eagle Claw stood back and listened in horror as Black Beak began talking about Timothy and how he was being held captive and how proud Black Beak was that finally his people had taken bold action against the white pony soldiers.

And before he stopped talking, he mentioned Zoe's being at the village, and how she and White Shadow were obviously enamored with one another. Even now she slept in his lodge with him as though she were his wife!

Carl listened intently until he had learned all that he needed in order to kill Zoe. He had killed her father; he had also gunned down her most prized deputy; she would be his last target before he moved on to another area, where there were more lawmen waiting to receive his bullets.

The sale of the stolen horses to crooked horse dealers would be his means of surviving until he tired of killing lawmen.

"I think it's time for you boys to get on home now," Carl said, his eyes locking with Eagle Claw's before Red Thunder and Eagle Claw turned and walked stealthily through the door.

Carl stabbed out his tenth cigarette. He shoved his chair back, went to help Black Beak from his chair, then led him outside where his friends waited for him with his horse.

"Take him home. Next time you'd better watch how much firewater he consumes," Carl said, lighting another cigarette. He chuckled. "I'd hate to have his headache tomorrow."

He watched them ride off, then he saddled his own horse and rode off behind them, keeping far enough back so that they were not aware that he was following them.

When the village came into view some distance away, Carl fell back. He drew a tight rein in the dark shadows of some trees and searched the bluff that overlooked the village. He spied a sentry there, and when he continued his search, he discovered three more sentries keeping guard on the village.

"Damn," Carl whispered, stabbing his cigarette out on his boot, and then tossing it over his shoulder. Apparently the Kiowa were keeping a close guard on everyone's comings and goings. The boys must have known of the sentries and ways to avoid being spied by them.

"But how can I get by them?" Carl whispered, nervously kneading his brow.

Suddenly he smiled. He had just remembered stories he had heard in town about Thunder Stick. It was known that the evil shaman would do anything for the shine of coins.

But getting to him was the problem.

"I might have to kill off one or more of the sentries," he said as he peered, evil-eyed, up at the one who sat on the bluff.

To get to Zoe he would do anything, kill anyone.

He recalled having seen Thunder Stick wandering in the forest gathering herbs. With any luck, tomorrow he would have the need of such plants for his hocus pocus medicines. Yes, tomorrow an opportunity might offer itself to him to get at the shaman without the risk of killing the sentries.

After dismounting, he unsaddled his horse, tied it deep in the thickness of the trees, and then lay on the ground on a blanket, his head resting on his saddle.

He lit another cigarette and waited for daylight to break along the horizon.

Chapter Twenty-five

I shut my eyes and turned them on my heart.
— Robert Browning

Having succeeded in explaining to White Shadow why she still felt compelled to continue searching for her father's killer, Zoe limped into her cabin and closed her door behind her. She had just come from the fort, where she'd learned that Timothy was still missing.

She gazed down at the moccasins that White Shadow had given her to replace the boot he had had to cut off her foot.

Oh, how she had hated leaving him this morning. Yet surely it wouldn't be too long before they could be together always.

The sound of someone arriving outside in a horse and buggy made her turn quickly, causing

her to stub her sore toe on the chair she was leaning against.

"Damn it," she whispered harshly, grimacing as
she leaned down to cradle her foot in her hand.

A soft knock on the door made her aware that
the person who had arrived was not a man. It was
the knock of a woman.

"Mary Ellen," she whispered, suddenly reminded of Timothy's sister's arrival in Gracemont.
"It is surely Mary Ellen."

Having no answers to give Mary Ellen about
Timothy, Zoe dreaded having to face her. Even
though Zoe was not to blame for Timothy's disappearance, her inability to find him made her
feel less than adequate as sheriff.

Sighing, Zoe went to the door and opened it.

Mary Ellen was standing there in a beautiful
lacy silk dress with the most feminine of hats on
her head.

"Have you any news of my brother yet?" Mary
Ellen asked, fanning her face with a lace-edged
handkerchief.

Zoe's eyes wavered as she gazed at Mary Ellen,
then looked past her at Rob, who had preferred to
stay in the wagon rather than take one step on
Zoe's precariously leaning porch.

"No, I have no news of Timothy," Zoe replied.

"I came to inquire yesterday but you weren't
here," Mary Ellen said snappishly. She lifted her
chin haughtily. "You were out looking for Timothy, I presume."

Zoe felt a heated blush rush to her cheeks. She
was suddenly self-conscious over where she *had*

been. In the arms of her Kiowa lover.

"Well, Zoe?" Mary Ellen persisted. "Were you out looking for my dear Timothy?"

"I'm sorry, Mary Ellen, but, well, yes, in a way I was, yet I was detained somewhat, or should I say sidetracked," Zoe said, her words sounding flustered and confused.

"What do you mean . . . detained? Side-tracked?" Mary Ellen asked, cocking a carefully plucked eyebrow.

Zoe laughed awkwardly as she looked down at her right foot. "Well, Mary Ellen, it seems that I came close to breaking a toe," she said, her eyes lifting when she heard Mary Ellen gasp.

When she saw what Mary Ellen was looking at Zoe knew that her horrified gasp was not because Zoe had injured her toe. It was apparent that Mary Ellen was aghast at the sort of shoes that Zoe wore today . . . moccasins.

"Where on earth did you get those things?" Mary Ellen asked, placing a hand on her throat; her eyes were as wide as saucers as she stared at the moccasins. "They are worn by . . . by . . . sav-ages, Zoe. Not white people."

The word "savage" caused Zoe's hair to bristle at the nape of her neck. She realized that Timothy's sister was no less a bigot than he.

"Mary Ellen, I have things to do, so I must ask you to leave," Zoe said, realizing how coldly she was speaking to the woman, and not caring.

"Leave?" Mary Ellen said, paling as she stared in disbelief at Zoe. "You are asking me to leave?"

"I do believe that's what I said," Zoe replied. She

grabbed the edge of the door and wished she could slam it in Mary Ellen's face.

"But you haven't told me what you are going to do about Timothy," Mary Ellen said, her voice tight. "I inquired at the fort. They said they have already searched for him until they are exhausted. They don't plan to look for him any longer. Is everyone just going to forget that my brother exists? Are you, Zoe? You were going to marry him."

"I never told Timothy that I would marry him," Zoe blurted out, haunted again by the promise that she had made to her father as he lay dying. "It was all a big misunderstanding. I plan to straighten it out as soon as I see Timothy."

"Then you aren't giving up on searching for him?" Mary Ellen persisted. "No, I haven't given up searching for him," Zoe said, sighing heavily. "But not today, Mary Ellen. I don't think I can ride one more minute on that horse with my throbbing toe."

"You'd let a toe stand in the way of finding Timothy?" Mary Ellen said, clenching her jaw. "Shame on you, Zoe."

Zoe was rendered speechless by Mary Ellen's attitude. She watched Mary Ellen stamp away to the buggy, huffing and puffing as her husband helped her into the seat.

"I'm leaving, Zoe," Mary Ellen cried. "I'm going back to Boston. I can't stand that flea-infested hotel another night!"

Zoe was taken aback when Mary Ellen said something else that cut her deeply.

"I never wanted my brother to marry you in the

225

first place," she shouted. "If he comes out of this alive, I'll tell him so, Zoe. I'll tell him you are a worthless tramp! That's why I bothered myself to come to Oklahoma . . . to tell my brother not to marry you. You and your family have never been anything but riffraff! Do you hear? Riffraff!"

Shocked by how Mary Ellen had turned on her, Zoe watched the wagon move away; then she went back inside and flopped down on a chair.

"Riffraff?" she murmured, tears coming to her eyes.

She became lost in thought, recalling the times she had walked past the Livingston mansion in Boston and had felt envious of those who lived in it.

Now she was glad that she had never been a part of that world. If living like that formed personalities like Mary Ellen's, Zoe felt blessed with her own parents.

She felt proud that she had not lowered herself to marrying Timothy just because of his riches.

"Timothy," she whispered, gazing at the window. "Oh, Timothy, where *are* you?"

She was puzzled at the way Timothy seemed to have dropped off the face of the earth.

Chapter Twenty-six

That loss is common would not make
My own less bitter, rather more.
—Alfred, Lord Tennyson

Having made sure Timothy was busy with several
warriors learning more Kiowa customs today,
Thunder Stick felt free to wander in the forest to
collect his various medicinal herbs.

Thunder Stick dropped his parfleche bag to the
ground, bent to his knees, and began digging
pomme blanche roots from the ground. He
stopped, startled, when he heard the crunching of
leaves close by.

"Don't be scared, old man," Carl said, stepping
out into the open for Thunder Stick to see. "I've
come to bargain with you." He placed a cigarette
between his lips and lit it, then rolled it with his

tongue over to the corner of his mouth.

Squinting his eyes, looking more closely at Carl as the outlaw stepped closer, Thunder Stick pushed himself up from the ground. "I know you. I have seen your Wanted posters everywhere. You are Carl Collins, the outlaw everyone is looking for," he said thickly. "What do you want with me?"

Thunder Stick inched slowly away from Carl. He glanced down at the holstered pistols hanging heavy at each of Carl's hips, then looked guardedly at the outlaw again.

"I want your help, that's all," Carl said, taking a long drag from the cigarette, then yanking it from his mouth and dropping it to the ground, grinding it out with the heel of his boot.

"What can this Kiowa Shaman do for an outlaw white man?" Thunder Stick asked.

"I want a man that your people hold captive," Carl said, frowning. "I want Timothy Livingston."

"Timothy . . . Livingston?" Thunder Stick gasped out, wondering how the white man had learned of his capture.

"I have heard that you are a lover of coins," Carl said, stepping closer. "I will pay you many if you will bring Timothy Livingston to me at my hide-out."

"You will pay me for him?" Thunder Stick said. He leaned his head forward and cocked an eyebrow. "How many coins?"

"Enough for you to chance placing yourself in danger by taking Timothy from your village," Carl said, smiling. "Is it a deal? If I show you my hide-out, can I trust that you won't bring anyone to it but Timothy? If I promise enough payment to you, can you be trusted to keep all of this to yourself?"

Thunder Stick rubbed his hands together. His eyes gleamed. "I will do anything for coins," he said, cackling. "*Ho*, white man. Show me your hideout. I will bring Timothy to you. But you must be patient. It will not be an easy task getting Timothy past the sentries. I must find a clever way to do it without bringing harm to myself. I do not wish to be banished by my very own people."

"I'll be patient," Carl said, lighting another cigarette. "I've got all the patience in the world if in the end I get what I want." He laughed throatily. "Take all the time you need. In the end, the waiting will be worth it."

"Tell me, white man outlaw, what worth this man has to you, that you would pay so dearly for him?" Thunder Stick asked, reaching down for his parfleche bag.

"The man is worthless to me," Carl ground out. "But in the end his capture will gain me a woman."

"Is this woman named Zoe?" Thunder Stick asked, leaning closer to Carl.

"Yes, Zoe," Carl said, chuckling. "Now, ain't she worth payin' for?"

Knowing how his chief felt about Zoe, Thunder Stick suddenly felt uneasy over bargaining with the devil . . . for he saw the outlaw as no less than the devil.

But Thunder Stick would chance anything to have the coins promised him. His chief's threats of banishment loomed over him now like a dark cloud! He could not help but believe that it would happen.

"We must be careful where we go today as you show me the way to your hideout," Thunder Stick said. "I do not want the sentries to see me with you. Like me, they all know your face . . . the face of a deadly outlaw. It would cause many questions should they see their shaman with such a man."

"But you know where the sentries are posted, so you should be able to elude them," Carl said.

"*Ho*, yes, I am good at eluding," Thunder Stick said, nodding. "Come. We will find a way around them."

Carl smiled smugly to himself.

Chapter Twenty-seven

Let me contend to the uttermost,
For his life's set prize, be it what it will!
                              —Robert Browning

White Shadow had decided to speak with his mother about revealing the truth to Timothy today.

From that point on it would be up to Timothy how things would be for him. If he accepted that his true mother was Soft Bird and he was able to see past his earlier prejudices and be proud of his Kiowa blood, then perhaps everyone's lives could move forward.

If Timothy did not accept that part of him that was Kiowa, then his captivity would continue until he did.

"*Ho*, I want it over with," White Shadow whispered to himself, doubling his fists at his sides. "He must be told today. I am tired of waiting for Zoe."

His jaw tight, White Shadow stood in the shadow of his tepee and slowly surveyed all who were outside their lodges, some doing their daily chores, others visiting.

Remembering that Timothy was being taught the Kiowa's "calendar of histories" today, the pictographic portrayal of important tribal events that were painted on skins by an artist of the tribe, White Shadow thought that perhaps his mother was there to observe Timothy's reaction to the painting.

For many years now the Kiowa had kept a record of their daring deeds on painted skins. Before the buffalo was all but annihilated, the paintings were done on buffalo hide.

Now it was done on deerskin.

Painted on the skins were such things as the yearly celebration of the great sun dance, which was denied the Kiowa now that they were isolated on a reservation.

Also on the earlier skins was the coming of the deadly smallpox, cholera, and measles, brought to his people by the whites. The broken treaties with the whites were also recorded there.

Painted in bright colors on the skins were depictions of fights with the Cheyenne and Osage, and with the United States cavalry.

The paintings being done today by the village artist were pictographs of the reservation upon which the Kiowa were housed. The boundaries were shown by a tall fence, with wolves showing bloody fangs guarding the perimeters of the reservation. White Shadow hoped that his brother would be touched by seeing through the eyes of the painter how much the Kiowa hated reservation life.

Shading his eyes with his hands, White Shadow looked more intently around him, then stopped when he found his mother standing among a crowd of his people who were observing today's paintings. The white man was standing beside the painter, watching each stroke of his brush on the buckskin canvas.

Ho, his brother was getting a lesson today about his true people that should affect him deeply, for surely somewhere inside his heart he was now aware of his true heritage and could feel compassion for his people.

White Shadow walked through the crowd until he came to his mother's side. When she looked up at him he saw tears in her eyes and knew that she, too, was touched by the depiction of the life she now knew on the reservation.

Sliding a comforting arm around his mother's waist, White Shadow drew her close to his side. Again she watched the artist, and then looked at Timothy. "I see much in your brother's eyes that I never saw before," Soft Bird whispered, wiping tears from her cheeks. "I see compassion. He seems captivated by the teachings today," she said softly. She gazed up at White Shadow again. "There is something in *your* eyes today, son, that

I cannot read. Do you wish to tell me what is on your mind?"

"*Ho*, I do," White Shadow said, nodding. "Mother, it is time to reveal the truth to my brother. I believe he is ready to hear it. I am ready to see that it is done. My life is at a standstill because Timothy is our captive. I wish to move onward. I wish to bring Zoe into our village as my wife. How can I when she is out there somewhere searching for a man who is right here in our midst? She must be told the truth soon, Mother, or she may be harmed while she rides all over the countryside searching for a man who is alive and well right here."

"But, son," Soft Bird said, her eyes wavering. "What if . . . ?"

"Come, Mother," White Shadow replied, gently placing an arm around her waist and ushering her away from the crowd.

He took her between two lodges and stopped and faced her. "Mother, what must be done must be done," he said. "Now is better than later. Each day we hold my brother captive we chance disaster for our people."

"But what if he does not accept what we tell him?" Soft Bird murmured.

"Mother, from the beginning this has been your plan," White Shadow said, his voice drawn. "I had hoped that you knew what to do should your first-born still deny you once he is told the truth."

"But you are chief," Soft Bird said. "Should not the decision be yours?"

"He is *your* son," White Shadow said. "Whatever

you say his fate is to be, it will be done."

Soft Bird turned and again stared through the crowd at Timothy. She watched as he willingly took the painter's brush in his hand and carefully painted part of the fence on the drawing.

She gasped when she saw how Timothy's hand trembled as he dipped his brush into red paint and then drew a drop of blood on the canvas, representing blood dropping from the fangs of one of the wolves that had been painted there.

"He understands," Soft Bird gasped out, covering her mouth with a hand. "He truly . . . understands . . ."

White Shadow's eyes widened as he watched Timothy hand the brush to one of the young braves who had been standing close by, watching.

White Shadow watched Timothy kneel and talk to the young brave, then nod toward the skin as the child took his turn painting.

"*Ho*, I, too, believe he understands," White Shadow said, turning to look at his mother. He lifted a hand and brushed tears from her cheeks. "Mother, I shall go and get Timothy. We will meet you in your lodge. There we will talk with him. When our discussion is over, he will know that you are his mother and that I am his brother."

Soft Bird gazed wistfully up at White Shadow, then flung herself into his arms and clung to him. "I hope I was not wrong to bring him here," she said, her voice revealing her fear. "But . . . I . . . had to."

"*Ho*, I know," White Shadow said, gently stroking her back. "I know."

She turned from him and went to her tepee while White Shadow stood awhile longer watching Timothy; then he went to him and placed a gentle hand on his arm.

When Timothy turned to face him, White Shadow saw much of himself in his features. Surely Timothy had seen it also when he looked into the mirror. Except for the color of his skin, he was Kiowa.

"My mother wishes to speak with you," White Shadow said thickly. "Come. I will take you to her."

"She wants to talk with me?" Timothy asked, walking beside White Shadow. "What is there about me that interests her so much? I have seen her constantly watching me. Why, White Shadow? Why won't anyone tell me why?"

"She is soon to tell you, herself," White Shadow said, nodding toward his mother's tepee. "Come. She awaits you inside her lodge."

"I hope she's going to tell me that she's decided to let me go," Timothy grumbled, yet he knew that there was something about being with these people that made him feel comfortable in a strange way. He was enjoying the lessons. He had learned more among the Kiowa about Indians than he had ever read in books or heard among the soldiers, who, for the most part, laughed and called Indians "savages."

Even Timothy had called them "savages." He had discovered, while among them, that they were anything but that. They were a unique, gentle, and caring people. Strange how he no longer felt alien to them.

"My mother will tell you what she has kept to herself for far too long," White Shadow said, causing Timothy to give him a puzzled look.

White Shadow turned to Timothy and placed his hands on his brother's bare shoulders. "Listen well to what my mother says to you," he said. "Listen with an open heart and accept what she tells you as truth. Show her that you understand and sympathize with her having been forced to give up her first-born those long years ago."

"Her first-born?" Timothy said, raising an eyebrow. "Why on earth do you think I want to hear any tales about her and her lost baby? White Shadow, I'm no priest who listens to confessions."

"This confession comes from the bottom of her heart, and it has everything to do with you," White Shadow said flatly.

White Shadow nodded toward the closed entrance flap. "Go," he said. "Mother waits."

White Shadow followed Timothy into the lodge, where Soft Bird sat at the back of the tepee.

White Shadow nodded at Timothy as he gestured with a hand toward a pallet of furs spread opposite Soft Bird.

He waited for Timothy to sit down, then sat down beside Soft Bird and gazed into Timothy's eyes as Soft Bird began telling Timothy the story of her first love.

With much emotion, she finally revealed to Timothy that she was his true mother, that he had been wrenched from her breast when he was only a few days old, her milk still wet on his tiny, hungry lips.

Timothy gasped and scrambled to his feet, then fell back to his knees when White Shadow reached for him and grabbed his hand.

"Sit, listen, and feel," White Shadow softly urged. "Reach inside your heart and feel what my mother feels. You will then know that she is your mother and that I am your brother."

Timothy glanced quickly at White Shadow. "You . . . are my brother?" he gasped out, pale.

"If Soft Bird is my mother and she is *your* mother, then does that not make us brothers by blood kin?" White Shadow said, his voice even and measured.

"I . . . am . . . Kiowa . . . ?" Timothy asked, his voice drawn. "All these years I was part Indian and . . . and . . . I was never told?"

"Your father made sure you weren't told," Soft Bird murmured. "Although I believe your father did love me, he could never look past the fact that I was Indian. Once he knew that I was with child, he kept me with him at his grand home, but only until I gave birth to you. I was allowed only a few days with you before he sent me away."

"You have been brought to our village to see how wrong you have been to be prejudiced against the very people who are blood kin to you, but also for you to learn the ways of your people," White Shadow said. "I have watched you. I have seen your interest. Today I saw you paint on the skins the depiction of blood dripping from the teeth of wolves. To the Kiowa, white men are, indeed, wolves. You have felt something, have you not, for your people? Have you not puzzled over how you have grown to feel close to those you have been among these past days? Do you not even now believe, wholeheartedly, that you are who my mother says you are?"

Timothy recalled the many times he had asked about his true mother; no one had ever given him any answers. His questions had always been ignored.

And his sister Mary Ellen. Was she only his half-sister?

Yes, although he found it all hard to comprehend, Timothy thought that what Soft Bird had told him was surely the truth, for why should she lie about such a thing?

Slowly he touched his face, scarcely breathing as he ran his fingers over his features. So often he had wondered about his high cheekbones, his Roman nose, his piercingly dark eyes, and the coal black hair that shone in the sun like a raven's wing.

When he saw that Soft Bird was holding a mirror out to him, he took it and gazed at his reflection, again seeing what he had seen throughout the years. He did, indeed, look like an Indian.

"It is true," Soft Bird murmured. "You are Kiowa. You can see it, can you not? You can feel it? Do you not see the resemblance between yourself and your brother White Shadow?"

Timothy shifted the mirror somewhat so that it captured White Shadow's reflection beside his own. He gulped; except for the color of their skin, they could almost be twins.

He dropped the mirror and lowered his eyes.

"Closing your eyes will not make the truth go away," White Shadow said. "You are what you are. Be proud of it."

"I understand many things now," Timothy said, swallowing hard. He slowly raised his eyes and looked first at Soft Bird and then at White Shadow. "I now know that the reason I always spoke out against Indians in such a harsh way was because I have been troubled often by dreams that *I* was an Indian. Yes, when I looked in the mirror, I always saw it. I fought the dreams and feelings by denying all feelings of sympathy for Indians.

"And I always wondered why Father went out of his way to preach against Indians," he said thickly. "And then he was killed by one."

"Forget your father. The Kiowa are your people now," White Shadow said, placing a gentle hand on his brother's shoulder. "Speak it aloud, brother. Say that you are Kiowa."

Timothy tried to, then closed his eyes and frantically shook his head back and forth. "I . . . can't," he cried. "I . . . just . . . can't."

"Then the lessons taught you were not effective," Soft Bird said, stifling a sob behind her hand.

Timothy heard her despair, and felt her disappointment inside his own heart.

Then suddenly he reached out his arms toward her.

White Shadow was startled by Timothy's abrupt

change of heart to accept the truth. He felt a lump in his throat when his mother fell into Timothy's embrace.

"Son," Soft Bird sobbed, clinging to him. "My son!"

White Shadow scarcely breathed as he watched Timothy's arms close around his mother.

"Your embrace feels like a mother's embrace," Timothy said, his voice trembling with emotion. "Your love feels like the sincere love of a mother. I have missed all of those things! It . . . made . . . me hard. It made . . . me . . . uncaring!"

"You are no longer denied anything that a mother can give a son," Soft Bird cried, gazing up at Timothy, their eyes locking in silent understanding.

White Shadow flicked tears from his eyes, and then placed a hand on his brother's shoulder. "Nor will you ever again be denied a brother's love," he said thickly.

Timothy looked past his mother's shoulder and smiled at White Shadow.

Chapter Twenty-eight

That I did always love,
I bring thee proof;
That till I loved you,
I did not love enough.
—Emily Dickinson

Having left his mother and Timothy talking, White Shadow reined in his horse outside Zoe's cabin. It was time to reveal the truth to her as well.

He knew that she would be stunned to know where Timothy had been these past several days, and why. He only hoped that she would be understanding about the fact that he had withheld the information until now.

Surely once she thought it through she would sympathize with Soft Bird and be happy that she now had the son she had been forced to give up so many years ago.

Dismounting and tying the reins around the hitching post, White Shadow gazed at Zoe's horse. He had not truly expected her to be home, because she was so determined to find her father's killer . . . and Timothy.

But now that he saw she was there, he was relieved. She would no longer have to worry about Timothy's whereabouts.

When the door opened and he saw Zoe standing there, he was filled with the same heated passion he always felt when he saw her. His love for her was so deep and true it was like a fire burning in his soul.

"White Shadow?" Zoe said, wiping sleep from her eyes. His horse's arrival had awakened her from a deep sleep. "I didn't expect you. Why are you here?"

"To talk," White Shadow said, going up the stairs and onto the porch.

When Zoe moved into his arms and their lips met in a long, deep kiss, she was filled with an intense happiness. Zoe clung to him, and although it had not been long since they had embraced and made love, at this moment it seemed like a lifetime ago.

White Shadow's lips slid away. He gazed intently into Zoe's eyes, then took her hand and walked her inside her cabin.

"You said you came to talk," Zoe murmured. "About what, White Shadow?"

"I have brought you news of Timothy Livingston," White Shadow said guardedly, his eyes searching hers when she seemed taken aback by what he had said.

"News of Timothy?" Zoe said, easing away from him. "What . . . sort . . . ?"

"He is alive and well," White Shadow said, now hesitant to tell her.

What if she didn't understand why he had kept this from her? What if she didn't understand why his mother had chosen to use abduction to regain her first-born?

"He is?" Zoe said, arching an eyebrow. "How do you know this, White Shadow? Have you seen him? Has he been rescued? Is he at the fort?"

Inhaling a deep, quavering breath, White Shadow took Zoe by the hand and led her to a chair before the cold fireplace, where gray ashes lay in heaps beneath the grate.

He urged her to sit down, then positioned a chair before her and faced her as he began his explanation. Each word seemed to cause her eyes to widen more, and her lips parted as she gasped.

When he was through, he could see the disbelief in her eyes, and then he saw something else that made him turn cold inside. He saw a flash of anger. He flinched when Zoe rose quickly from her chair and stood over him with an accusing stare.

"How could you have done this?" she asked, a sob lodging in her throat. "Taking Timothy captive in such a way and holding him against his will was a thing only an evil man would do."

His jaw tight, his eyes narrowed, White Shadow

jumped from his chair and towered over her. "Do you call my mother evil?" he said, his voice drawn. "I told you that she was the one who asked for the abduction! I told you why. She had a good reason."

"I just don't know," Zoe said, nervously raking her fingers through her hair. "Taking a man captive is wrong, no matter the reason."

White Shadow placed his hands on her upper arms. He gripped her tightly. "Did you not hear anything I told you?" he demanded. "My mother's child was wrenched from her arms . . . from her *breast* . . . while her milk was still wet on her child's lips. She was denied him all these years! He was raised as white in an environment of prejudice against all Indians! How else could she have gotten him to come to her? Do you think he would have believed that he was a half-breed if she had told him any other way?"

"But you knew that I was searching for him and . . . and . . . you still didn't tell me," Zoe said, her voice breaking. "Couldn't you have trusted me enough to share this with me?"

"You chose to wear the badge of sheriff," White Shadow said, dropping his hands away from her. "The badge makes you work for the best interest of whites, not Kiowa. If you had known about Timothy's abduction before he had the chance to truly experience being Kiowa, you would have ordered him set free. Do you think that my mother would have regained her son then?"

"I never would have gone against your wishes,"

Zoe said, swallowing hard. "I would have understood."

"Do you truly understand even now?" White Shadow asked, placing a gentle hand on her cheek.

"I want to," Zoe said, sighing.

"Come with me to my village and see Timothy and my mother together and then tell me that you still have trouble understanding," White Shadow said.

"Timothy has actually accepted this truth about himself?" Zoe asked, going to sit on the edge of the bed to put on her moccasins. She slid the first on easily, but winced when she slid her foot with the sore toe into the other moccasin.

"He seems to . . . unless . . . unless it is only a pose he assumes until he leaves and returns to the fort," White Shadow said tightly. "If he is only play-acting with my mother, and he then turns against her and brings the wrath of the pony soldiers down on my people, pity him. I will soon forget that he is my brother. I . . . will . . . fight him until one of us is dead."

"You truly think there is a possibility that he isn't being truthful about having accepted your mother as his blood kin?" Zoe asked, walking on outside to the horses with White Shadow.

"Only time will tell," White Shadow said.

Zoe mounted her steed as White Shadow swung into his saddle.

Still talking about Timothy, they rode off toward White Shadow's village.

"You know what this means, do you not?" White

Shadow asked as his village came into view.

"So much," Zoe said. She smiled at him. "But most of all, it means that once I tell Timothy that I can't marry him, we will have one more obstacle to our marriage behind us."

"You are still determined to find your father's killer before you marry me?" White Shadow asked guardedly.

"I would be much happier as your bride if that was behind me," Zoe said. She grew silent as they rode onward until they finally reached the outer perimeter of the village.

She gazed down the long line of tepees and looked at Soft Bird's lodge. Her pulse raced to know that Timothy was there, and why. He was, in part, Kiowa!

Recalling how Timothy had been such a bigoted person, she found it hard to believe that he would accept this truth so easily. But she did not want to voice aloud to White Shadow just how much she doubted Timothy.

Something else worried her, too. Once Timothy discovered that he was losing Zoe to a Kiowa chief, to his blood brother, how would he react?

She grew tense as she drew a tight rein before Soft Bird's tepee. She now dreaded facing Timothy. Yet she felt as though she knew him well enough to be able to read his expressions when she saw him. She would know whether or not he was lying about his feelings for the Kiowa.

Wanting to get this behind her, Zoe dismounted. She smiled a thank you to a young brave as he came and took her horse's reins.

Her pulse raced as White Shadow held back the entrance flap so that she could enter Soft Bird's lodge before him. She slid past him, and then stood, eyes wide, when she found Timothy sitting with his mother at the back of the tepee beside the rolled-up lodge skins.

She was stunned by his attire. He wore only a breechclout. Yes, except for the color of his skin, he *did* look like a Kiowa brave.

She was glad that he was so absorbed in what he and his mother were saying that he had not yet noticed Zoe standing there. She needed more time to compose herself, for she felt as though she would be talking with a stranger now instead of the man she had known before. She never would have thought that she would see him conversing in a friendly tone with an Indian. She never would have thought that he would willingly wear a breechclout.

White Shadow came into the lodge and took Zoe by the hand. She turned to him and was glad when he gave her a smile of reassurance. She needed that. Moments from now she would be adding to Timothy's discoveries. Not only was he part Kiowa, but also the woman he loved was marrying his Kiowa brother.

Zoe leaned closer to White Shadow. "I wish I didn't have to do this," she whispered.

"It is best that it is done now, not later," White Shadow whispered back. "Do you not agree that too many truths have been kept hidden for too long from too many people?"

"Yes," Zoe whispered, nodding.

"Then let us get one more truth out in the open," White Shadow said, leading her to Soft Bird and Timothy.

Timothy turned and was obviously taken aback when he saw Zoe with White Shadow. Zoe smiled awkwardly when he rose to his feet.

"Zoe, what are you doing here?" Timothy asked. "Did you know that I was being held captive? Were you in on this? Did you know that I was, in part, Kiowa?"

"No, I knew nothing about it and I have been almost mindless with worry over your disappearance," Zoe blurted out. "I thought perhaps Carl Collins might have taken you into hiding . . . or . . . worse yet . . . killed you. I only discovered moments ago where you really were, and why."

Timothy glanced down at his mother, and then smiled awkwardly at Zoe. "Soft Bird is my true mother," he said thickly. He glanced at White Shadow. "White Shadow is my blood brother."

"Yes, now I know," Zoe said, swallowing hard, amazed to see a more humble side of Timothy. She could not help believing that he had changed.

"And you truly cared when you thought I might have been kidnapped by Carl Collins?" Timothy asked, stepping closer to Zoe. "You do care that much for me, Zoe?"

"I do care, but . . ." Zoe began. She stopped and glanced up at White Shadow, then down at Soft Bird, whose dark eyes were on her.

"I need to speak with Timothy in private, please," she murmured.

White Shadow nodded. He went to his mother

and reached down and placed a hand on her elbow and helped her to her feet, then took one last lingering look at Zoe before walking his mother outside.

"You have something to tell me?" Timothy said, taking Zoe's hand. "You have reconsidered my proposal of marriage? You are going to marry me after all?"

"Your sister and husband have come from Boston," Zoe said. "Timothy, Mary Ellen said that you wired her several weeks ago about our upcoming marriage." She decided not to tell Timothy that Mary Ellen had not come for the wedding . . . but to stop it. His sister was gone now, and as far as Zoe knew she would never have to face the woman again!

"How could you have caused your sister and her husband such undue trouble?" Zoe said. "You know that I never promised to marry you."

"I had always thought that you would," Timothy said, lowering his eyes. When he did, he saw the breechclout. His face reddened with embarrassment. He looked slowly up at Zoe again. "Are you stunned by what I am wearing? And by the fact that I am part Kiowa?"

"I am surprised, yes," Zoe said. She inhaled a nervous breath. "But not stunned. I think it's wonderful that Soft Bird has found her long-lost son. I am touched that you seem to care for her. Do you, Timothy? Do you truly care? Or are you playing a game in order to be set free?"

"Are *you* playing a game?" Timothy asked softly. "Are you or are you not going to marry me? Is my being part Kiowa going to make a difference?"

"I'm sorry if it looked as though I was playing games with you when I made that promise to my father before he died," Zoe said softly. "I did it only for my father. Not for you. Not for me. I tried to explain to you why I told him I would marry you. Please try to understand now when I tell you once again that I won't be marrying you. And my decision has nothing to do with your being Kiowa. I had told you before I knew this that I wouldn't marry you."

She cleared her throat. "And, Timothy, your being part Indian never would have caused me to change my mind," she murmured. "For you see, Timothy, I am going to marry a Kiowa warrior. I'm going to marry a Kiowa *chief*. I'm marrying White Shadow."

"What?" Timothy gasped, paling. He took a shaky step away from her. "What . . . did . . . you just . . . say?"

"I'm in love with White Shadow," Zoe said, her voice wary. "I have loved him for so long, Timothy. But I could never allow my father to know. Therefore no one else knew. No one but me and White Shadow."

She waited for him to explode. Certainly, that was how he would have reacted only a few days ago.

But surprisingly, he seemed to accept the truth. He even reached a gentle hand to her face and touched it, a smile quivering on his lips.

"You think no one knew about you and White Shadow?" he said softly. "You were wrong. I saw it. Every time you two were thrown together in one way or another at the fort, or in town, or at the trading post when I was there to watch you, I saw it in both of your eyes. I just didn't want to accept the truth. I wanted you so badly; I wanted to think you were only interested in him because of some foolish girlish fantasy of forbidden love. I should have known that it was the real thing."

He dropped his hand away and held his face in his hands. "I feel so overwhelmed by everything that has happened," he said, his voice sounding drained. "I need to get some rest."

"Timothy, I have to ask . . ." Zoe said as she put a hand on his arm and walked slowly toward the entrance flap. "What are you going to do now? Surely you will be set free now. Are you going to stay here? Or go back to the life of a colonel at the fort?"

"Soft Bird has told me that I am free to go when I please, if that is what I wish to do," Timothy said, stopping and turning to gaze down at Zoe. "I even saw that the sentries were brought in from their posts. That means that I am truly free to go if I wish to."

"Will you?" Zoe prodded.

"I'm so bone-weary at having discovered so many things about myself today, all I can think about at this moment is getting some rest," Timothy said, kneading his brow. "Then I will decide what I must do next in my life. Without you at my side as my wife, I have nothing but my wealth waiting for me in the white world. But here, with the Kiowa, I feel such a bond, as though this is where I belong."

"It sounds like you have made up your mind," Zoe said, stepping outside the tepee with him.

"Yes, I think perhaps I have," Timothy said, smiling down at Soft Bird as she came to him and took his hands.

"I will walk with you to your lodge," Soft Bird said softly. "I will tell Thunder Stick to take all of his paraphernalia away so that you can now live in total privacy."

"Thank you, Mother," Timothy said, giving Zoe a sad look over his shoulder as he walked away from her. He then slid a slow gaze over at White Shadow. "I wish both of you well."

White Shadow was stunned by Timothy's reaction to the news of his upcoming marriage to Zoe. With each moment he was discovering just how much his brother had changed. And all for the good!

He watched Timothy and his mother until they went inside Soft Bird's lodge, and then he turned to Zoe. Smiling at her, he placed an arm around her waist and led her to his own lodge. As they sat down on blankets at the back of the tepee, White Shadow held Zoe next to him as they discussed all that had transpired today.

"I welcome my brother in my life," White Shadow said softly. "But only if he doesn't try to scheme to get you back."

"I truly believe that Timothy was sincere when he gave us his best wishes," Zoe murmured. "I do believe he is a changed man."

"Unless he is good at pretending," White Shadow said, his eyes narrowing at that possibility.

"At least it's wonderful to know that Timothy is safe and well," Zoe said, sighing. "I only wish I knew where to find my father's killer. While I am with you like this, so wonderfully alone, it is almost possible for me to forget Carl Collins and the need for vengeance. I'm not even sure if I want to go on with the search. So much in my life has changed since I vowed to find him."

"You just say the word and we can be married," White Shadow said, pulling her down on the pelts beside him. "Perhaps I should try harder at persuading you?"

"And how would you do that?" Zoe teased, already feeling her heartbeat accelerate as White Shadow unbuttoned her shirt.

She closed her eyes in ecstasy when he slid aside her shirt and cupped her breasts in the heat of his hands.

"By making love," White Shadow said huskily.

"Yes, yes . . ." she whispered.

Their hands trembled with excitement as they undressed one another in a blaze of urgency.

White Shadow's mouth slipped down to her shoulder and then fastened gently on one of her breasts, his tongue making large, swirling circles around her nipple.

He swept his arms around her and lifted her soft, pliant body next to his. His knee urged her legs apart as he entered her in one deep thrust.

Zoe closed her eyes in ecstasy and slowly moved

her head from side to side as White Shadow began his rhythmic thrusts. She felt herself being enveloped in heat and brightness as the pleasure spread throughout her. She arched her back so that she was closer to his heat. She whimpered softly against his lips when his mouth came to hers.

"Feel how I want you?" White Shadow whispered huskily against her lips as he shoved himself even deeper inside her. "Feel my need? Does it match yours?"

"Yes, yes," Zoe whispered.

She swept her arms around his neck and drew his lips more tightly against hers.

Their kiss became long and deep, his hands all over her now, touching her, stroking her, and softly pinching her until she wanted to melt on the pelts spread beneath her.

White Shadow felt the pleasure so intensely, it was as though flames were roaring in his ears. The passion spreading through him was growing hotter, like an all-consuming fire.

He fought to bring his breathing under control when he felt himself close to the edge. His body stiffened.

He slid his mouth from her lips and buried it in the soft column of her throat, his hands holding her breasts, his thumbs grazing her nipples. Then he made one last deep plunge inside her and welcomed the euphoria that came with total release. He felt her simultaneous release as her body trembled against his, her moans revealing to him the depths of her own pleasure.

And then they lay there, clinging, the moon having replaced the sun in the sky.

"Stay the night?" White Shadow whispered against Zoe's cheek. He kissed his way slowly down her body, leaving her trembling in the wake of his mouth, tongue, and lips.

"If you continue to do that, I will be sorely tempted to stay forever and ever," Zoe whispered back, crying out with renewed pleasure when she felt his tongue flick over the tender mound of her woman's center. She closed her eyes and, for now, lived only for the moment.

Content that Timothy was restfully sleeping, Soft Bird left his cabin and went to her own.

She hadn't seen Thunder Stick as he stood in the shadows, watching her. She hadn't seen Thunder Stick move stealthily through the darkness toward Timothy's cabin.

Chapter Twenty-nine

Heard, have you? What? They have
told you he never repented his sin.
—Alfred, Lord Tennyson

A noise in the cabin awakened Timothy. "Who's
there?" he asked. He felt disoriented as he leaned
up on an elbow to look around him.

When he saw a dark figure looming over him in
the darkness, he flinched.

"It is I, Thunder Stick," the shaman whispered.
"You are to come with me."

Before Timothy realized what was happening,
Thunder Stick had Timothy's hands tied in front
of him, and a gag placed over his mouth.

Timothy tried to fight back, but the old man had
the advantage of surprise.

Timothy was utterly bewildered. Just hours ago

257

he had been reunited with his true mother. He had accepted a new way of life. Why was he being gagged and tied?

Something was quite wrong, for it did not seem logical that a gentle women like Soft Bird would be deceitful in this way. Why would she pretend to love him, and then treat him once again like a prisoner?

Timothy gave Thunder Stick a shove. But it was not enough to get away from him. Thunder Stick's hand was instantly on Timothy's arm, yanking him up from the pallet of blankets.

A fierce anger roared through Timothy to think that all of this had been a ploy to make him look small and foolish in the eyes of the Kiowa. Even soft Bird telling him that she was his mother! That had surely been done to make him look ridiculous to the Kiowa. Probably they wanted to make him pay for all of the times he had wronged them in the past. He expected to find everyone outside, waiting to laugh at him and to torment him.

But as Thunder Stick led him outside, Timothy found the village quiet. The large outdoor fire had burned down to sparkling, orange embers. Even the village dogs were asleep. It seemed that only Thunder Stick and Timothy were awake.

And as Thunder Stick hurried Timothy behind the cabin, and then to the dark shadows of the forest, where two horses were saddled and waiting, Timothy knew that it was only the shaman who was playing games with him. Thunder Stick was probably betraying his people, too. For why else would he be sneaking around while everyone else was asleep?

Again Timothy tried to yank himself free, to fight back, but to no avail. He glared at Thunder Stick when the old man gave him a sly smile.

"Get on the horse," Thunder Stick whispered harshly, shoving Timothy toward it. "White man, you are more valuable to me tonight than you are to your Kiowa mother." He cackled. "Do not attempt again to get away from me," Thunder Stick warned. "I would not hesitate to kill you. You are as valuable to me dead as alive."

He took the reins of Timothy's horse as he eased up into his own saddle.

"We do not have far to travel before we get to the outlaw's hideout," Thunder Stick said, leading Timothy through the forest. "Once I get you there, I will be paid many coins."

He was being taken to an outlaw's hideout? Timothy's spine stiffened. He knew only one outlaw. Carl Collins!

As Thunder Stick led his horse onward, traveling by the light of the moon, Timothy gazed around him, hoping someone would see them. If only his mother hadn't removed the sentries!

Timothy was alone at this midnight hour with a madman, being taken to a madman.

They rode onward, and Timothy's eyes widened when just up ahead, in a clearing, he could see the glow of lamplight in a cabin. Fear struck at his heart, for he doubted he would survive this captivity.

Surely Carl Collins planned to kill him, to send

some sort of twisted message to the fort. Perhaps Carl wanted to show everyone just how much power he had over the entire community.

Carl stepped outside and gazed at Thunder Stick; then his lips twisted into a smug smile when he saw Timothy. He lit a cigarette and waited for Thunder Stick to bring Timothy to him.

As his eyes locked with Timothy's, he laughed. "You ain't such a powerful man now, are you?" he said, giving Timothy a shove so that he fell clumsily to the ground.

Timothy grimaced when Carl placed a foot on his abdomen and dug his heel in as he held him there with brute force.

"I'll take care of my prisoner," Carl said, sliding Thunder Stick a sour glance. "Shaman, you know what you've got to do now. Before I'll pay you one damn cent, you've got to bring Zoe to me. Then, Shaman, I'll make you rich."

"You told me you would pay me if I brought Timothy Livingston to you," Thunder Stick said, glaring at Carl. "Pay me now. Then I will go for the white woman."

"Do you think I'm stupid, or what?" Carl said, laughing loosely as he yanked Timothy up from the ground. "Go and get her, Shaman, or forget our deal."

"She is staying the night with my chief," Thunder Stick said in a growl.

"Then go and watch for her to start home. When she does, grab her," Carl said flatly. "Tell her I have Timothy. That's one hell of a way to get her to come with you. Tell her if she doesn't come, and come alone, Timothy will die."

Timothy paled. He now understood what was behind this scheme. The outlaw was setting a trap for Zoe.

He struggled to get free of Carl's tight grip, but his mind went blank when the outlaw knocked him on the head with the butt end of his pistol, rendering him unconscious.

"Now, Shaman! Leave now!" Carl said, dragging Timothy toward his cabin door.

Thunder Stick frowned, then nodded and mounted his steed again. His thin shoulders were slumped and his eyes were filled with an angry fire as he rode away.

"The stupid sonofabitch," Carl mumbled.

He flipped his half-smoked cigarette over his shoulder and then dragged Timothy inside the cabin.

Chuckling, Carl tied Timothy in an upright position in a chair facing the door so that Zoe could see him the minute she entered the cabin.

"One more lawman . . . or should I say law *woman* will soon bite the dust," Carl said, laughing boisterously.

He stretched out on his bed and crossed his legs at the ankles.

Smiling, he took a cigarette from his shirt pocket, stuck it between his lips, lit it, and enjoyed another smoke as he waited for his moment of glory.

"Yep, I'll take much delight in killin' 'er," he said, his eyes squinting as the smoke from his cigarette spiraled into them. "I ain't never had the opportunity of killin' a law *woman* before."

He lay there wondering what was the best way to do it. One thing was certain; since she was all *woman*, he would have some fun with her first.

Chapter Thirty

O breathe a word or two of fire!
Smile, as if those words should burn me.
> —John Keats

Knowing that White Shadow needed time with his mother and Timothy this morning, Zoe had left the Kiowa village early and was now at home going through her father's belongings.

Tears came to her eyes as she once again recalled her father lying on the street, dying from the killer's bullet. Never had she felt as helpless as then.

Even now she felt ashamed that she had not been able to do anything to save her father. She took the badge and ran her fingers over it. Should she give up the job of sheriff?

Would it be fair to her father if she did? Would

it be right to turn her back on all of her plans to hunt down the killer and make him pay for the destruction he had left across the countryside?

Wiping tears from her eyes, she laid the badge down on a table.

"I truly hate what my father's death has done to me," she whispered. A sob lodged in her throat. "I'm eaten up with bitterness."

No, she did not want that, any more than she really wanted to wear his badge. She wanted happiness, and she could only have that if she went to White Shadow and never looked back again at this life she had left behind her.

A knock on the door drew her quickly around. "White Shadow?" she whispered, her pulse racing to think that he had finished his business with Timothy and had come to encourage her to leave today for his village and be his wife.

Now that Timothy was no longer an obstacle to their marriage, it would be so easy to fling herself into White Shadow's arms. How easy it would be to ride out of Gracemont and never return.

It was a town with bitter memories. Even now her father's blood still lay baked into the earth on Gracemont's main street.

Filled with the sudden peace of her decision to go with White Shadow, Zoe went to the door and jerked it open.

She paled and gasped when she discovered who was standing there. It most certainly wasn't someone she adored.

A sudden fear gripped Zoe's heart. She could think of no reason for Thunder Stick to be at her doorstep unless . . . unless . . . something had happened to White Shadow!

"What do you want?" Zoe blurted out, searching Thunder Stick's old eyes. "Why are you here?"

"To talk," Thunder Stick said solemnly. "I have brought you a message."

"From whom?" Zoe said warily. "White Shadow? Has he sent you here with a message?"

"No, I have not come with news from my chief," Thunder Stick said; then he shoved her aside and walked into her cabin.

Stunned by the Shaman's rudeness, Zoe looked at him guardedly.

"I ask you again. What do you want?" she persisted, leaving the door open behind her. She took slow steps away from Thunder Stick when he stared back at her with a strange gleam in his eyes.

"You are to come with me," Thunder Stick said solemnly.

"Where? Back to your village?" Zoe asked.

"No, not to my village," Thunder Stick said. He reached for the badge she'd left on the table and stared at it. Then he smiled ruefully up at Zoe. "You are to go with me to Carl Collins's hideout."

"What?" Zoe gasped, taking another step away from him. "What are you talking about?"

"If you ever want to see Colonel Timothy Livingston alive again, you will do as I say," Thunder Stick said.

He gazed down at the badge and chuckled. "You thought you were so powerful because you wore a badge?" he asked mockingly.

He looked slowly up at her, his lips twisted in a

half smile. "A woman who wants to be a man because she does the job of a man?" he taunted. "I do not see why my people's chief would want you as his wife. You are not deserving."

"Timothy," Zoe said, aghast at what the shaman was saying. "What about Timothy? Are you saying that he is no longer at the Kiowa village? That he is now Carl Collins's prisoner?"

"*Ho*, and not because Carl Collins wanted *him*, but because he uses Timothy Livingston to lure *you* to him." Thunder Stick dropped the badge on the table. "I will be paid many coins by the outlaw once I take you to him. My taking Timothy there was only a part of the outlaw's scheme."

"Are you saying that you are responsible for Timothy being with the outlaw?" Zoe asked, paling. "That you went against your own people to get paid a few meager coins?"

"My payment will not be a few coins," Thunder Stick said. He went to Zoe and grabbed her by an arm. He leered into her eyes. "I will be paid many."

"You are sick," Zoe said, trying to wrench herself free, but discovering that his grip was too tight.

She swallowed hard as he leaned his face into hers, his peyote breath causing her to flinch.

"Get away from me, you stinking old man," Zoe said, once again trying to get her arm free. "I'll have no part in your scheme. Do you hear? I'll do nothing you say."

"Then Timothy will die the moment I tell Carl Collins you refuse to come to him," Thunder Stick threatened.

"You won't get as far as his hideout, because I will ride to your village and tell White Shadow about all that you have done," Zoe said, glad when he released her.

Out of the corner of her eye Zoe saw the rifle that she always left standing beside the door, loaded, for just such moments as this.

"No, you will not have that opportunity," Thunder Stick said, withdrawing a knife from a sheath that he had hidden beneath the folds of his robe.

He grabbed Zoe and twisted her around so that her back was to him, enabling him to place the sharp edge of the knife against the delicate column of her throat.

"Go with me or die *now*, not later," Thunder Stick growled out.

Zoe was afraid to move. Yet she could not let him know that she was so afraid, her knees were weak. She had to prove to him that she was brave enough to defy him.

"You are a deceitful man," she hissed. "When your chief finds out how evil you are, you will be banished from the tribe, or perhaps even killed."

"My chief will never know about any of this," Thunder Stick said, cackling. "There will be no trace left of you . . . or Timothy."

Timothy! Zoe thought desperately to herself. Oh, Lord, she had to try to do something to save Timothy! Surely when she got to the hideout she could find a way to best Carl Collins before he killed her *or* Timothy!

Yes, she had to give it her best shot, or die now at the hands of the evil shaman. If she had more time, surely things would work out in her favor.

"I'll go," she said, relieved when he dropped the knife from her throat.

She reached a hand up and found a drop of blood on her neck. She knew now just how close she had come to dying. The shaman would not have flinched while drawing the knife across her throat.

"Do not try to escape," Thunder Stick said, stepping around her and grabbing her loaded rifle. "Get outside and mount your horse. Ride beside me and remember that this rifle will be aimed always on you. One wrong move and I will shoot you."

Chapter Thirty-one

You have taken back the promise!
—Adelaide Anne Procter

White Shadow and Soft Bird walked together to
Timothy's cabin. Soft Bird carried a wooden platter of food. White Shadow carried a medicine
bundle holding several sacred objects of his and
his mother's family.

The bundle was small and made of leather. Inside were small pictographic representatives of
Kiowa myths, as well as small bits of cloth,
leather, and other objects that had meaning only
to White Shadow and his family.

These sacred fetishes were regarded with awe
and reverence by the Kiowa. One could not whistle near a medicine bundle, or play a gambling
game in its immediate vicinity.

Timothy would be taught to pray with the aid of this bundle if there was something he wanted. He wouldn't be praying to the bundle but to its power.

White Shadow hoped that this gift would sway his brother to stay among their people rather than return to the life he had known.

White Shadow stood stiffly beside his mother as she gently spoke Timothy's name through the closed door.

When there was no response, White Shadow and Soft Bird exchanged questioning glances.

"He still sleeps?" Soft Bird said, staring at the closed door.

"If so, I shall awaken him," White Shadow said, lifting the latch on the door and stepping inside the cabin.

The sun was pouring through the windows, giving enough light for White Shadow to see things clearly around him. When he saw that the bed of blankets was empty, and that there were no signs of Timothy anywhere inside the lodge, he stiffened.

Soft Bird moved to his side. She gazed around her with wide eyes.

Then she looked up at White Shadow. "You left instructions among our warriors that Timothy would have no lessons today?" she asked softly. "You told Thunder Stick to stay away from Timothy?"

"I did both those things," White Shadow said, laying the medicine bundle aside. He went to the blanket that hung on the wall, behind which was hidden the secret room. He lifted the blanket, opened the door to the small room and peered inside.

"He is not there," he said thickly. "My brother is gone, Mother."

Soft Bird's face was filled with hurt. She set the tray of food down on the floor, and then rushed from the lodge.

White Shadow stepped outside and watched his mother going from warrior to warrior, from lodge to lodge, desperately inquiring about Timothy. When she came back to White Shadow, her eyes were filled with soft tears. He took her hands and gazed solemnly down at her.

"He is gone," Soft Bird said, sobbing. "No one has seen him. Nor did anyone see him leave. White Shadow, that can only mean that Timothy did not want to be seen leaving. He wanted no one to question him as to where he was going because he was too cowardly to tell us he did not want to accept his heritage."

She yanked her hands free and ran blindly toward her tepee. Her choked sobs wrenched White Shadow's heart. His jaw tightened, and hatred rose within him.

Given his freedom, Timothy had taken advantage of it. He cared nothing for his mother . . . for his Kiowa people.

White Shadow rushed to Soft Bird's lodge and knelt down beside her where she lay on her blankets, her body racked by deep sobs.

"Mother, do you want me to go for him?" he asked, placing a soft hand on her hair.

"No!" she cried. "Do not go for him. Let him go! It is no different from before. I never had Timothy for my son, nor will I ever. Let him go, White Shadow. Finally in my heart . . . he . . . is dead."

Feeling her hurt deep inside himself, for he had found in his heart a place for his blood brother, White Shadow leaned down and drew his mother into his arms. He cradled her next to him as she cried, his anger toward his brother suddenly turning to fear for his people.

What if Timothy went to the fort? What if he told the pony soldiers where he had been . . . that he had been held captive these past days by the Kiowa?

No. White Shadow still did not believe that his blood brother would do this.

"*Nuakolahe*, mighty creator, put feelings into my brother's heart that will make him do right by his people!" White Shadow softly prayed.

Chapter Thirty-two

My spirit is too weak—mortality
Weighs heavily on me like unwilling sleep.
　　　　　　　　—John Keats

It was the time of the year when the wild turkeys were plentiful in the area. Black Beak, Red Thunder, and Eagle Claw rode northward on a turkey chase toward the canyon where Carl Collins lived.

"We should steal horses instead of hunting for turkeys," Eagle Claw growled as he frowned at Black Beak.

"I told you," Black Beak said, "no more stealing horses. That is final. Do you hear? Final. If you wish to steal horses, find someone else besides Black Beak to befriend. I have lost too much respect already in the eyes of our people. I will not shame my chieftain cousin again by getting into mischief."

"Turkeys," Red Thunder said, laughing sarcastically. "When we could have horses? Do you think Carl Collins would pay us even one coin for a turkey?"

"I am not thinking about coins or Carl Collins today," Black Beak said solemnly. "I think only of taking food home to my mother for her cooking pot."

"I see one!" Eagle Claw shouted. "See? It is a big gobbler! See it running beside the creek?"

"It is headed for the canyon!" Red Thunder said, yanking an arrow from his quiver. "We must head it off or lose it!"

"Let it go," Black Beak said, watching the turkey as it flew off. "Follow it instead of killing it. It will lead us to many more. Each of us will have turkey tonight for our families."

They rode hard into the canyon, their eyes on the turkey as it continued flying low over the ground, gobbling.

Black Beak suddenly realized just how far they had gone when he saw a familiar bend in the canyon wall, around which lay the straight stretch of land where Carl Collins had made his hideout.

"Stop!" Black Beak said, looking quickly from Eagle Claw to Red Thunder. "I do not want to draw Carl Collins's attention. Let the turkey go."

"Let us kill turkeys and take them to the outlaw," Red Thunder suggested, his eyes anxious. "Perhaps he will play a game or two of cards with us and give us some of his whiskey. Surely he is a lonely man."

"A man who deserves to be lonely," Black Beak said tightly. "We have been wrong to align ourselves with that cold-blooded killer. I cannot believe that I did. I even told him things I should not have told him about Timothy being at our village. No. Let us turn around and ride back home. Forget the turkeys. Forget the outlaw."

"I will go alone and drink with him," Eagle Claw said, riding off. "My tongue is not loosened by firewater. You can be a child all of your life, Black Beak. I am a man."

"Eagle Claw, do not go!" Black Beak cried, galloping after Eagle Claw. "This man cannot be trusted!"

As Black Beak made the turn into the canyon, he saw that Eagle Claw was no longer on his horse, but hiding behind a thick stand of trees, looking toward the outlaws' cabin.

Black Beak drew a tight rein and leapt from his horse. He quickly led his steed over behind the trees beside Eagle Claw. "Why did you not go all the way to the cabin?" he asked as he sidled up close to his friend. "What are you looking at?"

"Carl Collins is not alone," Eagle Claw whispered, frowning over his shoulder as Red Thunder rode up on his horse, making far too much noise. "Down, Red Thunder! Get off your horse! Quick! Hide!"

Red Thunder dismounted and bent low as he ran to where Black Beak and Eagle Claw were hiding. "What is wrong?" he whispered.

"There are three horses reined at the outlaw's hitching rail," Eagle Claw whispered. "That means that there are two people inside the cabin with Carl Collins. Perhaps it is other outlaws? Perhaps they are planning to murder more white lawmen?"

"More than likely they are planning to murder a law *woman*," Black Beak said, immediately thinking of Zoe.

"Let us watch and see who comes and goes from the cabin," Eagle Claw said.

"We are placing ourselves in danger," Red Thunder said, glancing from Black Beak to Eagle Claw.

"I thought you were braver than that," Eagle Claw said, frowning over at Red Thunder. "I stay. Black Beak stays. If you wish to leave, Red Thunder, leave now and be quiet about it."

Black Beak scarcely heard what was being said between his friends. He had seen movement at the window inside the lodge.

Then he gasped when the cabin door opened and he saw Carl Collins shove someone he recognized from the cabin.

"My cousin's breed brother!" Black Beak said, drawing his friends eyes back to the cabin. "How can it be? I thought Timothy Livingston was at our village. How did he leave without being seen? When? Why is he there with the outlaw?"

"He is not with the outlaw because he wishes to be," Eagle Claw said. He nodded toward Timothy, who was half staggering away from the porch. "His hands are tied."

They watched Carl Collins untie Timothy's hands long enough for Timothy to relieve himself next to the small porch. They watched Carl tie Timothy's hands again when Timothy was finished, and then shove Timothy back inside the cabin.

"Timothy is the outlaw's captive," Black Beak said, puzzled as to how the outlaw had managed to get Timothy from the village, and what his motive might be for keeping him captive.

"We must go and save him," Black Beak said without further thought. "Timothy Livingston has proved to our people that he is worth saving. He has accepted his Kiowa heritage. He is not the man he was before he was taken captive by the Kiowa. He is my cousin's blood brother. He is *my* cousin by blood ties! We . . . must . . . save him!"

"We cannot go alone to the cabin to save our chief's brother," Eagle Claw said, again looking at the other horses reined at the hitching rail. "There is more than one outlaw today to deal with, for you see there is another horse besides the outlaw's and Timothy's at the hitching rail. We must go home and get help for the rescue."

"We cannot go for anyone," Red Thunder argued. "Do you not see that if we go to our village and tell our people about what we have seen, they will realize that we know too much about where the outlaw's hideout is?"

"You are right," Black Beak said, nervously kneading his brow. "And if we bring our warriors here and the outlaw sees that we are responsible for his capture, he will tell everything he knows about us . . . about how we steal horses for money, how we drank and gambled with him . . . how I told him that Timothy was at our village. He used the information for his own evil purposes! We would be condemned forever in the eyes of our people, I, especially."

"Let us not be hasty in doing anything," Eagle Claw said, turning his back on the cabin. "We must not be connected in any way with this white man criminal. It will prove that we are guilty of too much wrongdoing. Let us go into Gracemont. Tonight is the first night of the Fourth of July celebration. Tonight there are to be fireworks. Tomorrow and tomorrow night there will be many more exciting things happening in the town. Why jeopardize our chances to see such excitement for the first time in our lives, by telling about the outlaw holding Timothy hostage at his cabin? Surely the outlaw is not going to kill Timothy right away?"

"*Ho*, let us wait at least until after we see the fireworks before we disclose Timothy's whereabouts to my cousin," Black Beak said, nodding. "What favor did Timothy Livingston ever do for us, anyhow? He cared nothing for our people until he discovered that he had Kiowa blood running through his veins. Let him suffer a day or two longer with the evil white outlaw, and then we will find a way to disclose the truth of his whereabouts to White Shadow. Let us have some fun while we can, for perhaps after we become involved in Timothy's rescue, and everyone learns of our connection with the outlaw, we may never be free to have fun again. We might even be banished from our tribe."

"*Ho*, let us have fun while we can," Red Thunder mumbled, glancing from Black Beak to Eagle Claw. "I have waited too long to see the fireworks. I will let nothing stop me from seeing them now."

"I would like to go and look through the window and see just who the other outlaw is," Black Beak said, staring at the cabin once again.

"Perhaps it is not an outlaw at all," Eagle Claw said, laughing. "Perhaps it is a woman."

"A woman?" Red Thunder said, arching an eyebrow. "Do you think it might be?"

"What woman would be caught dead with the likes of Carl Collins?" Black Beak said, chuckling. "No. There is no woman inside his lodge. Just two evil gunslingers . . . and . . . my own cousin by blood ties."

"You are not softening, are you?" Red Thunder said, leaning his face into Black Beak's. "You are not thinking of going and trying to save Timothy? You are not forgetting the fireworks?"

Black Beak swallowed hard.

He lowered his eyes, then jerked his head up and glared from Red Thunder to Eagle Claw. "No, I am not softening," he said. "Come. Let us go. We will decide after the fireworks what we should do about Timothy."

Their eyes eager, Red Thunder and Eagle Claw nodded.

On foot they led their steeds past the bend in the canyon, and then mounted them.

Just before they rode off, Black Beak looked

back in the direction of the cabin. A shiver ran up his spine to think that he was being a coward . . . that he was placing his own selfish needs before those of an innocent man being held captive.

But he would make it up to Timothy by saving him . . . after the fireworks demonstration in the sky!

As he rode off he could not get the third horse at the hitching rail off his mind. Something told him that the third person in the cabin did not belong there. Carl Collins had never spoken of friends who frequented his cabin.

That meant that whoever was there was not there by choice.

"Could he have two captives?" Black Beak whispered to himself. "If so, who?"

He brushed such thoughts from his mind and was glad when they left the canyon behind and were riding across land that would soon lead them into Gracemont.

Tonight.

All that he would allow himself to think about were the wonders of tonight when the sky would be lit up with flaring colors.

No. Nothing would get in the way of his seeing something so rare and beautiful.

Nothing!

Chapter Thirty-three

Hope is the thing with feathers
That perches in the soul.
—Emily Dickinson

Not able to accept the cold-hearted way that Timothy had hurt his mother by leaving without an explanation, White Shadow was on his way to Fort Cobb. He wanted to ask Timothy how he could be so cruel to the woman he knew was his mother. Had his tenderness toward her all been a hoax to assure his freedom?

White Shadow stiffened, knowing that he might be riding into danger at the fort. Had his brother told everyone where he had been, and why? That he had been held against his will?

Perhaps even now Timothy was preparing his soldiers to attack the Kiowa village, to wipe out the truth of a heritage he was too ashamed to accept.

That thought caused a feeling of bitterness that he fought with all his might. He did not want to think that anyone who was blood kin to him could be so vindictive . . . so evil.

No, he would think no more about what his brother might be doing, until he saw for himself that Timothy was planning to betray his people. He would risk danger to see whether his brother was evil to the core, or just too cowardly to admit that his life should be lived with the Kiowa, not whites.

As he caught sight of the guards who stood on each side of the fort's open gate, White Shadow's heart was thundering like a drum inside his chest. He had faced many challenges in his life, but not when his mother's well-being was at stake. He had left her at home with a mournful emptiness in her eyes.

White Shadow could hardly bear thinking of her hurt, knowing that there was nothing he could do to make Timothy return to her if he did not want to.

He knew that this loss would be harder to bear than the first, for this time her son would have turned his back on her by *his* choice, not because his father did not want him to be a Kiowa brave.

As White Shadow drew a tight rein beside one of the guards, the young lieutenant stared up at him, a rifle clutched tightly at his side.

"I have come to inquire about Colonel Timothy Livingston," White Shadow said, looking past the lieutenant at Timothy's two-storied stone house.

He searched for a horse at Timothy's hitching rail. When White Shadow saw none there, nor any movement at the house, he once again gazed down at the lieutenant.

"The colonel has been missing for several days now," the lieutenant said tightly. "The search has been called off. It is everyone's belief now that . . . that Colonel Livingston is dead."

White Shadow was taken aback by the fact that Timothy wasn't there. Where could he be?

At Zoe's cabin!

Surely he had gone directly to her to talk her out of marrying White Shadow. His behavior when he had been told of Zoe's intentions had seemed forced. Surely, he had felt a deep resentment toward White Shadow for having taken her from him.

That alone might be why Timothy had fled the Kiowa village. He had wanted to go to Zoe to persuade her against marrying White Shadow. Did Timothy want Zoe so much that he would place everything second to her?

Leaving the young lieutenant staring after him, White Shadow wheeled his horse around and rode hard toward Zoe's home. But when he arrived there and discovered that neither she nor Timothy was there, he became more puzzled than before.

"Where can Timothy be?" he whispered. "Where is Zoe?" Was she at the jail, or had she gone out searching for Carl Collins?

White Shadow rode quickly down the main street of Gracemont toward the jail. He wheeled his horse to a quick stop before it and slid out of the saddle.

Not even taking the time to tie his reins to the hitching post, he ran inside the jail. He stopped abruptly when he discovered the cold silence of the room. Zoe was not there. Nor was Timothy.

"Where can Zoe be?" he whispered.

He moved slowly around the room, sliding his hand first over her desk, and then running his fingers through the keys that hung from a nail on the wall.

"Where is Timothy?" he whispered, going to the door to stare at the bustling activity in town. He watched children running around, their faces lit with excitement.

"The fireworks," he whispered.

He knew that the fireworks were to be displayed in the dark skies tonight over Gracemont. He knew that the children at his village would come into town to see the fireworks, for this would be the first time ever for them to see something so magical.

Zoe had spoken of the fireworks herself, of how she had seen them in the town of Boston. When she had described them to White Shadow, he had seen the excitement in her eyes. He knew that she would want to see the fireworks tonight.

I'll wait for her here, he decided. He sat down on the chair behind her desk. Surely wherever she had gone, she would make it a point to return for the fireworks.

But what of Timothy? Was he with Zoe? If so, did she want to be with him?

Or had Timothy turned to the dark side of his character and taken her away? Was she even now his captive until she promised to marry him instead of White Shadow?

He prayed to *Nuakolahe* that he was right to wait for her, that she was not a captive, after all, but was free to return to Gracemont when she wished.

Once again he listened to the excitement outside. The final preparations for the fireworks were being made, and he heard the arrival of many horses and buggies as settlers came from their homes to view the wonders in the sky. White Shadow went to the door and searched the faces, hoping to find Zoe among them.

When he still did not see her, he looked heavenward at the darkening sky. A stark fear came into his heart to think that Zoe might be in danger somewhere out there. He had never felt as helpless as now, knowing that he could do nothing to help Zoe.

It was as though she and Timothy had disappeared into thin air.

Finally he rode back to her cabin, in the hope that she had returned. But his heart sank when he discovered that she still was not there.

"Zoe, where are you?" he cried, nervously raking his fingers through his hair. "Where . . . are . . . you?"

Chapter Thirty-four

My first thought was,
he lied in every word.
—Robert Browning

Zoe was tied to a chair, totally helpless. She still couldn't believe that both she and Timothy were prisoners of Carl Collins.

But what stunned her the most was that White Shadow's shaman was responsible for both her and Timothy's abductions. She couldn't believe that Thunder Stick had betrayed his own people.

But Zoe now knew that Thunder Stick would sell his own soul to the devil if it meant that he would be paid, for she had watched in utter disbelief as Carl gave the shaman many coins in payment for the abductions.

Thunder Stick had been gone now for at least

an hour. And after Timothy had been taken outside to relieve himself, he had been brought back inside Carl's cabin and tied and gagged again.

Hearing Timothy sigh, Zoe looked over at him. As he gazed at her, she could see a quiet apology in the depths of his eyes. He must know that he had been used as a decoy to lure Zoe there.

Surely they both were going to be killed by the vicious outlaw. They just did not know when. . . .

"Well, now, don't you two look pretty sittin' there next to one another," Carl said, coming to stand over them. He puffed on a cigarette, then took it from between his lips and ground it on the grungy, wooden floor with the heel of his boot. "Two *Injun* lovers. That makes neither of you fit for much, now does it?"

Carl leaned down into Timothy's face and gripped him tightly by the shoulders. "I know why Zoe likes bein' among the Kiowa, for she's head over heels in love with the chief," he said tightly. "But what puzzles me is why *you* were there. Have you had a change of heart about Injuns, Colonel? I know by your reputation that you hated Injuns. What's the connection, Colonel? Why were you with the Kiowa?"

He yanked Timothy's gag off. "Speak up or forever hold your peace," he said, laughing boisterously.

"You sonofabitch, I'm not telling you anything," Timothy growled. He glanced over at Zoe, and then stared into Carl's eyes. "Let her go, outlaw. I'll pay you triple what you paid the shaman if you'll let Zoe go."

"And I was born yesterday," Carl said. He began pacing the floor, his eyes moving slowly back and forth between Timothy and Zoe. "If I set you free you'll go straight to the fort and come back here with something besides coins. You'll bring the whole cavalry here and kill me."

"I promise you I won't do that," Timothy said. "I'll bring you the money, take Zoe with me away from here, and forget we ever set eyes on you."

"You'd do all of this for a woman who betrayed you?" Carl said, chuckling. "I've seen the two of you horseback riding like people who are in love. That is until she got goofy-eyed over the chief. Ain't that right, Zoe? You played Timothy for a fool over that Injun."

Not about to explain her actions to the outlaw, Zoe pursed her lips tightly together.

"That's all right," Carl drawled out, laughing. "Just sit there like a stubborn mule. I don't care. But, Miss Prissie, listen to what else I have to say and see how high and mighty you'll feel then."

He stopped and leaned down into Zoe's face. "Did you know that your pa and I were in cahoots?" he asked, his eyes gleaming.

Zoe paled. Then she firmed her jaw and reminded herself that this outlaw would lie just to torment her. She would not believe anything he said. Especially about her father.

Suddenly Carl reached for the badge on Zoe's shirt and yanked it off. He spit on it, then dropped it to the floor and ground the heel of his boot into it, crushing it flat.

"That's what I thought of your cheatin', lyin' father," Carl growled. His eyes narrowed as he again stared into Zoe's eyes. "I shot your father because he reneged on me. He came to me one day and said he'd no longer be able to stay quiet about me, no matter how much I paid him not to send his posse after me and arrest me. He was paid well for his silence so that I could stay here in my hideout during my killin' sprees across the countryside. But then he said he had to come clean for *you*, because he didn't want to lose your respect, and he told me he was going to give me a day's head start before the posse came gunnin' for me. I didn't take much to bein' betrayed by the likes of him. I killed him before he could kill me."

Zoe was at a loss for words. She felt completely numb inside, for she couldn't help believing what the gunman had said. It was the sort of thing someone couldn't just make up in the blink of an eye. And she couldn't help recalling that White Shadow, too, had said her father was corrupt!

She had a sick feeling in the pit of her stomach. Her father had looked the other way while this evil gunman went around killing people. She fought against tears.

"Don't believe him, Zoe," Timothy blurted out. "He's lying—"

Timothy's words were cut short when Carl backhanded him across the face, drawing blood from his nose and the corners of his mouth.

"She knows what I'm saying is the truth," Carl said, wiping Timothy's blood from the back of his hand on his pants leg. He leered at Zoe. "Don't you, law woman? Your father was stashing the money away. He was waitin' for you to marry Timothy and then he was goin' to go to California and live high on the hog on my money. He was no good, Zoe. Absolutely no good. You don't know the delight I got in shootin' him."

Still Zoe said nothing, for a part of her heart was torn in shreds at the knowledge of the role her father had played in this gunman's life.

"I think your father kind of felt sorry for me, for the sort of life that drove me to killin' lawmen," Carl said, lighting another cigarette.

He took several puffs, then slid the cigarette to the corner of his mouth and once more leaned into Zoe's face and continued talking.

"Like I said, your father knew my past as well as me," he gloated. "He felt for me. And he should've. He sympathized with me because he knew of my past hurts."

He straightened and sat down on a chair at the table. He poured himself a shot of whiskey, yanked the cigarette from his mouth, and then drank the whiskey in one deep swallow.

He slammed the glass down on the table and turned and glared at Zoe. "You see, Zoe, my father was a sheriff," he said, his voice drawn. "He was a mean man who hanged outlaws by day and beat his son and wife by night. My killing days began when I was eighteen. I shot my very own pa. Ever since then I've shot every lawman I set my eyes on. I hated them even more when my best pal was gunned down by a lawman. It's been good for my soul to see lawmen dropped by my bullets."

Zoe was horrified by his tale of murder and

mayhem. She knew now that neither she nor Timothy would ever get out of this madman's clutches alive. Her heart ached when she thought of how close she had come to having a life that would make her content. To be White Shadow's wife would have been the ultimate of happiness!

She jumped when Carl came suddenly to her and grabbed her hair. He yanked her head back so that she was forced to stare up into his cold, lifeless eyes.

"You're the first law *lady* I've run across," he said, sneering. "You bein' a lady changes things. Now I'm not certain what I should do with you." He chuckled. "Of course I'll get my jollies by raping you. Then, and only then, will I decide if you should be made accountable for wearing a badge."

He released his hold on her hair and laughed boisterously. "Yeah, it might be enough for me to have told you about your lousy, sonofabitch father," he said, once again going to pour himself a shot of whiskey. "It gave me pleasure seein' the disbelief in your luscious green eyes when you discovered the lout your father was, and knew why he had to die."

Zoe watched guardedly as Carl swallowed several gulps of whiskey.

She then looked over at Timothy, whose eyes were on her. "What can we do?" she whispered. "How can we—"

Her words were cut short when Carl came to her and suddenly grabbed the front of her blouse. He ripped it open, the buttons popping and flying.

Zoe screamed and tried to wrestle her arms free

of the ropes that held her in bondage. Carl's lips were suddenly on one of her breasts, his tongue sucking at her nipple.

"Get away from me, you fiend!" Zoe cried, feeling sick when his hands went to her breasts, cupping them.

Carl laughed throatily as he jerked himself away from her. "That's just a taste of what I'm goin' to do to you," he said, folding the shirt back over her exposed breasts. "You cain't tell me you didn't enjoy it."

"You're nothing but slime," Zoe hissed, her eyes brimming with tears. "I hate you."

"Sure, that's what they all say," Carl said, shrugging his shoulders. "But in the end? The women enjoy my ways of makin' love. So will you."

He sauntered toward the door. "Miss Prissie, I won't rape you just yet," he said, jerking the door open. He turned and glared at Zoe. "I'm going to make you suffer by waitin' and wonderin' when I'm going to defile your lily-white body. First I have some fireworks to watch. I'm going to ride to a close-by butte and get a look at the fireworks they are shootin' off in Gracemont. They should show up well enough in the dark sky."

He stepped outside, hesitated, and then went back inside to Zoe. "On second thought, you might want to see the fireworks, yourself," he said, chuckling. He untied her from the chair, yet left her hands tied behind her as he shoved her toward the door.

"Come on outside with me, Zoe," he said. "I've

got better plans for you than leavin' you sittin' next to pretty boy here."

After he shoved her outside, Zoe screamed and kicked at him as he yanked her blouse off, and then ripped the rest of her clothes from her body.

"Now won't you be a pretty sight out here all alone whilst I go and take a look at the fireworks?" Carl chuckled as he tied her naked body to a porch post, her nudity a soft gleam beneath the moonlight.

He stood back and stared at her. The look in his eyes told Zoe that she would soon lose everything. She knew that once he raped her he would kill her.

She tried to wriggle free of her ropes, but succeeded only in rubbing her wrists raw.

"You cain't get free so why bother tryin'?" Carl said, running his fingers down her thigh. "Hmm, perhaps I should forget the fireworks. What I have here can light up my insides more than the fireworks can light up the sky."

Zoe fought the urge to beg him to release her. She knew that she was in the presence of a madman, someone who listened to nothing but the anger that ate away at his insides.

"Naw, you'll be here when I get back," Carl said, sauntering away from her. "It's been a long time since I saw fireworks. I'm not going to miss them tonight."

Zoe watched him ride away, and then gazed out across the canyon.

"Oh, White Shadow, please find me," she sobbed. "Please . . . find me . . . before it's too late."

Chapter Thirty-five

Virtue, how frail it is!
Friendship, how rare!
—Percy Bysshe Shelley

The fireworks were blasting up into the sky, spraying the dark heavens with splashes of bright color.

Black Beak stood holding his horse's reins as he gazed at the beautiful display overhead, yet he found himself unable to truly enjoy it. Although the fireworks were something he had never seen before, brilliant and beautiful, he couldn't get Timothy off his mind.

Black Beak was guilt-ridden over having ignored Timothy's plight. Nor could the young brave forget how Soft Bird must be feeling, thinking that Timothy had left of his own free will.

Wanting to continue watching the fireworks, yet

knowing that he just couldn't, Black Beak quickly mounted his horse.

"Black Beak, where are you going?" Red Thunder asked, rushing to him. "Do you not enjoy the colors in the sky? Do you not find them fascinating?"

"*Ho*, I find them fascinating, but I cannot enjoy them," Black Beak said, frowning down at Red Thunder. "It was wrong of us to keep Timothy's abduction a secret. It is not fair to Timothy or to his mother and his chieftain brother. I must go now and report his abduction."

"But you will miss the fireworks," Eagle Claw said, stepping up beside Red Thunder. "Black Beak, we have waited for many sunrises to see the fireworks. How can you just ride away as though they are not there?"

"Tomorrow night they will be in the sky again," Black Beak said solemnly. "I hope I shall earn the right to see them then."

"You are foolish," Eagle Claw said, his eyes narrowing. "Why should you do anything for that man who never did anything for the Kiowa?"

"Because he is, in part, Kiowa, and he is my blood kin," Black Beak said. "And because I do not want to add another disappointment to the long list of disappointments that my chieftain cousin has had in me. I will attempt to make up all wrongs tonight by getting Timothy released so that his mother will see that he is alive and well . . . and will know that he did not leave because he chose to turn his back on her."

"Do you not remember why we decided not to

tell anyone about Timothy's abduction?" Red Thunder asked, grabbing Black Beak's reins from him. "Get down from your horse, Black Beak. You are not going anywhere. I will not allow you to reveal to everyone that we aligned ourselves with the filthy outlaw."

Black Beak's jaw tightened angrily. He yanked his reins back from Red Thunder. "Do not ever again try to coerce Black Beak into doing wrong," he hissed. "Do not think you can order Black Beak around. Black Beak is his own person! He is cousin to our chief!"

"Your cousin will disown you once he discovers that you have taken payment for stolen horses sold to the outlaw," Eagle Claw said heatedly.

"He may never know," Black Beak said, swallowing hard. "Just because I lead White Shadow to the hideout does not mean that I have been there for the wrong reasons. I will tell White Shadow that we just happened onto the hideout when we were chasing wild turkeys. That, in itself, is not a lie. He need never know that we were there before the turkey chase."

"Your chieftain cousin is a very wise man and will learn the truth one way or the other," Red Thunder said, sighing deeply. "You are foolish to put yourself in the position of being found guilty of dealing with the outlaw, which might eventually get you banished from our tribe. And not only you, Black Beak, but also myself and Eagle Claw."

"Whatever shall be, shall be," Black Beak said thickly. "I do tonight what I must do. I cannot rest another moment, knowing that I should do something to help Timothy."

Eagle Claw glowered at Black Beak, then turned and stamped away. He was soon lost in the crowd.

Red Thunder's eyes wavered as he stared up at Black Beak; then he too walked away.

Black Beak gazed sadly at Red Thunder for a moment and then rode off. As he passed the jail, he saw lamplight through the window and decided to go there first to tell Zoe of Timothy's abduction.

They could ride to the village together and alert everyone. Then they would ride in force to the hideout. The outlaw wouldn't have a chance to escape.

"But what of Timothy?" Black Beak whispered to himself.

He was afraid that once the evil outlaw realized he was surrounded by the Kiowa, he might end Timothy's life before allowing him to be set free.

What puzzled Black Beak the most was why the outlaw had abducted Timothy in the first place. What good was Timothy to him? And why had he kept him alive? It was well known that the outlaw killed his enemies unmercifully, even shooting some in the back.

Black Beak wheeled his horse to a halt in front of the jail. He slid from the saddle, tied his reins quickly to the hitching post, and ran inside.

When he saw who was sitting behind the desk, he was at a loss for words.

White Shadow was equally taken aback by Black Beak's arrival. He'd expected his cousin to be outside enjoying the fireworks. That was all the youngsters had talked about since the news had spread to the reservation about the fireworks display in Gracemont.

As for White Shadow, he had not been able to enjoy the fireworks, for he couldn't get Zoe and Timothy off his mind. He had returned to the jail, hoping she would appear there to watch the fireworks.

"Black Beak, why are you here instead of outside with your friends?" White Shadow asked, slowly rising from the chair when he saw a wary look in his cousin's eyes.

"White Shadow, I . . . I . . . thought Zoe would be here," Black Beak said guardedly. He looked slowly around him, and then gazed again at White Shadow. "But I find you here and not Zoe. Why? Why are you here? Where is she?"

"I do not know where my woman is," White Shadow said, stepping around the desk to stand before Black Beak. He gazed down at his cousin and placed a hand on his lean shoulder. "Nor have you yet told me why you are here."

"I came to tell . . . to tell . . . Zoe . . ." Black Beak stammered. He suddenly felt dwarfed beneath his cousin's steady stare.

If White Shadow jumped to the right conclusion about how Black Beak knew of the outlaw's whereabouts, then all would be lost. Even the fact that he had come purposely to help save Timothy's life might mean nothing if White Shadow discovered the truth about Black Beak's horse-stealing and his dealings with Carl Collins.

Black Beak was so frightened, his knees trembled.

"Tell Zoe what?" White Shadow asked, his eyes narrowing as he saw the fear in his cousin's eyes.

"That I know where Timothy is," Black Beak blurted out.

White Shadow took an unsteady step away from Black Beak, and then he stood tall and straight over him, his spine stiff. "How would you know this?" he asked tightly.

"Is how I know so important?" Black Beak asked, wincing when he saw a quick leap of fire in his cousin's eyes. He felt it best to tell everything now and worry about being punished later.

"I . . . I . . . me and Eagle Claw and Red Thunder were out on a wild turkey hunt so that we could bring home fresh meat for our mothers' cooking pots," Black Beak said in a rush, his heart hammering like pistol shots within his chest. "We chased this one turkey into a canyon. It . . . it . . . led to a valley. In this valley was a cabin. We spied and saw . . . and saw . . . Timothy taken from the cabin to relieve himself. The man who was with him was the one on the Wanted posters. Carl Collins. Timothy is his captive, White Shadow. His captive!"

For a moment White Shadow was stunned speechless.

Then he sorted through all that Black Beak had said and was relieved to know that at least Timothy had not fled the truth about his family, but had been taken away by force.

Then White Shadow's insides grew cold when

he thought of someone else, and how she seemed to have disappeared from the face of the earth.

Zoe! His precious Zoe! If Timothy was a prisoner of the outlaw, might his Zoe also be?

White Shadow clasped both hands on Black Beak's shoulders. "Did you see anyone else there?" he blurted out.

"No," Black Beak said, his eyes wide. "But we did see more than one horse at the hitching rail. We thought someone besides the outlaw and Timothy might be at the hideout. We did not venture close enough to see."

White Shadow's eyes narrowed again. "When did you witness all of this?" he asked warily. "It is dark now, but you surely saw Timothy at the hideout when it was daylight. Does that mean you did not come right away to report what you saw?"

White Shadow's hands tightened on his cousin's shoulders. "Did you first go to our village to report the news?" he asked, his teeth clenched. "Or, cousin, did you come to see the fireworks instead? Was it guilt that finally caused you to come and tell Zoe?"

Black Beak lowered his eyes. "I know that too much time has passed since we witnessed Timothy at the outlaw's hideout," he gulped out. "But . . . but . . . we have waited so long to see the fireworks. We did not want to miss them! We were going to watch them and then return home to tell you about Timothy. At the time, we saw no harm in that. Now . . . I . . . know we were wrong. I should have gone immediately to our village and told you . . . but . . . you would not have been

there, anyhow. You were here! Do you not see that
it is best that I came first to tell Zoe? I found you
here! You now know! Now you can do something
about it."

"*Ho*, I will do something about it all right,"
White Shadow said, turning to walk quickly toward the door. "Come. You will ride with me to
our village. We will gather together many warriors
and then you will lead us to the hideout."

"But what about Zoe?" Black Beak asked, hurrying out of the jail with White Shadow. "Where
is she?"

"I do not know," he said. "Perhaps she is also a
prisoner of the outlaw's."

Black Beak's eyes widened. He gulped hard,
knowing that if Zoe was a prisoner of the madman
outlaw and she had been harmed by him, Black
Beak would most certainly be punished for not
having told anyone what he had seen.

He prayed silently to himself that White
Shadow was wrong, and that Zoe wasn't a prisoner along with Timothy. Black Beak could almost feel the wrath of his cousin if Zoe had been
harmed in any way by Carl Collins. Black Beak
would be banished from the tribe, to walk forever
alone without a people!

Tears came to his eyes at that thought, for he
did love his people with all his heart. He had just
found it hard to quell his rebellious nature once
his people had been forced to live on the reservation.

He swung himself into his saddle and rode away
with White Shadow. He heard a loud blast over-

head and knew that more fireworks were lighting the heavens, but he refused to look. He blamed his fascination with the fireworks for the trouble he was in tonight. How could he have allowed a white man's invention to cause him to put his people's best interests from his heart and mind?

Never again would he make such a mistake. From now on his people and their laws came first. *If* he was given the chance to prove his worth again to them, he thought wearily to himself.

He pushed his horse into a gallop and rode beside White Shadow, proud that someone like him was his blood kin. He gazed over at White Shadow and felt truly sorry for having deceived him these past months.

White Shadow glanced at Black Beak. He knew that his cousin had not told him the full truth tonight. White Shadow could see concealed lies in his cousin's eyes.

Nonetheless, White Shadow was proud of Black Beak tonight for having been brave enough to risk shame by telling White Shadow where he had seen Timothy.

For now, White Shadow would concentrate on rescuing Timothy and learning Zoe's whereabouts. He would know soon whether or not Zoe had been taken prisoner along with Timothy.

And if she had been, pity the outlaw whose filthy hands had touched White Shadow's beloved woman. White Shadow would not be able to end Carl Collins's life soon enough.

Chapter Thirty-six

Struck to the heart by this pageantry,
Half to myself I said, "And what is this?"
—Percy Bysshe Shelley

Black Beak led the many warriors into the canyon and rode for a while longer. Then he drew a tight rein and turned toward White Shadow. "So many horses make too much noise," he said. "We must go the rest of the way on foot."

White Shadow nodded. He turned to his warriors and gave them their instructions.

They proceeded through the narrow passage on foot. When they finally reached the meadow, Carl's corralled horses and cabin were plain to see beneath the bright glow of the full moon.

But something else was quite visible to White Shadow as he peered toward the cabin. His heart cried out to Zoe when he saw her tied, naked, to the post of the porch.

Nothing could hold White Shadow back. He couldn't bear to see his woman mistreated in such a way another moment. Without waiting for his warriors to accompany him, he ran stealthily through the open meadow, his rifle held poised, ready to fire should Carl suddenly appear at the door of the cabin, or at one of the windows.

When White Shadow came close enough to the cabin for Zoe to see him, Zoe's eyes lit up. "White Shadow!" she cried. "Oh, White Shadow, I knew you would find me somehow!"

An instant fear leapt into White Shadow's heart. He was afraid that Zoe, in her excitement at seeing him, had forgotten about Carl, for surely he was inside the lodge. White Shadow expected the outlaw to rush from the door at any moment, firing, and a stray bullet might possibly hit Zoe.

"Say no more!" White Shadow said, his eyes still watching the door as he came closer to the porch.

"Carl Collins isn't here," Zoe cried. "He went to a bluff to see fireworks. Thank the Lord he went in a different direction from the way you just came or else he might have seen your arrival."

White Shadow hurried to the porch. He dropped his rifle and quickly untied Zoe, then drew her into his arms.

Zoe clung to him. "Thank God," she sobbed. "Oh, thank God you came. Carl . . . was going to rape me, then—"

White Shadow leaned away from her and gently

placed a hand over her mouth. "Do not say it," he said thickly.

He swept her up into his arms, scooped up her clothes, and carried her inside the cabin. He stopped with a jerk when he caught sight of Timothy, tied to a chair. His eyes locked with his brother's in a silent apology, then he went to Carl's bed and yanked a blanket from it.

He slid the blanket around Zoe's shoulders and then eased her to the floor.

He took his knife from a sheath at his side, then went to Timothy and sliced through the ropes and released his brother.

Timothy reached up and removed the handkerchief that had been tied around his mouth. He dropped it to the floor, wiped at his dry lips with the back of his hand, and gazed at White Shadow.

"White Shadow, how did you know where we were?" he asked, turning his head away from Zoe as she dropped the blanket to the floor to hurry into what was left of her clothes.

"My cousin Black Beak," White Shadow said. "He just happened along while chasing a wild turkey into the canyon when Carl took you from the cabin for a moment or two. He came and told me. It was terrible to hear that you had been abducted by the outlaw, but good to know that you had not left on your own without saying goodbye to our mother."

Zoe went to White Shadow, fully dressed, yet having to hold her shirt together in the front since Carl had torn the buttons from it.

Recalling the moment that Carl had yanked the

blouse off Zoe, and growing angry at the memory of how Carl had placed his lips and tongue on Zoe's breast, Timothy went to a peg on the wall and yanked one of Carl's shirts from it.

He took the shirt to Zoe and slipped it around her shoulders. "Wear this," he said thickly.

She smiled a quiet thank you at Timothy.

She turned her back to him, removed her blouse, and slipped quickly into the shirt, although the stench of the man clung to the cotton fabric.

But it would do until she could exchange it for something else. The thought of soon wearing the soft, white doeskin dress that White Shadow's mother had made comforted her.

After tonight, if everything went as it should, she would feel truly free to go with White Shadow to his village.

She turned at the sound of many footsteps. She found Black Beak standing just inside the door, and many of White Shadow's warriors crowding into the small confines of the cabin.

"And so it is true," Lightning Flash said as he stared at Timothy. "Timothy was abducted by the outlaw." He looked questioningly at White Shadow, then back at Timothy. "But how could the outlaw have entered the village without being detected?"

"Because it was not Carl who came and got me," Timothy said, stepping closer to Lightning Flash. "It was Thunder Stick. He is responsible for my being here."

Everyone gasped.

Then White Shadow placed gentle hands on Timothy's shoulders. "How can this be?" he said, his voice drawn. "Why would Thunder Stick do this?"

"For money," Timothy said thickly. He glanced over at Zoe as she joined White Shadow. "Thunder Stick even went as far as coercing Zoe into coming to the hideout."

"But why would the outlaw pay money for *you*?" Lightning Flash asked.

"It was not me the outlaw wanted, it was Zoe," Timothy said, glancing at Zoe. "My being here was the bait that brought Zoe to him."

Silence filled the room. This revelation of the shaman's evil deeds made White Shadow cringe, for he, himself, had wondered about Thunder Stick and had done nothing to stop him. Because of his mother's feelings for the shaman, White Shadow had always looked the other way.

Now he understood just how wrong he had been not to send Thunder Stick away long ago. He was a disgrace to all Kiowa.

"I was brought here for the criminal to rape, then murder," Zoe said softly.

"No one will ever get near my woman again," White Shadow said. "She will be with me."

"But what about Thunder Stick?" Lightning Flash asked. "Will he be punished severely?"

"He will be banished from our tribe," White Shadow pronounced. "That is the worst punishment of all for any Kiowa."

Zoe looked at Black Beak, then went to hug him. "Thank you for telling White Shadow about seeing

Timothy here at Carl's hideout," she murmured. "If not for you, both Timothy and I would soon be dead."

Black Beak looked over Zoe's shoulder and found White Shadow staring at him. Black Beak's eyes wavered, for if White Shadow discovered just how much Black Beak and his friends had done behind his back, they would also be candidates for banishment. Black Beak only hoped that this good deed tonight would erase all of the wrong that he had done.

"We must not delay any longer what must be done," White Shadow said, looking from one warrior to the other. "We must capture Carl Collins. We must make him pay for his wrongful deeds."

Every man raised his rifle and shouted the war cry. Zoe's spine tingled at the sound.

She started to leave the cabin with the others, but stopped long enough to get her sheriff's badge from the floor. Although Carl had attempted to ruin it, the pin was still intact, leaving the badge wearable.

But knowing White Shadow's feelings about the badge, Zoe thrust it inside a pocket instead of wearing it. Then she ran outside just as the horses were being brought from hiding.

"Let us go and make a trap for the outlaw!" White Shadow shouted.

They all mounted their steeds. Zoe gazed at Timothy. He seemed proud to be among the warriors. *She* was proud of the change in him. She was glad to ride beside him when White Shadow gave the order to follow him. Everyone rode in the direction that Zoe had pointed out to him, toward the butte where Carl had gone to look at the fireworks.

"He will be dead before sunrise!" Lightning Flash shouted, raising his rifle in the air as he rode alongside White Shadow.

Clasping a rifle that she had found in Carl's cabin, Zoe could hardly quell her excitement. At last she would have the chance to avenge her father's death.

At this moment, Zoe remembered how her father had told her that he would always be with her, looking over her shoulder. She hoped that was true, and that he was with her now, and would see the demise of the evil outlaw who had left a trail of blood everywhere he traveled.

Yet another part of her feared that something might go awry tonight and that Carl would escape, to murder again.

If Carl had seen the Kiowa enter the canyon that led to his hideout, he would already be long gone without a trace left behind to find him. He had proven that he was not only a vicious killer, but clever, as well.

"Please let it be over tonight," Zoe prayed, gazing heavenward.

Chapter Thirty-seven

Some silent laws our hearts will make,
Which they shall long obey.
          —William Wordsworth

Zoe lay on her belly on the ground beside White Shadow watching the valley below, where Carl would have to travel to return to his cabin. She glanced on all sides of her and smiled when she saw that White Shadow's warriors were ready and waiting, as well.

Her gaze lingered on Black Beak, grateful that he had told White Shadow about Timothy's abduction, which in turn had led White Shadow to her. She would find a way to repay him for his kindness.

Without a doubt she would always speak in his behalf when someone talked about his being nothing but a rebellious teenager who cared for no one but himself.

Tonight Black Beak had proved that he had the same blood flowing through his veins as his cousin White Shadow. He might even follow in White Shadow's footsteps and be a powerful, admired warrior.

The sound of a horse drawing close down below made Zoe's heart race with excitement. She jumped up with White Shadow and Timothy, Black Beak following close behind, and scrambled down the side of the bluff, while the other warriors went in other directions so that Carl would find himself surrounded.

The rifle clutched tightly in her right hand, Zoe stopped beside White Shadow and hid behind a thick stand of cottonwoods as she waited in the moonlight for her first glimpse of Carl. Her fingers trembled as she raised the rifle, taking aim as she heard the horse drawing closer and closer.

And then Carl came into sight.

Zoe's heart pounded as she glared at the ruthless outlaw. She wanted to squeeze the trigger and have her revenge.

But she knew that the plan was only to stop him.

Then, since she was still sheriff, she would take him to jail. There was no question that he would be sentenced to hang.

Afterward she would gladly lay the badge aside for someone else to wear.

It saddened her to know that she couldn't offer the title of sheriff to Harold Hicks. He had proved, in the end, that he was worthy of the job.

Now she didn't care who had it. Once she left that jail, she would not look back again. Her future was all that she would think about . . . a wonderful future with the man she loved!

She smiled when suddenly the Kiowa warriors stepped out into the open on all sides of Carl, their presence causing him to draw a tight rein.

She laughed out loud when he saw her as she stepped into the open with Timothy and White Shadow. She wondered only for a second why Black Beak hadn't come out into the open with them.

But at that moment, Carl suddenly sank his heels into the flanks of his horse and broke through the chain of Kiowa warriors, trampling two of them.

Zoe's insides froze when she saw Carl riding toward her, his right hand going for his firearm. In the time it took her to take a deep breath, she saw in her mind's eye how Carl had managed to escape after having fired the fatal shot.

She shuddered as she relived the shame of the filthy outlaw's vile hands and mouth on her breasts! She cringed when she recalled just how close he had come to raping her.

She thought of all of the women whose bodies he had surely ravaged . . . all of the men he had murdered in cold blood!

No! She couldn't allow Carl to escape again, to continue his bloody rampage across the land! She wouldn't allow him to take another lawman's life—*hers.*

"No!" Zoe cried aloud. She raised her rifle and took steady aim.

Again she felt herself freeze!

She . . . couldn't . . . pull the trigger!

She had never killed a man.

She couldn't now!

Not even this fiendish outlaw.

Suddenly there was a volley of gunfire all around her. Her lips parted in a loud gasp when she saw Carl's body lurch this way and that as the bullets slammed into him.

Zoe's eyes widened as she watched Carl fall from his horse, his body bouncing a few times along the ground until it finally stopped, dead still, his sordid misdeeds finally over.

For a moment longer Zoe stared at Carl's body. Then she lowered her rifle to her side and turned slowly to gaze up at White Shadow, whose rifle was still smoking. "I . . . couldn't . . . pull the trigger," she gasped out, her heart racing. "White Shadow, I just couldn't do it."

White Shadow took her rifle, then handed it and his own to Timothy. He drew Zoe comfortingly into his arms. "I never thought that you could," he murmured, slowly caressing her back. "You have never killed a man. It is not in your character to kill."

"But he deserved to die," Zoe said, swallowing hard. "He killed my father in cold blood. And so many more . . ."

"*Ho*, I know," White Shadow said, gently gripping her shoulders, easing her away from him. His eyes locked with hers. "But that does not mean

Cassie Edwards

that you should be the one to take his life."

"But I wanted to avenge my father," Zoe said, sighing deeply.

"It was best that you did not kill the outlaw," White Shadow said. "That act would haunt your dreams when you should be dreaming of your husband."

"My husband," Zoe murmured, tears burning at the corners of her eyes. "I am free to marry you now, White Shadow. We are free to begin the rest of our lives together."

"*Ho*, feel blessed for that," he said. "Forget this man who for too long has tortured your heart. It is over, Zoe. Done and over."

White Shadow lifted Zoe into his arms and carried her to her horse. "Let us leave this place of death and go home," he said, gently placing her in the saddle.

Zoe got a glimpse of Black Beak as he slunk away toward his own horse. Again she felt that something was wrong with him. He acted as though he was a man filled with guilt.

Her attention was drawn elsewhere when Lightning Flash came to White Shadow. "There are many horses in the outlaw's corral," he said. Black Beak froze in the act of mounting his horse.

"*Ho*, I saw them," White Shadow said, kneading his brow. "I wonder how he, one man, could have possession of so many steeds? I do not believe he has them legally."

"You think he stole them?" Lightning Flash asked.

"Or someone stole them and sold them to him," White Shadow said.

Black Beak's spine was stiff as he went to White Shadow. "I heard you discussing the horses," he said. "Are they not ours now that the outlaw is dead?"

"Your interest in the horses seems somehow more than it should be," White Shadow said. "Why is that, Black Beak?"

"You know my love of horses," Black Beak said, shuffling his feet nervously. "We cannot just leave them in the corral. They would not be cared for. They should be ours, White Shadow. Our people's."

"You are right, my cousin," White Shadow said, clasping a hand on Black Beak's shoulder. "Go. Help round them up. See that they are taken to our village. Place them in our corrals."

He paused, and then dropped his hand to his side. "Then, my cousin, you know that you and your friends must be punished for having kept information about my woman and my brother silent for too long," he said dryly. "Your punishment will be decided soon."

Black Beak lowered his eyes, then raised them and looked at Zoe when he felt her gazing at him. He felt as though she could see into his soul and knew the truth about him. Yet surely it was only his guilt causing him to imagine things. He had been wrong to wait so long to see that this lovely woman was set free.

That was more cause for guilt than the fact that

these very horses he was taking home had been stolen by him and his friends.

He stared at Zoe for a moment longer, feeling awful that she had come close to being raped and killed; then he ran to his horse and swung himself into his saddle and rode toward the corral.

Zoe had watched Black Beak with much interest. She had seen the guilt in his eyes and hoped that it was only over how he had kept her and Timothy's abduction a secret for so long. But it seemed as though something else was eating away at him.

White Shadow and Lightning Flash still stood together. "We now have someone else to deal out punishments to," White Shadow said, his voice tight. "Thunder Stick. He must pay for his role in the abduction of my brother and my woman. He must be banished."

"Your mother has such deep feelings for Thunder Stick," Lightning Flash said, his voice drawn.

"She will have no feelings except hate for the shaman once she hears of his deceit," White Shadow said, smiling at Timothy as he came and stood beside him. He reached a hand to his shoulder. "My brother, it is good to know that you did not leave our village because it was your wish to do so. The hurt caused our mother would be great were that so."

"I shall go and speak to her now," Timothy said, nodding. "I would never hurt her. It is so good to finally know my true mother."

"Even if she is full blood Kiowa?" White Shadow asked, arching an eyebrow.

"*I* am Kiowa," Timothy said, proudly squaring his bare shoulders.

"You say that with much pride, my brother," White Shadow said, his voice breaking. His own pride in his brother was deep. Not long ago he had seen all Indians as non-persons.

"I *am* proud," Timothy said, swallowing hard. "I shall ride ahead and meet my mother."

"It is best that you ride with us," White Shadow said, lowering his hand to his side.

"Because you still do not trust me?" Timothy said, taking a step away from White Shadow.

"No, because I do not trust white men who might see you dressed as an Indian and feel that you are someone who betrays his own race," White Shadow said, his voice drawn. "Now, after having just saved you, I do not wish to chance losing you again. Our mother deserves two sons arriving home, not just one."

Timothy smiled, and then went to Zoe. He reached for her hand. "I'm sorry about what you had to endure in that damnable cabin," he said, his voice filled with emotion. "How . . . how . . . he unclothed you and tied you outside, to the post."

He hung his head, and then gazed up at her again. "I never felt as helpless in my life as I felt when I saw that louse touching and kissing you," he said, his voice breaking. "Zoe, know that I would have protected you had I not been disabled by the ropes."

"I know, Timothy," Zoe said, squeezing his hand affectionately. "Please don't blame yourself. The shaman is at fault. Only the shaman."

"And he is going to pay," Timothy said, his jaw tight. "For everything, Zoe. He . . . will . . . pay dearly for what he did to both you and me."

"And I will be the one who sees that he does," White Shadow said as he stepped up to Timothy's side.

Timothy eased his hand from Zoe's.

"Timothy, what are you going to do now that you have been given your freedom, not only from the outlaw, but also the Kiowa?" Zoe asked softly. "Are you going to stay with the Kiowa, or return to your post at the fort?"

White Shadow gazed intently at Timothy as he awaited a response.

"I need time to think," Timothy said. "But first things first. I want to go to Mother and explain things to her. Then, White Shadow, is it true that I am free to make my own decision as to where I wish to be?"

"*Ho*, my mother said that you are free, did she not?" White Shadow said, his eyes narrowing. He truly expected now that Timothy would return to the white man's world. Or else why would he even be talking about it?

"I shall make my decision soon," Timothy said, nodding. "Please understand that I must do what my heart tells me to do."

"That is the way it should be for everyone," White Shadow said, nodding.

Timothy clasped his hand on White Shadow's shoulder. For a moment their eyes locked, and then he spun around and went to his horse and mounted it.

White Shadow turned to Zoe and their eyes held. A moment later he swung himself into his saddle.

They rode off toward the village, leaving the body of the outlaw for the hungry, roaming animals of the night.

Chapter Thirty-eight

O, how much more doth beauty beauteous seem
By that sweet ornament which truth doth give!
                              —William Shakespeare

The Washita River's current was slow, and the warm, brown water seemed to be standing still as Zoe and White Shadow swam side by side in it. It was a secret place in the dense, overhanging growth of the banks, and as day broke along the horizon, Zoe laughed softly when a dragonfly flew past her nose.

"It is good to see the morning awakening while I am with you in this way," White Shadow said, reaching over to gently grab Zoe by an arm and pull her into his embrace.

Her wet breasts pressed into his chest as she

twined her arms around his neck. Her nipples were hard from aroused passion.

"I couldn't have slept a wink had you taken me to your bed," Zoe murmured. She gazed warmly into the deep, jet black of his eyes. "And I needed a bath, so why not share one together in the river with you?"

"We shall share more than that in the river," White Shadow said, chuckling. "Our bath is over. Now we make love."

His lips crushed hers beneath them in a deep, long, meltingly hot kiss. His hands slid over her body, one cupping a breast, the other stroking her woman's center. He had waited so long for them to be together without interferences. There was no one now to come between them. They were free to love and to share their dreams of the future. Without Zoe, there would have been no future for White Shadow.

"I love you so," Zoe whispered against his lips, gasping with pleasure when she felt him shove his manhood inside her and start his rhythmic thrusts.

She wrapped her legs around his waist and rode him, the water soft and wonderful against her tired flesh.

The sun was an orange disc, rising slowly from behind the distant mountains. Eagles had awakened and were soaring overhead.

Zoe could hear the yapping of dogs back at the village and knew that the Kiowa people were stirring. She could even smell the first signs of smoke as the women lit their cooking fires for breakfast.

"Are you hungry?" White Shadow whispered into Zoe's ear.

"Only for you," Zoe whispered, throwing her head back and sighing when his lips went to one of her breasts, which lay just above the surface of the water, his tongue licking.

And then he swept his arms fully beneath her and carried her to the shore and laid her on a thick bed of grass.

Again they kissed with a fierce, possessive heat, their bodies tangling as his manhood once again found her hot, moist place and entered her with his throbbing hardness.

Husky groans rose into the air.

White Shadow plunged into Zoe, withdrew, and plunged again with insistent thrusts. He rolled her nipples with his tongue, and then his fingers, as he kissed her again, this time with a raging hunger.

Zoe moaned as she felt her pleasure mounting. Waves of liquid heat seemed to be pulsing through her. She thrust her aching breasts into his hands as he cupped them.

She twined her fingers through his hair and brought his lips more powerfully against hers, his lean, sinewy buttocks moved tirelessly, driving her deeper into the mystique of their magical moments together.

And then White Shadow kissed her with an easy sureness, his mouth cool and soothing, his hands taking in the roundness of her buttocks, stroking.

His tongue brushed her lips lightly, and then he

again swirled his tongue around first one nipple and then the other.

"I feel it rising . . . rising . . ." Zoe cried, her hair thrashing as she tossed her head from side to side. "Oh, White Shadow!"

White Shadow gazed down at her and smiled as he moved inside her with fast, quick, sure movements, his own excitement like hot, ecstatic waves rushing through him. He clung to her, sank himself more deeply into her in one last plunge, then gritted his teeth and closed his eyes as his own body reached the ultimate of pleasure.

Afterward, they lay beside one another on their backs on the sweet, soft grass.

"It's so peaceful here," Zoe murmured. "I would think that everyone would come here for their baths . . . or just to enjoy a leisurely moment with nature."

"Baths are taken closer to our village," White Shadow said. "And that is for a particular reason."

"What reason?" Zoe asked, gazing at White Shadow.

"Ghosts," he said, his eyes twinkling as he smiled mischievously at Zoe.

"Ghosts?" Zoe said, her eyes widening. "What ghosts?"

"Long ago, women gathered wood close by here," White Shadow said. "While they gathered wood, the children would swim. After the children got out of the river, their mothers would go down to the sandy shore and take sticks and cover their children's tracks. The oldest woman of the group would call back towards the river. She would call the names of all of the children who had been swimming there and would say, 'You had better all go home! *We* are going home!' "

"But the children were already gone from the river," Zoe said. "Who was the woman talking to?"

"The reason the woman would call back toward the river was to call the voices of the children to them. That way the ghosts of the river couldn't get hold of the children's voices and make them sick."

"And they covered their children's tracks because . . . ?"

"Because the mothers did not want the ghosts to come around at night and follow the children's tracks to their home and cause them to get sick."

"You truly believe in ghosts?" Zoe asked softly.

"When I was a very young boy, *ho*, I was afraid," White Shadow said, nodding. "When I was small my mother took two dry walnuts and bored holes through them. She took a strip of buckskin and put it through the nuts and tied it around my wrist. She believed they would protect me from ghosts at night and would prevent me from getting ghost sickness."

"How interesting," Zoe said.

White Shadow chuckled, and then looked heavenward along with Zoe when the eagles they had seen joined together, soaring overhead in what appeared to be a mating ritual.

"They are so lovely," Zoe murmured, her cheeks flushed from the aftermath of their lovemaking.

"They are a spiritual bird," White Shadow said, his gaze taking in how the morning sun lit the underside of the eagle's wings, making them seem translucent. "They deserve the freedom of the sky that the *Nuakolahe* has blessed them with. I just wish it could have been the same for the Kiowa, that the land we were blessed with could still be solely ours."

"Things change and not always for the best," Zoe said, turning and leaning on an elbow to gaze at White Shadow. "But nothing will ever change for the eagles. They have the sky as their own, forever."

"*Ho*, they are truly the blessed ones," White Shadow said, nodding.

"We are also blessed," Zoe murmured. "We now have each other as our own, forever."

"*Ho*, forever," White Shadow said, placing a hand on her cheek.

"White Shadow, I wish there was something I could do for your people," Zoe murmured.

"You have," White Shadow said, smiling at her. "You are becoming as one with us. You make a wonderful addition to our family of Kiowa."

"And I so look forward to my life with you and yours," Zoe murmured. She sat up and plucked a blade of grass and began running it between her fingers. "I wonder what Timothy is going to do."

White Shadow sat up beside her. He gazed into the rolling river. "He will do as his heart leads him," he said. He looked over at Zoe. "But it is enough for now that he went to Mother and showed her that he had left the village because he was forced to, not because that was how he wished it to be. It has made my mother's heart sing again to know that her first-born truly cares for her."

"I hope he decides to live with the Kiowa. I know that is what your mother wants," Zoe said, scooting over to sit closer to White Shadow. He slid an arm around her waist and pulled her against him.

"And how would you feel to have him there so close to you when you become my wife?" White Shadow said, lifting her chin until her eyes met his. "Will his presence make you uncomfortable?"

"Never," Zoe said, smiling. "Why should it? He has accepted that I never loved him. We are at peace with each other over the way things have turned out."

"Then I, too, wish that he will stay," White Shadow said, nodding.

"Are you saying that you weren't sure how you felt about Timothy staying or going?" Zoe asked, her eyes wide. "Even if his staying would make your mother so happy?"

"It is your happiness that I concern myself with," White Shadow said, brushing a soft kiss across her lips. "I love my mother, *ho*. But I love you more."

Touched by this confession, which she knew must be hard for a man who had devoted so much of his life to making things right for his mother, Zoe flung herself into his arms. "I shall never disappoint you," she murmured. "I promise to make you a good wife . . . and a good mother to our children."

"Children," White Shadow said huskily. "We shall have many."

The mention of children reminded Zoe of Black Beak and his friends, who were now in isolation in a cabin at the far side of the village. White Shadow had decided that the council would deal with their reckless, wrongful behavior.

"Are you truly going to leave Black Beak and his friends locked up away from the Fourth of July excitement at Gracemont?" Zoe blurted out, moving to sit before White Shadow and gazing into his eyes.

White Shadow's jaw tightened. He said nothing.

"That wouldn't be fair, White Shadow," Zoe murmured. "This is the first Fourth of July celebration we've ever had in Gracemont. Today and tonight there will be so many things for young people to see and enjoy. Please allow Black Beak and his friends to join the fun. Wasn't Black Beak responsible for your finding Timothy and me? If he hadn't told you, I doubt that Timothy and I would be alive this very minute."

Still White Shadow said nothing.

"Your shaman is truly the one who is at fault," Zoe said, moving again to his side. She reached for her clothes and began dressing. "It is a shame that he was gone when you went to Thunder Stick's lodge. Thunder Stick has proved that he is a coward by leaving in such a way. He has been nothing but a disappointment to your people. He has disappeared, and good riddance. Black Beak has proved that he is brave. Please see the difference and show forgiveness to Black Beak. He promised never to do anything again that would disappoint you."

"And I have heard that countless times before," White Shadow finally said.

"But this time I truly believe he has learned his lesson," Zoe pleaded, standing as she ran her fingers through her hair. She flinched only a little when she placed her full weight on her sore toe. Finally, she sighed to herself, her toe was almost well.

"I will think about it," White Shadow said reluctantly.

"Didn't Black Beak even confess to stealing horses and selling them to the outlaw?" Zoe said, watching White Shadow dress in his fringed buckskins. "I saw that his secret was eating away at him. When he suddenly blurted out that the horses that you have now in your corral were horses that he and his friends had stolen, it took a lot of courage. He didn't have to tell you. No one else would have ever known. Carl was dead. He was the only one who would have told."

"I do see the courage it took for him to make such a confession," White Shadow said, nodding as he slid his feet into his moccasins.

"Then please reconsider about keeping him locked away like a terrible criminal," Zoe murmured. "I truly believe he has learned his lesson."

She thought back to what Carl had said about her father. She hadn't decided whether or not to tell White Shadow, recalling the one time White Shadow had called her father a cheat. It would take courage to tell him that he was right, wouldn't it? He admired courage, and it would be like lifting a heavy burden from her shoulders if she talked it out with him.

"White Shadow, about my father . . ." she murmured, looking almost bashfully at him.

"What about your father?" he asked, raising an eyebrow.

She broke down and told him the worst about her father, relief surging through her as she did.

When she saw a look in White Shadow's eyes that told her he knew it all already, she was stunned that he had never told her the worst about her father, himself.

"Why didn't you tell me?" she blurted out. "You knew all along what my father was involved in, yet you didn't tell me."

"You carried enough hurt in your heart over his death. I did not wish to make it worse," White Shadow said. He placed his arms around her waist and drew her against him. "My woman, I love and protect you in all ways."

Tears came to Zoe's eyes.

White Shadow lifted her into his arms and walked away from the river. "Now I want you to go to my lodge and eat, then sleep," he said. "This afternoon and tonight, do you not wish to join the excitement at Gracemont?"

She snuggled against his chest. "*Ho*, I wish to join the fun," she murmured.

Her eyes slowly drifted closed in contentment. It was easy to sleep now, knowing that everything in her world was suddenly right. She could not see how anything could tip the scales against her again, not with White Shadow there as her protector.

She was enjoying being protected!

Chapter Thirty-nine

Take heed of hating me,
or too much triumph in the victory!
—John Donne

People had come from all over to see the fireworks in Gracemont. The streets were crowded with civilians and soldiers alike. The white settlers were even mingling with the Kiowa people without confrontation.

It was a day of fun . . . of wonder, as innovations like lemonade were introduced to the people. Then when the skies darkened, there would be another night of magical fireworks.

Zoe had seen many fireworks and street carnivals while living in Boston, but today's meant more to her. She was with the man she would soon marry.

331

As she walked beside White Shadow, taking in the excitement, it was as though she were walking on clouds. Never had she been so happy or so at peace with herself. She was entering a new phase in her life. She had never felt as needed, or as pretty.

She didn't even care when the white doeskin dress she wore brought stares from people passing by her. She smiled prettily at those who gazed in alarm at her companion . . . a powerful Kiowa chief.

She was proud to be with White Shadow. She had waited so long to be with him. At times she had wondered whether she would ever be able to show her love for him to the world.

"Let's have a lemonade," Zoe said, stopping to stare at the delicious pink liquid in a large glass container. "It's *pink* lemonade, White Shadow, my favorite."

"I am not familiar with lemonade," White Shadow said. He stared questioningly at the open-air stand where a canvas had been draped, tent-like, over the top to ward off the hot rays of the afternoon sun.

"It's made from lemons. Sugar is added to take away the tartness," Zoe said, tugging on his arm. "Come on. Please? For me? I'm sure you will find it quite tasty."

She gave him a pleading smile.

White Shadow gazed down at her, filled with so much love for her today, he felt as though he might burst. He had watched her out of the corner of his eye as she had mingled with the crowd today. It pleased him to see so much joy in her lovely face and eyes. It was good to see her no longer troubled by worries. He would make sure she would have no more cause for unhappiness. He would protect her and her feelings with his life.

"And so you wish for me to drink the white man's drink called lemonade?" he said, chuckling. He produced a small leather pouch and shook out a few coins into his palm. "Then I will drink it."

Zoe giggled as though she were the eight-year-old girl she had been when she first tasted lemonade. She read the sign on the front of the stand and saw that a cup of lemonade would cost a nickel. She reached over and plucked two nickels from White Shadow's hand, then put them down on the counter.

"Two lemonades, please," she told the bald, frail-looking vendor.

When he didn't respond right away, but instead took a handkerchief from his pocket and dabbed at the sweat on his brow while staring at White Shadow, Zoe tried not to become annoyed. She told herself that it was only the perspiration he was dealing with, not his feelings toward Indians.

She sighed with relief when he finally ladled out two tin cups of lemonade and handed one to Zoe, the other to White Shadow.

Zoe swung around and smiled at White Shadow. "I'm sure you will enjoy the lemonade," she murmured as she watched him take his first sip.

White Shadow's lips puckered at first but then the sweetness overwhelmed the sourness and he found himself enjoying the lemonade. He gulped the rest of it down in two deep swallows.

Seeing just how much White Shadow liked the lemonade, Zoe smiled up at him as she emptied her own cup.

She started to ask for refills but stopped when she saw a cluster of Kiowa children walk past, giggling, their eyes showing how much they were enjoying the party the town was throwing for everyone.

Zoe was happy for those children, but she could not help thinking again of Black Beak and his friends and how they were still locked up in a cabin at the village, missing the fun.

Zoe set her empty cup down on the counter.

White Shadow placed his beside hers. He was aware of the change in her mood. She was quiet and pensive now, whereas moments ago there had been such joy in her eyes.

He took her hand and walked her away from the vendor to a quiet place between two buildings. Holding her hands, he gazed down at her. "What is wrong?" he asked. "Why are you so quiet suddenly?"

"White Shadow, how can I have fun when . . . when . . . I know that Black Beak and his friends aren't able to?" Zoe murmured. She gave him a pleading look. "Please, *please*, reconsider and send someone for them. Didn't you say that there will be a council tomorrow to choose their punishment?"

"*Ho*, that is so," White Shadow said, nodding.

"Then why not allow them to come today and

enjoy themselves and *then* hand out their punishments tomorrow?" Zoe said. "This is the first time Gracemont has had such a party. And I'm sure it won't happen again for many years. It isn't fair that anyone should be kept from it."

White Shadow eased his hands from Zoe's. He stepped from between the buildings and gazed at the Kiowa children, who were enjoying themselves immensely. Some of them had even been joined by white children. It was a time when the two peoples could come together as though they were one, and he knew that it was wrong to forbid his cousin and his companions the wonder of witnessing this moment. Surely it would be many years before it would happen again.

He turned back to Zoe. "*Ho*, you are right," he said thickly. "I shall see that the braves are released. They will join the fun. Then tomorrow their future will be decided in council."

"Thank you," Zoe said, flinging herself into his arms. "I'm so glad you see the importance of the braves being here today. I truly believe the young men will repay your generosity with actions that will please you."

"Horse-stealing? Gambling?" White Shadow said, holding her hands as she stepped away from him. He gazed down at her. "It will be hard for these young braves to put so many vices behind them. They have practiced them so freely for so long."

"People grow up," Zoe said, slipping a hand free to reach up and gently touch his face. "I feel grown up. You've turned me into a woman, my darling."

White Shadow swept his arms around her and walked her backward until they were in the shadows of the buildings again; then he pulled her to him and took her lips in an all-consuming kiss.

When he released her, Zoe raised a hand to her burning cheek. "My, oh, my," she said, laughing softly. "I believe I just saw fireworks, and the sky isn't even dark."

White Shadow chuckled, and then took her hand. "Come," he said. "Let us find someone who will be willing to leave the celebration long enough to release the young braves."

Soon a warrior was riding from the town, on his way to the reservation to give the young braves the good news.

"I feel so much better now," Zoe said, sighing.

The smell of popped corn drew her attention. She looked over at a street vendor who was popping corn in a glassed-in container, giving everyone the opportunity to watch the corn as it popped into huge, white morsels.

"Now I'm hungry," she said, tugging once again on White Shadow's arm. "I want some popcorn. Would you share a sack with me?"

White Shadow smiled down at her. "Popcorn I know," he said. "Lemonade I did not know. *Ho*. I would enjoy popped corn today."

Again he removed some coins from his pouch.

She and White Shadow mingled with the crowd, the corn salty and buttery on their tongues. When Zoe saw several soldiers standing together and holding their horses' reins, she was not only reminded of the horse races that the men were preparing for, but also of Timothy.

He had not said yet what he planned to do with his future—return to Boston, or stay with the Kiowa. One thing was certain; his command had been stripped from him. Word had spread to the fort that Timothy was with the Kiowa, and that he was, in part, Kiowa, himself.

Only this morning Timothy had received the official orders that he was no longer in command at Fort Cobb. A new colonel would soon arrive to replace him.

Zoe had been with Timothy when he had received the message. He had been sitting with his mother and brother when a lieutenant had arrived at the village. The lieutenant had been invited into White Shadow's lodge. Everyone fell silent when the message was handed to Timothy and he read it aloud.

Zoe had seen the hurt in Timothy's eyes when he realized that he could be stripped of his command so easily, after both he and his father had been so dedicated to their country for so long. Ever since Timothy had been old enough to walk, he had been trained by his father to be a soldier! He had carried his title of colonel well, until the day of his abduction.

And then everything had changed for him.

"Everyone is being urged to step to the side of the street for the horse races," White Shadow said, jolting her back to the present.

She went with him to one side and stood amidst the crowd as several soldiers and Kiowa warriors brought their horses to the starting mark.

"You should have joined the race," Zoe said, gazing up at White Shadow. "Your steed is surely the fastest of them all and you are the most skilled at riding."

"There is someone else whose skills might out-shine mine," White Shadow said, his eyes dancing as he watched Timothy ride up on a black mustang. "I have watched him and admired his skills when I have seen him riding alone across a wide stretch of meadow. He knows how to surpass the speed of most riders."

"Who are you talking about?" Zoe asked, then followed his line of vision and gasped when she saw Timothy position the black mustang at the starting line.

It was not only his presence that surprised her, but his attire. He wore only a brief breechcloth. Even his feet were bare.

And with his long black hair blowing back over his shoulders in the afternoon's brisk breeze, oh, how he did look like the half-breed Kiowa that he was!

"What does he think he's doing?" Zoe said in a loud whisper, a hand at her throat.

"He is going to race and beat the whites who took his command away from him," White Shadow said, laughing throatily. "Zoe, he will win."

Understanding what Timothy was doing, Zoe smiled and snuggled closer to White Shadow. "I damn well hope he does win," she said. "He'll show 'em. What they did to him is a disgrace."

Her heart racing, Zoe examined those who were lined up on their horses with Timothy, some Kiowa, some soldiers, and some civilians. Zoe said a quiet prayer that Timothy would win. He had lost a lot these past weeks: his title of Colonel, and the woman he had always wanted to marry.

Yet, she reminded herself, he had gained much, too: a mother he had been kept from since birth, and a people whose dignity surpassed any of those he had mingled with throughout his life.

Yes, in truth, he had won more than he had lost.

But still, she wanted him to win one more thing today. For his pride as a Kiowa, she hoped he would win!

A man standing at the side of the road lifted a pistol in the air. Everyone grew quiet. And then the gun was fired and the horses were off.

Zoe held her breath when Timothy got a slow start, his steed lagging behind the others. And then her pulse raced and her eyes brightened when Timothy lay low over the horse and soon overtook the others.

He stayed in the lead until he reached the end.

Smiling triumphantly, Timothy turned and smiled smugly at the soldiers, whose horses were panting and pawing at the ground.

Timothy gave a mock salute to the soldiers, then rode off and stopped where his prize was waiting for him. He slid from his horse and gazed at the blue ribbon and the fancy saddle that were being held out for him.

His chin held high, ignoring the cold stare of the man who was forced to give him what he deserved, Timothy accepted the ribbon and the saddle, then turned and smiled down at the Kiowa children who came in clusters around him, some chatting, some hugging him.

But then he looked past them and smiled at White Shadow.

Zoe was touched deeply by the look she saw in Timothy's eyes. It was the look of someone who truly loved his brother.

She turned at the sound of approaching horses. She smiled as she watched Black Beak and his friends arrive. The excitement in their eyes revealed just how right she had been to encourage White Shadow to give them this day.

Again she walked the streets with White Shadow, enjoying the games and the friendliness of the crowd as most people forgot their prejudices.

The fireworks were the most wondrous she had ever seen. She sat on a blanket with White Shadow, looking heavenward. When his hand encircled hers, she felt as though she was glowing brighter than the colors bursting against the dark sky.

But still at the back of her mind was some unfinished business. She had to officially resign as sheriff of Gracemont!

Chapter Forty

No more be grieved at that which thou hast done.
                                        —William Shakespeare

The council house was crowded with Kiowa people. Today was much different from yesterday. There was none of the excitement that had been contagious among the Kiowa as they arrived in Gracemont to be a part of the Fourth of July celebration.

Today there was a strained silence as Black Beak, Eagle Claw, and Red Thunder stood before their elders to learn of the punishment for their misdeeds in recent weeks.

Zoe sat at the back of the room beside Timothy, while White Shadow sat among the elders, although he had decided not to be a part of the decision-making today.

Cassie Edwards

Zoe's eyes wavered as she gazed at Black Beak. She knew that he was frightened, yet he stood tall and straight-shouldered. There was courage in his eyes and in the way he held his chin high and confident. He knew, as did Zoe, that today might be his last day among his people.

Zoe just wished that White Shadow would be making the final decision about his cousin's fate. She felt as though she had reached him with her pleas for Black Beak, reminding him over and over again of how the youth was responsible for Zoe and Timothy being alive today. White Shadow had agreed with her that he deserved no punishment as severe as banishment from the tribe.

Yet he had still said that it was up to the elders to make such decisions about the young people of their village. White Shadow respected his elders. They were wise beyond his years. They had been making critical decisions for the Kiowa long before White Shadow was born.

White Shadow sat among his elders, his legs crossed before him, his hands clasped tightly on his knees. Every so often he would give Black Beak a glance, and then look straight ahead again, focusing on nothing in particular as his thoughts filled with memories. He could not help recalling the times he had sat amidst the council elders beside his beloved grandfather. If he closed his eyes even now, he could hear his grandfather's powerful voice. He, too, always gave the elders the rights of decision-making over the young of their village who occasionally walked the wrong road of life.

Ho, his grandfather, the powerful Chief Brave Charger, would not speak his opinion today, although if he were there he would surely be feeling the same as White Shadow about Black Beak. Black Beak had shown his courage more than once these past two days, but most of all when he had spoken up in behalf of Zoe and Timothy.

If Black Beak changed his direction in life, and walked the straight road of good, White Shadow would favor his cousin being chief once he, himself, could no longer perform the task . . . but only if White Shadow had no sons!

But it all depended on today . . . what the elders would say.

He glanced over at Eagle Claw and Red Thunder. White Shadow didn't have much hope for those two braves. Today, when they had entered the council house, they had shied away from Black Beak. Even now they did not stand beside Black Beak.

White Shadow knew why. It was because Black Beak had opened up his heart and soul and confessed to horse-stealing, which had brought blame to Eagle Claw and Red Thunder. They perhaps saw him as a traitor, whereas, in truth, his confession was another act of courage on Black Beak's part.

His attention was quickly drawn to Dreaming Wolf, the oldest of the elders, as he slowly pushed himself up from the mat-covered floor. With a blanket hanging loose from his lean shoulders,

Dreaming Wolf went and stood first in front of Black Beak, and then in front of the other two braves. He was soon joined by the others in council as they came and stood on both sides of him.

"Today, we elders have considered the deeds done by these three Kiowa braves. We have looked into their futures and seen strong, courageous warriors who may help defend our children from the ravages of the whites who crowd more and more onto the land that once was our people's. Weighing past wrong against future good, we elders could not find it in our hearts to send tomorrow's warriors into banishment," Dreaming Wolf said in his deep-throated voice.

Dreaming Wolf stepped away from the other elders and went to each young brave. He clasped a hand on each one's shoulder, his eyes locked with theirs in silent communication. Then he stepped back again and joined the others as they, in turn, did the same thing.

Once the elders were again standing together, Dreaming Wolf raised a hand in the air and gazed heavenward. "*Nuakolahe*, oh, great creator of all things, hear my plea for these young braves," he cried. "Send them from our council house today with dreams of a future of *good*, not bad. Develop them into great warriors who will make our people proud, not ashamed."

White Shadow smiled and found Zoe smiling at him when he gazed over at her. *Ho*, they both were glad for Black Beak, but White Shadow had something else ahead of him that would take much courage on his part. Today, after the council, Zoe was leaving for a while, to set things straight in her life. He knew that she would return, but it gave him an uneasy feeling for her to be away from him for even a short time.

White Shadow's gaze shifted to Timothy.

White Shadow couldn't help feeling somewhat uneasy over Timothy's decision to leave today, also to put things in order in his life. Although Timothy had said that he would return to be a part of his mother's and brother's lives, White Shadow was afraid that once his brother returned to that other world, he might decide not to return to his Kiowa life, after all.

After everyone had left the council house, to go on with the business of the day, White Shadow stood with Zoe and Timothy watching Black Beak being shunned again by the two young braves who had been his best friends.

"I am filled with much gratitude over the council's decision today," Black Beak said as he came to stand before White Shadow. "I feel that my life has been handed back to me. I will repay you all by being the sort of brave you wish me to be. I will soon be a warrior who will prove his worth to his people."

White Shadow clasped a hand on his cousin's shoulder. "And do not let Eagle Claw and Red Thunder interfere in your plans ever again," he said tightly. "Cousin, they have their lives. You have yours. Be glad that you will be living yours separate from theirs. Although they were pardoned today along with you, I do not trust that they intend to turn their lives around. But the elders had to give them a chance. *And* you. Prove to the elders that you were worthy of this second chance."

"*Ho*, I will," Black Beak said. He lowered his eyes, and then gently removed White Shadow's hand from his shoulder. "But for now I need time alone. I want to ride and think. I want to see into the future. The only way I can do that is on my horse, riding beneath the blue heavens."

"Then go, my cousin," White Shadow said, nodding. "Think pure thoughts. Commune with *Nuakolahe*."

Black Beak suddenly flung himself into White Shadow's arms. "Thank you, cousin, for everything," he murmured, and then stepped away.

For a moment Black Beak gazed into Zoe's eyes; then he hugged her. "I am so glad that you are all right," he said, his voice breaking. "Had anything bad happened—"

"Shh," Zoe said, interrupting. "Nothing did. And because of *you*, Black Beak. I will forever be grateful."

He eased from her arms and smiled at Timothy. "I am also glad that you are all right," he said, then turned and ran to his horse and swung himself into the saddle.

He took one last look at Eagle Claw and Red Thunder, who continued to stand together, glaring at him; then he thundered away on his steed out of the village.

"He is so troubled," Zoe said, watching Black Beak until he made a turn in the road, which took him out of viewing range.

She turned and stared at Eagle Claw and Red Thunder, whose heads were together as they laughed and talked. "And it's because of them," she said tightly. "I hope Black Beak realizes soon that their friendship has only harmed him and that he is better off without them."

"In time he will," White Shadow said, nodding. "It is just that he has been best friends with the young braves for so long, it does not seem right that they would turn on him so quickly."

Zoe saw Soft Bird come from her lodge and walk toward Timothy; in her eyes was a hurt look. Zoe understood. Timothy was leaving today. And even though he had promised to return soon, it was evident that Soft Bird did not believe him. It was in her eyes that she felt as though she was losing her son again. Only time would prove that she was wrong.

Timothy went to Soft Bird and embraced her. "Mother, I shall return soon," he said, his voice filled with emotion. "But I have things to do in my other world to make things right."

"You are returning to soldiering for a while, my son?" Soft Bird asked, easing from his arms to gaze up at him.

"No, I am not returning to soldiering," Timothy said, glancing down at his attire . . . a breechclout and moccasins. He then again looked at his mother. "I have another life elsewhere besides soldiering. In Boston. I must go there and set things right. *Then* I shall return and stay, Mother."

"I fear someone will stand in your way again," Soft Bird said, placing a gentle hand on his cheek.

"Son, do not let anyone stop you from returning to the life that you were born to live. You were meant for the Kiowa life. Not the white."

"*Ho*, I know that now and I won't let anything stop my return," Timothy said, again sweeping her into his arms and hugging her. "How could I allow anything to keep me from your sweetness?"

"Another woman maybe?" Soft Bird murmured.

"There has been only one special woman in my life and . . . and . . . she is taken, Mother," Timothy said, his voice breaking.

"Zoe?" Soft Bird asked, again easing from his arms, to gaze into his eyes.

"*Ho*, Zoe," Timothy said softly.

He gave his mother one last hug and then joined Zoe as two young braves brought their horses to them.

Zoe went to Soft Bird and hugged her, and then gave White Shadow a lengthy hug. "Darling, I will return before nightfall," she promised. "And thank you for allowing me this time alone. I need it. I will not only resign as sheriff; I also need to visit my father's grave." She swallowed hard. "I have some things to talk over with him, don't you think?"

"About the secrets he kept from you?"

"*Ho*, about the secrets he kept from me."

"Forget them, Zoe," White Shadow said, taking her hands. "They died with him."

"It doesn't always work that way, especially if you have a daughter who has to live with the truth," Zoe said, finding it hard to believe that her father had had a dark, sinister side.

White Shadow hugged her again, and then walked her to her horse. He held her at her waist and lifted her into the saddle, then turned to Timothy. He gave him a long look, then went and shook his hand. "Return home soon, brother," he said, swallowing hard when Timothy suddenly hugged him tightly.

"I shall," Timothy said. "Thank you, White Shadow, for wanting me. Thank you for being my brother."

"I shall always want you, as I will always be your brother," White Shadow said. He stepped away from Timothy and watched him mount his horse.

Farewells were once again said, and then Timothy and Zoe rode off together.

They rode in silence for a while; then Timothy sidled his horse closer to Zoe's.

"Zoe, have you done away with your father's clothes yet?" he asked.

"What?" she asked.

"Have you gone through your father's things yet?" Timothy asked softly. "Are his clothes still at your house?"

"Yes, they are, but why do you ask?" Zoe asked, lifting an eyebrow.

Timothy nodded toward his breechcloth. "I think I'd draw undue attention on the train to Boston if I wear what I have on, don't you?" he said seriously. "I know that I am a half-breed, but I don't think announcing it to the world in such a way is safe, do you? I might get my throat slit before I get one mile into my journey."

"Yes, you're right," Zoe said, gazing at his attire

and then at his long, black hair. "We'll go to my house. You can choose whatever you wish of my father's."

She paused, and then said, "But what of your clothes and personal possessions at the fort? Aren't you going to go and claim them?"

"I don't want to go anywhere near the fort," Timothy said.

"Why? Because they know you are in part Kiowa?" Zoe asked.

"No, it's nothing like that," Timothy said solemnly. "I'm proud of my Kiowa heritage. It's just that I don't trust my temper around men who'd strip a man of his rank just because he is part Indian."

"But, Timothy, those who did that only acted as you would have a few weeks ago," Zoe said. "You were the most prejudiced man I have ever known."

"Then you never knew my father," Timothy said flatly. "He was the one who taught me my prejudices."

"And he once loved your mother, who was a full-blood Kiowa," Zoe said softly.

"I doubt that," Timothy said. "He loved no one but himself. She was just someone to bed. That was all. There was no love involved or he wouldn't have sent her away and kept her child. To me that was the ultimate sin . . . to take a child from a mother's arms."

"You aren't going to hurt your mother, also, are you, Timothy?" Zoe asked guardedly.

"Why do you ask that?" Timothy asked.

Savage Heat

"You will return to the reservation, won't you?" Zoe asked. "You aren't fooling yourself into believing that you will, when deep down you know that once you get back to your affluent life in Boston, you won't want to leave again?"

When Timothy didn't respond, Zoe paled. "No, Timothy," she said, her voice drawn. "Please don't do that to Soft Bird. I believe it would cause her to lose faith in humanity."

Timothy's eyes wavered as he looked quickly away from Zoe.

Chapter Forty-one

One against one, or two, or three, or all—
—John Keats

Finally able to put behind him the hurt over his friends shunning him, Black Beak rode with a proud heart. He was going to put his restlessness behind him and become a warrior, one whom all would look up to, as they did White Shadow.

Often Black Beak had watched how his people followed White Shadow with their eyes, in awe of his very presence.

"*Ho*, I will be admired, too," Black Beak whispered to himself.

He flexed the muscle in his right arm and stared at it. He laughed when he saw how far he had to go to have the kind of muscles that attracted attention.

But he would. By the time he reached the age of twenty he would be all muscle and brawn, someone the Kiowa maidens would wish to have in their blankets . . . someone perhaps as lovely as Zoe?

He arched an eyebrow when he thought of the color of Zoe's skin. Could he, himself, be attracted to a girl with such skin coloring? Or would he, in the end, find someone of his own kind to marry?

"I will not wonder about such things until I have become a mighty warrior," he said, his breath catching when he saw something a short distance away that made his heart skip a beat.

A horse.

A horse all alone, grazing on tall, sweet grass, and tethered by a rope to a low cottonwood tree limb near a creek.

Black Beak yanked on his horse's reins and slowed his mount down to a slow lope as he studied the lone steed up ahead. It was a powerful rust-colored mustang with white spots on its rump.

The mustang was sleek and beautiful. Its mane was thick and shiny.

"Never have I seen anything as beautiful," Black Beak whispered, his heart racing as he came closer to the horse.

Again he looked at the rope that held the horse. He then looked slowly around him for the owner and saw no signs of anyone.

Curiosity getting the best of Black Beak, he stopped beside the grazing mustang and reached over and stroked his mane.

"Where is your owner?" Black Beak whispered,

again looking guardedly from side to side.

He then looked farther ahead, where a butte rose chimney-like from the ground. Around it were green, flowering shrubs, growing thick and clinging to the rock.

Cautiously he looked over his shoulder to see if anyone was approaching on the road. He was relieved when he saw that he was alone with the mighty steed.

His heart pumped hard within his chest. It seemed that someone had abandoned the horse, though he didn't understand how anyone could.

But the fact was . . . the horse was alone. No one was there to claim it except Black Beak.

He could not be accused of stealing a horse that had been abandoned by its owner. When he took it home with him, surely everyone would understand that he had not stolen it.

He was anxious to have the mustang. Black Beak felt strangely dizzy as he slid out of his saddle and reached for the rope that was around the horse's neck.

His heart pounded as he began untying the knot. The mustang's dark eyes watched him trustingly as he softly neighed and pitched his head from side to side.

"You will soon be free," Black Beak murmured. "And once you are home with me you will never be mistreated like this again. I shall feed you regularly. I shall brush you every day. And I shall take you on long rides. . . ."

His words died on his lips when he found himself suddenly surrounded by men he quickly recognized. They had apparently been hiding in the bushes near the butte.

It was clear to Black Beak that he had just stepped into a trap. The horse had been tied there purposely to lure him into danger!

Anyone who knew him would know that he could never ride past a horse that was alone, whether it was tied, or loose. His love for horses was rooted in the time when his ancestors stole horses as a way of counting coup, a common practice among his people when they lived free. That was one way his ancestors had won their war honors!

Black Beak dropped his hands to his sides and turned slowly to gaze at the men, recognizing them all. He had gambled with these men in Muddy and Gracemont. He had even cheated them.

"Sam, Roy, Clem," Black Beak said, his spine stiff.

He stared at their pistols, which were aimed directly at his bare belly, his breechcloth blowing around his thighs in the brisk breeze.

"What are you men doing out here?" Black Beak asked guardedly. "Why are you aiming your guns at me?"

"You have to ask?" Clem said, laughing throatily. He spat a thick wad of chewing tobacco over his shoulder, some of the tobacco clinging to his thick, black beard. "If so, you don't remember warnings very well."

"That's because he's a dumb savage," Roy said,

his yellow buckteeth protruding from between his thick lips. "Ain't you dumb, Injun?"

Black Beak refused to answer.

His jaw tightened and his eyes narrowed as Sam stepped closer. His clothes were soiled and smelled of dried perspiration and whiskey.

"Hold yer hands in the air so's I can take your knife away from you," Sam said, his greasy hair blowing around into his face. He looked over his shoulder at Clem. "If he makes a move for me, shoot 'im."

"He ain't goin' nowheres," Clem said, spitting another mouthful of tobacco over his shoulder. "Are you, Injun? We've got you. We can do anything we want with you and there ain't no one here to help you."

Clem screwed his face up into a frown. "Where's your friends, savage?" he asked, taking a plug of tobacco from his pocket and biting off a piece.

Still Black Beak refused to answer.

He grimaced when his knife was yanked from its sheath. He groaned and doubled over with pain when Sam punched him with a fist in his stomach.

"That's just the beginnin' of your beatin' today," Roy said, laughing boisterously. "You're goin' to be taught a lesson about cheatin' white-eyes. I doubt you'll ever want to gamble again."

Roy grabbed Black Beak by an arm and shoved him to the ground. He kicked him with his boot, then rolled Black Beak over so that he was lying flat on his back.

Black Beak glared up at Roy as the man placed his foot on Black Beak's stomach and began slowly grinding the heel of his boot into his flesh.

But Black Beak refused to let out another sound. Never would he allow these white men to know that they were causing him pain. He would prove that he was a much better man than that. He would prove just how strong a Kiowa brave was!

Clem knelt down beside Black Beak. "You certainly are a dumb Injun, all right," he said, leaning into Black Beak's face. "Don't you know about how the United States cavalry uses horses like we did today as bait to catch Indian horse thieves? We saw you ridin' alone today, Black Beak. We saw an opportunity to finally get back at you for all those times you cheated at the crap tables. We used the same trap as the soldiers use."

"Yeah, we knew that no Injun could go past a stray horse without stealing it, especially you, Black Beak," Sam said. He yanked on Black Beak's long, black hair. "You've bragged about stealin' horses enough times while gamblin' with us. But that ain't why we're here. We've been hell-bent for some time on makin' you pay for cheatin' us."

"Clem, stand the savage up. You hold him on one side, and Roy, you hold him on the other," Sam said. "I'm first at gettin' in the blows. Clem, you can be second."

Sam laughed as he gazed over at Roy. "If he's still standin', Roy, you can have the honors of knockin' him to the ground and spittin' on him," he said huskily.

Black Beak fought the pain of the blows that

began to pelt his face and all along his body. His groin was on fire when Roy kicked him unmercifully there.

He closed his eyes and held himself rigid as the blows continued. He could feel the blood gushing from his nose and mouth. His eyes were now swollen so much he couldn't open them if he tried.

Half conscious, the pain so severe he could hardly stand it any longer, Black Beak fell to the ground. His body jerked this way and that as the men took turns kicking him.

He was aware enough to know that more than one bone was broken. And then he fell into the dark, deep void of unconsciousness. . . .

When he awakened, he listened for sounds of the men. He waited for someone to hit him again. But he heard nothing, and felt only the pain of what had been done to him. Although he could not see through his swollen eyes, he knew that he was alone.

He fought to remember who had attacked him, but his head pounded so severely it was hard to think clearly about anything.

"Roy . . . Clem . . . Sam . . ." he gasped out between bruised, swollen lips. "I must remember. Roy . . . Clem . . . Sam. Zoe. She knows them. Zoe. She . . . can . . . find . . . and punish. . . ."

Again he fell into a mindless sleep.

When he awakened he still felt pain. It was so severe, it threatened to make him sink into the void of unconsciousness again.

But he knew that to save himself he must find a way to get back home. It was apparent that his horse had been taken by the men or it would be there, nickering and nudging at him. He and his mount were the best of friends. He had raised and cared for his steed since it had been only a foal.

"I am alone," he whispered. "I must find help."

Although every move he made pained him, Black Beak forced himself to start crawling along the ground. He wasn't aware of which direction he was going, for he couldn't see. He wondered if he would ever see again.

He became aware of the sound of water flowing over rocks. The creek. He was crawling alongside the creek he remembered seeing.

Suddenly, he was aware of just how thirsty he was. His throat was as dry and parched as a road on a summer day when rains are scarce.

He felt around himself for something to scoop up the water. A wave of gratitude washed through him when he found an empty turtle shell.

His hand trembling, his fingers swollen and bloody, he lifted the shell into his hand and slowly lowered it into the water. When he felt that it was filled with water, he slowly lifted it out again. He stretched out on his back and let the water drip from the shell into his mouth.

But he couldn't hold the shell for long. It was as though it was a dead weight between his painful fingers. He let it fall to the ground.

Taking a deep breath, Black Beak moaned as he turned over on his belly again.

Slowly, each movement filled with pain, he began crawling, praying to *Nuakolahe* to lead him toward home. Inch by inch he went along the ground.

When the pain was too much for him, he fought against it, but he fell once again into the deep void of unconsciousness. He wasn't aware of an approaching horse as he lay out in an open meadow for anyone who passed by to see.

Flies buzzed around his open wounds. Bees dove toward him, and then flew away. An eagle soared overhead, shadowing Black Beak's body, its eyes watching the rider stop beside Black Beak to stare down at him.

Chapter Forty-two

Ah! Who shall lift that wand of magic power,
And the lost clue regain?
                    —Henry Wadsworth Longfellow

Returning to consciousness and finding that he
could see a little more than before, Black Beak
looked up and thought he was seeing a vision. The
woman leaning over him was too beautiful to be
real.

"Who are you?" Black Beak asked, as he reached
a weak hand toward the copper face.

"My name is Scarlet," the woman said, softly
smoothing a hand over Black Beak's bruised and
bloody face. "I will not ask what happened here. I
do not want to know. Tell me where your home
is. I will take you there."

Although Black Beak's senses had been almost

knocked from him, he could never forget such a name as Scarlet or the woman to whom it belonged. He had heard many rumors about her among his Kiowa friends. This woman was ten winters older than Black Beak, and she was known for her lust for life and her sexual appetite. She was surely on her way home even now from a tryst with a lover.

Black Beak had been fascinated by this woman for many moons after having seen her once with one of the older unmarried Kiowa warriors from his village. He had come across them making love beside the river. He had watched, wanting the woman so much that his groin ached.

"I . . . am . . . Black Beak," he said, the strength of his voice almost drained from him. "I am Kiowa. White . . . Shadow . . . is my cousin . . . our people's chief."

Scarlet's eyes lit up. She smiled. "I know of your chief," she said softly. "He is a handsome man."

"He . . . is . . . soon to marry," Black Beak put in so that this woman would not get any ideas about seducing White Shadow.

"How terrible," Scarlet said, her lips curving into a pout.

When she left Black Beak's side, he panicked, for he was afraid that she had decided to go on her way and leave him there, helpless. "Do . . . not . . . leave me!" he said with the last of his strength.

Again he drifted into unconsciousness, only aware moments later of being transported on a travois, which Scarlet had hurriedly made for the rest of his journey back home.

He felt blessed that she had found him. Even if she did raise the eyebrows of his people when she entered the village, it would be only for a moment. Soon they would learn of Black Beak's attack and that Scarlet had probably saved his life by bringing him home.

He smiled as he once again relived that day when he had seen her nude, voluptuous body as she had been making love. It was easy to place himself in her arms in his thoughts.

"Scarlet . . ."

And even though she was of Comanche descent, he loved the way the name felt against his lips as he whispered it so low that she could not hear him.

Chapter Forty-three

Mad with demand and aching with despair,
It leaps within my heart and you are . . . where?
—Ivan Leonard Wright

White Shadow paced at the edge of his village as
he gazed at the setting sun. Black Beak had not
returned home and White Shadow had already
alerted his warriors that if Black Beak had not
come home by nightfall they would all go out and
search for him. He might be in trouble. He had
surely made many enemies while participating in
the white man's gambling games.

White Shadow would not allow himself to believe it was something more than that . . . that
Black Beak would go back on his word. If he was
somewhere gambling, that would be the last of
White Shadow's patience with his cousin. This

time Black Beak would be banished and forgotten as though he had never existed.

White Shadow stopped and cupped a hand over his eyes. He stared when he saw someone approaching in the distance. Against the setting sun he could only see that the person on the horse was a woman, and then he saw that she transported a travois behind her.

"Black Beak?" White Shadow whispered. "Could that be Black Beak on the travois?"

He broke into a run and met the rider's approach. As he drew closer he recognized the woman. It was the shameless hussy Scarlet of the Comanche tribe.

He recalled how long ago she had been sent from his village and was no longer welcome there. She was known, with her beauty, to lure married men to her blankets.

Never had White Shadow known such a woman as Scarlet and he most certainly did not want Black Beak to be near her. If Black Beak was being truthful about wanting to be the best man that he could be, Scarlet would quickly destroy his good intentions. She could cause him to think of nothing but her.

White Shadow stopped beside Scarlet as she reined her horse to a stop. He was momentarily taken by her intense loveliness, her slightly slanted eyes dancing as she gazed down at him from her horse.

Then White Shadow was shaken from his reverie when Black Beak called his name in so weak a voice that White Shadow could scarcely understand him.

White Shadow hurried to Black Beak's side. He knelt beside the travois, gasping at the sight of his cousin's bruised and battered body.

"Who did this to you?" White Shadow said, his voice drawn. "Black Beak, who . . . ?"

"I knew them," Black Beak stammered out. "So does Zoe. Go . . . to . . . her. Tell her to find Roy, Sam, and Clem. They are gamblers. She . . . will . . . know where to . . . find them. Make them pay, White Shadow. Make . . . them . . . pay."

White Shadow's heart lurched when Black Beak's eyes closed and he seemed to have stopped breathing.

"He is all right. He sleeps, then awakens, then sleeps again," Scarlet said from her saddle. "Let me take him to his home. His mother can care for him. If you will permit it, I will also stay with him and care for him. I know many things even shamans do not know."

White Shadow frowned up at her. "I know you well, Scarlet," he grumbled. "And I do not doubt that you know tricks shamans do not know, since you are familiar with so many ways to trick men. But you cannot stay with Black Beak once we get him to the village."

His frown deepened. "I do not want to embarrass you by saying more," he said tightly.

"Scarlet does not embarrass easily," Scarlet said, her perfectly shaped lips tugging into a knowing smile.

Again White Shadow fell under the spell of her

wickedly slanted eyes; then he shook his head and cleared his thoughts as Black Beak groaned and reached up to grab White Shadow's arm.

White Shadow reached for Black Beak's hand, eased it from his arm, and then nodded to Scarlet. "Take him to my village," he said tightly. "I will follow."

"I will do what you say only if you promise to allow me to sit with Black Beak and help his mother care for him," Scarlet said, lifting her chin stubbornly. "While you go and tell the white woman sheriff about the men who did this to Black Beak, I shall sit with him and make him comfortable. How can you refuse me? Was it not I who found him and took the time to bring him home instead of leaving him for the wolves to feed on tonight?"

"It is true that you found him and brought him home, but it is also true that you are a woman who preys on men," White Shadow said, rising from the ground. "You dare not cast your wicked spell on my cousin. He has the marks of a true warrior."

"He is but a boy," Scarlet said, tossing her long, black hair back from her shoulders. The motion was enough to reveal the abundance of her breasts to White Shadow as they pressed tightly against her lovely white doeskin dress.

White Shadow's jaw tightened as he looked quickly away from her. "Ride!" he said. "Take him home! We are wasting time discussing your morals!"

"Kiowa chief, I shall behave myself," Scarlet purred. "I am hungry for men, not boys."

White Shadow watched her ride away, and then stared at Black Beak.

A quick anger grabbed him at the thought of the three white men giving his cousin such a heartless beating. He could guess why. Surely it had to do with Black Beak's gambling. He had wronged the men somehow.

But that did not give them the right to beat him unmercifully. They had left him for dead!

After he saw that Black Beak was in his parents' lodge and was being taken care of by his mother and Scarlet, White Shadow gathered together many warriors and led them toward Gracemont.

He would go to the jail first. Zoe had said that she was going to leave the badge there. He cast his eyes heavenward. The sky was now dark. Zoe had promised to be in his lodge before night fell.

A feeling of dread swept through him to think that perhaps the same men who had harmed Black Beak might have done something to Zoe. They surely knew that Zoe would know them and arrest them should Black Beak have lived long enough to speak their names.

He sank his heels into the flanks of his horse and rode onward, and when the town of Gracemont came into view he drew a tight rein.

He studied the buildings of the town. Lamplight glowed from the windows. He could hear the faint sound of men laughing and pianos playing in the saloons and gambling halls.

Then his eyes went to the jail. Lamplight also poured through its windows. Surely Zoe was there, unless a new sheriff had already been appointed.

White Shadow did not want to ask Zoe to help him find the men in question. But he must. She knew them. She could go into the establishments and point them out to White Shadow.

But then what? he wondered to himself. If he and his warriors took it upon themselves to punish the men in the Kiowa way, the white pony soldiers would come down hard on the Kiowa. They might even take this opportunity to start a war with the Kiowa.

Always in the past, the white men had needed only the slightest excuse to come to the Kiowa village with their firearms and kill not only the warriors, but also innocent men and women.

White Shadow had to prevent this from happening at all costs. Even if it meant having to give up the white men so that the white man's law would punish them.

And even if it meant that he had to see Zoe act out her role as sheriff one last time.

Lightning Flash edged his horse close to White Shadow's. "Why do you stop?" he asked.

"I must go on into Gracemont alone," White Shadow said, giving Lightning Flash a guarded look.

"But you will be putting yourself in danger by doing that," Lightning Flash argued. "You are chief. You must not act alone to take care of such matters as this. Your warriors are here to protect you. Let us go into town and find the men. We will see that justice is done."

"I will go into Gracemont alone," White Shadow persisted, not taking the time to explain why he felt that he must. "Stay. If you hear me fire three shots into the air, *then*, and only then, do you come to assist me."

"White Shadow, you—" Lightning Flash began.

"Do not question White Shadow's judgment," White Shadow said, interrupting Lightning Flash.

White Shadow rode off alone. He knew that this was the only way. One man arriving in town would not arouse suspicions or alert the guilty men that their freedom was short-lived. White Shadow could mingle with the other riders on the street and not look as though he had come seeking vengeance.

He rode onward until he reached the jail. He stared at Zoe's horse, glad that she was still there.

Still not wanting to draw attention to himself, he rode to the back of the building and dismounted. He tied his horse to a hitching post, then moved stealthily along the side of the building, made a quick turn, and ran across the porch until he was finally at the door.

He slipped quickly inside, his eyes locking with Zoe's as she jumped up from behind the desk. His sudden entrance had startled her.

"White Shadow, I was just about to leave," Zoe said, hurrying to him. She twined her arms around his neck. "You just couldn't wait, could you? You are impatient to have me with you tonight, aren't you?"

"I am always impatient for you," White Shadow

said, having to resist the temptation of her body as she leaned it against his. "I—"

Before he could explain why he was there, Zoe slipped away from him and picked up a piece of paper from her desk. "I'm sorry I didn't come to you before night fell, as I promised," she murmured. She held out the note toward White Shadow. "But . . . but . . . when I found this and read it, I . . . I . . . became caught up in painful memories."

"What is it?" White Shadow asked, taking the paper. He knew not how to read or write, but he saw that someone had written something on the page.

"It's a note left for me by my father," Zoe said, caught up in the emotion of how she had felt when she had first read it. "I found it in a desk drawer. It was in an envelope addressed to me. I . . . opened . . . it. I read it."

She swallowed hard and gazed at the badge on the desk. "Father was going to resign the very day he was shot," she murmured. "He was going to go away. He . . . could . . . live no longer with the disgrace of what he had done . . . of how he had protected criminals. The letter was an apology to me for all the wrong that he had done. He . . . said . . . he never wanted me to find out, but Carl Collins had said that he would tell me if my father ever duped him. Seems Father went back on his word to the outlaw. That was why my father was gunned down, not only because he was a lawman, but because he had—"

"You need say no more," White Shadow said,

laying the note on the desk. He drew Zoe into his arms. "Your father paid with his life for his misdeeds. And he tried to make it up to you by writing this letter. Let it go now, Zoe. Let it rest. There is something else tonight that must be tended to."

"What?" Zoe asked, stepping away from him. She wiped tears from her eyes with the back of her hand. "What needs to be done tonight?"

White Shadow gazed at the badge on the desk, and then looked into Zoe's eyes. "I never thought I would ask you to wear that thing, but, Zoe, tonight I must," he said thickly.

"You want me to put the badge back on?" Zoe asked, her eyes wide. "Why, White Shadow? You know that I didn't plan to."

"I need your help," White Shadow said, picking up the badge. He turned it over in his hand and saw that the clasp was still in place, even though the badge itself had been mashed flat.

His eyes locked with Zoe's as he held the badge up to her shirt. "One more time, Zoe," he said softly. "Please wear it one more time."

"I still don't understand," Zoe said, taking the badge and reluctantly pinning it on her shirt.

He explained about Black Beak's beating and told her who Black Beak had accused of the evil deed.

He explained why he felt that she must handle it instead of himself and his warriors.

"Those men did that to Black Beak?" Zoe said, paling at the thought of how badly Black Beak was injured. Thank heavens, his injuries were not so bad that he would die from them.

"And the guilty parties must pay, but by the white man's law, not the Kiowa," White Shadow said, placing a gentle hand on her cheek. "Will you arrest them and place them behind bars? Will you see that they are punished for the crimes they committed tonight against my cousin?"

"*Ho*, I will make sure that no other lawman steps in and makes the punishment less than what they truly deserve," Zoe said thickly.

She went to the case of firearms and opened it. She took out her father's favorite rifle, loaded it, then went and stood before White Shadow.

"We'll check Gracemont's gambling establishments first, and if the men aren't there, we will go on to Muddy," she said. She looked past him, and through the open door. "Your warriors. Are they near?"

"They are waiting at the edge of town in case I need them," White Shadow said. "I hope I do not have to bring them into this."

"Then we won't," Zoe said, her jaw tight. "Come on, White Shadow. Let's get this over with."

Together they left the jail.

Silence in the saloons and gambling houses followed them as they checked first one and then another. In each establishment everyone stared at her and White Shadow.

"One more saloon, and if they aren't there, we'll have to go on to Muddy," Zoe said, walking along the wooden sidewalk.

"Injun lover, that won't be necessary."

Zoe stiffened when she heard Sam speak up from the alley.

Recognizing a deadly ambush, Zoe lifted her rifle, swung around on a heel, and fired as Sam jumped out into the open, his firearm leveled at her. She watched him clutch at his stomach and then fall to the ground, dead.

Clem was the next gambler to jump out from the shadows, growling like an animal, his firearm ready. White Shadow swung his rifle up and shot him.

Roy threw out his rifle, and then moved slowly out into the open, his arms raised in the air.

"I would've taken you for the dumbest of the three of you," Zoe said, bending to pick up Roy's rifle. She chuckled. "Guess I was wrong."

"Don't kill me," Roy begged, his eyes wide as he looked from White Shadow to Zoe. "I didn't do anything to Black Beak. Honest. It was them two. They did it all. I told 'em they shouldn't have done it. They wouldn't listen."

"And you think I'm going to believe such hogwash as that?" Zoe said. She took a step toward Roy and gave him a hard nudge in his chest with the barrel of her rifle. "Walk, Roy. I have a jail cell waiting just for you."

"I thought you weren't sheriff any longer," Roy said, stumbling along ahead of her with his hands over his head.

Zoe smiled over at White Shadow. "I won't be as soon as I send a wire to the authorities in Washington that they need a sheriff here, pronto . . . that they have a filthy bushwhacker waiting here in Gracemont to be dealt with."

Everyone had come out from the gambling establishments. They stared at the two dead men, and then at Zoe, who walked proudly beside White Shadow, prodding Roy toward the jail.

"Someone go and get the mortician," Zoe shouted. "Seems a couple of ornery polecats bit the dust tonight."

Everyone crowded over the two dead men.

"Got what they deserved," Zoe heard more than one man say. "The other one should be hanged. He's rotten to the core, that one."

She and White Shadow went on to the jail with Roy. Zoe locked him in a cell. Then, for the final time, she removed the badge and placed it on the desk.

"After I send the wire to Washington, I will finally be free to go with you," Zoe murmured. "But if I am asked to testify later against Roy, I'm sure you won't object, will you?"

"Not if it gets him the punishment he deserves," White Shadow said. He took her elbow and ushered her outside.

When they reached the dark shadows of the porch, White Shadow swept his arms around Zoe's waist and drew her into his arms. "My *manyi*, my woman," he said, and gave her a long, deep kiss.

Zoe twined her arms around his neck and returned his kiss, oh, so happy at finally being free of her past.

There was only one thing troubling this moment of bliss. Timothy. She had watched him board a stagecoach that would take him to a train station in a nearby larger town.

That train would return him to Boston and the life he had known since he was a child. Would that life-style be like cotton candy for him? Would he savor it and never want to give it up?

Or did he truly love his mother and brother . . . his people?

She hoped that he wouldn't wait too long to make his decision. There was a special person whose heart could easily be broken. Soft Bird. It seemed Soft Bird's life still was one of waiting. . . .

Chapter Forty-four

Come live with me, and be my love,
And we will some new pleasures prove.
                                    —John Donne

Zoe could not believe that she had been a part of
the Kiowa's lives now for several months . . . that
she was, indeed, married to their powerful, handsome chief.

White Shadow had built Zoe a two-room cabin
so that she would be warm in the winter and comfortable during the long months of summer when
the heat became unbearable. Zoe even had her
own cow for fresh milk.

Best of all, she was heavy with child, as was
Scarlet. Although Black Beak had been only seventeen and Scarlet was so much older, they had
fallen in love.

At first everyone had been skeptical . . . had even tried to talk Black Beak out of making the mistake of marrying a woman whose reputation was soiled.

But nothing would dissuade him. As soon as he was well, he went against all warnings and married Scarlet, who seemed to adore him.

Zoe's thoughts went to Thunder Stick and how his body had been found shortly after Zoe's marriage to White Shadow. An overdose of peyote seemed to be the cause, for there were no other signs of foul play on his body.

White Shadow gazed at Zoe as she slowly ran her hands over the ball of her stomach; her buckskin dress was stretched tight over it. "Your thoughts are many this morning," he said, putting another piece of wood into the fireplace.

The winds whistled and howled around the corners of the cabin as winter drew close with its fierce snows and freezing temperatures.

"My woman, are you thinking about our baby, whether it will be a boy or girl?" White Shadow asked.

Zoe smiled at him, then reached out and took one of his hands. She placed it on her stomach. "No, I wasn't thinking of the child," she murmured. "But I do feel it moving inside me this morning. Do you also feel it, my husband?"

White Shadow placed his palm flat on her stomach. Suddenly he felt the twitch against his hand, and then a rolling sort of motion. "I do feel it," he said, his eyes gleaming proudly. "Is it not a miracle?"

"*Our* miracle," Zoe said, turning toward him and twining her arms around his neck. "I can hardly wait, White Shadow, to hold our child. Never in my life have I been as happy as now. And think of how much happier the child will make us."

She saw a sudden sadness flood his face, erasing the smile. She knew the look well, and what caused it.

"My darling, there is nothing more we can do about Timothy," she said, her voice drawn. "I've wired him time and again from Gracemont. He just doesn't respond."

"It has made an ache inside my mother's heart that I fear will send her to her grave," White Shadow murmured. "If Boston was not so far for me to travel, I would go and confront my brother with what he has done to our mother. He is a selfish man, after all."

"Perhaps we are all wrong about Timothy," Zoe said softly, smiling a thank you to White Shadow as he placed a warm blanket around her shoulders. "Perhaps something has happened to him which makes it impossible for him to contact us. It *is* a long journey to Boston. Anything could have happened to him on his way there."

"I am so proud of Black Beak," White Shadow said, purposely changing the subject from Timothy. "I am so proud of Scarlet. I thought it was a mistake for them to marry. But they have settled into a life that makes them both happy."

"I never thought Scarlet would be the sort who would cook and clean for *any* man," Zoe said softly. "And now she is going to be a mother?" She laughed softly. "I am truly, truly amazed at the change in her."

"I try to trust her, but sometimes I find myself watching her while she is walking among our people, to see if her eyes wander to the men," White Shadow said, drawing a blanket around his own shoulders. "I suppose I cannot put from my mind how she once described her feelings . . . that she is hungry for men, not boys. In a sense, Black Beak is still just a boy."

"A boy who has won the heart of a woman and who is soon to father that woman's child," Zoe quickly added.

She scooted over on the blanket spread out on the floor before the fireplace and leaned against White Shadow. She sighed with pleasure when he put an arm around her and held her close.

"*Ho*, sometimes women make men of boys," White Shadow said, chuckling.

"And I would say that Black Beak is quite a man now," Zoe said. "No boy could keep Scarlet happy. She's known for her voracious sexual appetite. Seems Black Beak is feeding that hunger just fine."

Loud shouts outside the lodge and a noise that sounded like distant thunder drew them quickly to their feet.

"Whatever can it be?" Zoe said, her eyes wide as she stepped outside with White Shadow.

She hugged the blanket around her shoulders as she went with White Shadow to stand with a crowd of his people at the far edge of the village.

She gasped at the sight of what was approaching them.

Buffalo! Many buffalo! Several horsemen were riding along with the buffalo, keeping them from separating.

"Who is that? Where on earth did the buffalo come from?" Zoe asked. It had been years since anyone had seen them in this vicinity.

White Shadow studied the lead rider. Then his heart leapt inside his chest. "It is my brother Timothy," he said, startled by the sight of his brother riding with the buffalo in full buckskin attire, his flowing raven-black hair now grown long past his shoulders.

"Timothy?" Zoe said, straining to look more closely at the lead horseman. "Is it truly Timothy?"

"Timothy?"

Zoe turned when she heard Soft Bird's voice. Her eyes were filled with hope, her cheeks flushed with excitement.

Zoe watched Soft Bird walk on past her. Then although she was lean and stooped with age, she began running toward the approaching men and buffalo.

"Mother, stop!" White Shadow cried, going after her. "The buffalo! You might be trampled by the buffalo!"

"Buffalo," Zoe whispered to herself, still stunned. "Where on earth did Timothy find so many?"

But it didn't matter where he had found them. The fact was that he had returned to his true roots, to his true people. He had returned to his mother and not empty-handed. Somehow he had managed to bring a gift of buffalo not only to his mother, but to all of his people!

Now knowing that Timothy truly cared, and that he hadn't forgotten his promise to return home, Zoe felt her eyes mist with tears of gladness. Everything was going to be right in the world now that Timothy had come home. And . . . and . . . who was that riding at his side on a palomino?

It wasn't a man.

It was a lovely bronze-skinned woman dressed in a buckskin dress.

Surely she was Timothy's woman!

Zoe giggled. "Well, well," she whispered to herself. "It seems that Timothy has managed to put *all* of his past prejudices behind him."

Zoe guessed that he had met the woman on the trail from Boston to Oklahoma. Surely he had taken her as his wife, for the closer they came to Zoe, the more evident it was that the woman was quite pregnant.

Unable to hold herself back any longer, Zoe left the crowd of Kiowa people.

She ran to White Shadow and watched as Timothy dismounted and swept his mother into his arms.

She watched as White Shadow went to the pregnant woman and helped her from her horse. The buffalo were stopped by the men while the family became reacquainted.

"Why did it take you so long to return home?" Soft Bird cried, her hands moving over her son's face as though reassuring herself that it was truly he. "Zoe wired you. You did not respond. We thought you did not care for us and were going to remain in Boston."

"As soon as I arrived at Boston I liquidated my assets and immediately made plans to return to you but I was sidetracked," Timothy said softly.

"Sidetracked?" Soft Bird asked, her eyes wide. "How were you sidetracked?"

Timothy gently clasped his fingers on his mother's frail shoulders. He gazed warmly into her eyes. "Mother, I know how important the buffalo is to the Kiowa," he said thickly. "I know how the Kiowa have missed having buffalo. When I heard about a man who had seen the vanishing of the buffalo and had caught as many as he could and begun raising them, I went to him. With the money I received from the sale of my mansion in Boston I bought up a whole herd of buffalo. It has taken this long to bring them to Oklahoma."

"You did this for your people?" Soft Bird said, tears streaming from her eyes. "For your mother?"

"When I was a Kiowa captive I listened to everyone speaking so sadly of the loss of the buffalo," Timothy murmured. "I wanted to change that."

He looked over his shoulder at the buffalo, and then smiled down at his mother again. "And I made sure I brought many male and female," he said. "In the spring our herd of buffalo will have grown."

Timothy looked over at his wife. He held a hand out for her. "Smiling Heart, come to me," he said, motioning for her.

"Smiling Heart?" Soft Bird asked, turning to

watch the lovely pregnant woman walk toward Timothy. "Who is this woman Smiling Heart?"

"She is my Comanche wife," Timothy murmured, gently sliding an arm around his wife as she came and stood beside him. "I met her on my way to Boston. We shared a stagecoach for many miles. It did not take long for us to know that fate had drawn us together. We were married even before I arrived in Boston."

He slid a hand down her abdomen. "And the spring will not only bring us many new buffalo, but also a child born of mine and Smiling Heart's love," Timothy said proudly.

"Then there will be many new babies to smile upon in the spring," Soft Bird said, looking at Zoe.

Zoe took White Shadow's hand and went to stand beside Soft Bird. She had purposely given Timothy and his mother time to be alone together.

White Shadow gazed into his brother's dark eyes, then he reached his arms out and gave him a hug. "My brother, you have come home," he said thickly. "Welcome. Welcome home."

"It is good to be back," Timothy said, returning the hug. He took in Zoe's pregnancy, and then winked at Zoe over his brother's shoulder. "My brother, I see that you've been busy while I've been gone."

"Kiowa chiefs are always busy," White Shadow said, stepping away from Timothy.

Timothy reached a gentle hand out and touched Zoe's tummy. "I do not mean busy with the duties of a chief," he said, chuckling. "But with the duties of a husband."

"As were you," White Shadow said, smiling down at Timothy's wife.

"Seems we brothers think alike," Timothy said, chuckling.

Then he grew serious. He again swept an arm around his wife. "White Shadow . . . Zoe . . . this is my wife, Smiling Heart," he said softly. "Smiling Heart, this is my brother, White Shadow, and his wife, Zoe. My brother is chief."

"I know of your brother," Smiling Heart said, looking up at White Shadow. She then smiled at Zoe. "And I am also familiar with the white woman who was for a short time sheriff of Gracemont."

"You knew me then?" Zoe asked, lifting an eyebrow.

"My sister Scarlet spoke of you to me," Smiling Heart said. "She admired you so much . . . how you took on the job of a man."

"Scarlet is your sister?" Zoe asked, in almost the same breath as White Shadow.

"And so you know her?" Smiling Heart said.

"Do we know her?" Zoe said; she laughed softly. "Smiling Heart, we know her very well."

"She is married to my cousin Black Beak," White Shadow explained, amazed at the coincidence.

"Black Beak is married?" Timothy said, his eyes wide. "He is only seventeen."

"Now eighteen," White Shadow said. "He celebrated a birthday while you were gone."

"A boy eighteen married my sister who is . . ."

Smiling Heart began, then stopped before mentioning her sister's age.

"They are very happy together," Soft Bird said, taking Smiling Heart's hand. "Come. I shall show you their happiness."

Everyone laughed, and then followed them as they walked toward the village while the buffalo were herded toward the corrals.

"Buffalo!" Soft Bird said, her voice revealing her awe that the Kiowa had buffalo again. "My son, you bring miracles today to your people."

Timothy smiled at White Shadow, then at Zoe. "*Ho*, in life there is sometimes such a thing as miracles," he said.

"Timothy, we can double the herd of buffalo in a year," White Shadow said, edging closer to his brother so that they could talk.

"We can triple it in three," Timothy said, his eyes revealing his excitement at the prospect.

Zoe listened to her husband and his brother talking together, no longer finding it hard to believe this change in Timothy. His mother's plan had worked. Timothy's heart was a kind and generous one now, because the Kiowa in him had been awakened.

Suddenly she went to Timothy and stopped him to hug him. "Thank you for everything," she murmured. "Coming home . . . the buffalo . . . everything!"

White Shadow stood back and watched his woman in the arms of a man who once claimed her as his, and he was not jealous. Zoe carried

White Shadow's child in her womb, not his brother's.

His eyes shifted to Smiling Heart and he saw no sign of jealousy in *her* eyes, for it was she who carried Timothy's child.

"We will have a great celebration tonight in the council house," Soft Bird said, her eyes filled with joyous peace now that her son had returned home to her. She went to Timothy and took his hands. "Thank you, my son, for everything."

White Shadow slid an arm around Zoe's waist and drew her close to him. Their eyes locked as they exchanged warm, contented smiles.

"The long, hard winter won't be so bad," Zoe murmured. "We have much family to fill up the cold days and nights."

"*Ho*, family," White Shadow said, nodding. "I only wish I had known my brother sooner."

"But you know him now and I can see that you are proud," Zoe said, smiling up at him.

"*Ho*," White Shadow said, nodding. "Finally I can believe in my brother. I am proud."

Chapter Forty-five

Love and harmony combine,
And around our souls entwine.
　　　　　—William Blake

Zoe stood at her bedroom window. She was thinking about how quickly the years had passed since she had become White Shadow's wife. Ten sweet years, made even sweeter by having shared the happiness with their five children.

"All girls," she whispered, glad that White Shadow had shown no disappointment in not having a son. Each time Zoe had given birth, he had accepted the tiny daughter in his arms no less proudly than if it were a boy.

He had accepted that they would never have a son. Because of complications during the last birth, Zoe knew she didn't dare have any more children.

Sighing, waiting for White Shadow to come into the bedroom for their usual moments alone in mid-afternoon, while their children were outside playing with their friends, Zoe gazed contentedly out at the grazing herd of buffalo. It was late spring and many of the cows had newborn calves. She smiled when she saw a calf lying in the tall grass. It was red-orange in color, delicately beautiful with new life.

Zoe's attention was drawn quickly to Black Beak's ten-year-old son Red Wolf, and Zoe and White Shadow's ten-year-old daughter Moon Shadow, as they played near the buffalo herd. She gasped and watched in horror as Red Wolf teasingly tugged on the tail of one of the buffalo bulls.

"No, Red Wolf, don't do that," Zoe whispered, knowing that Red Wolf could not hear her warning through the closed window.

Zoe froze inside when the bull turned and glared at Red Wolf, its great, dark, shaggy head low and fearful-looking.

"Run!" Zoe cried as the bull started pawing at the ground.

Zoe breathed a sigh of relief when Red Wolf and Moon Shadow took off in a mad dash and clambered over the fence.

She tightened her jaw and placed her hands on her hips as she stared at Red Wolf and Moon Shadow, who were now rolling in the grass in a fit of laughter.

"And so you saw it also, how our daughter and Black Beak's son are up to their same old mischief?" White Shadow said as he came and stood beside Zoe to look out of the window. "Red Wolf is truly his father's son. He reminds me so often of when Black Beak was that age. Long before you knew Black Beak as a mischievous boy of seventeen, he was getting in all sorts of trouble with his antics."

He slid an arm around Zoe's waist. "But now he is a great warrior who will one day be chief," he said thickly. "Since we have no sons to be chief, Black Beak will be next in line after me."

"Late Fire still won't consider being chief?" Zoe asked, turning to face White Shadow. She gazed up at him as she recalled the day that White Shadow had offered Timothy the Indian name Late Fire and he had willingly, proudly taken it. That name had been chosen because Timothy had learned of his Indian heritage later in life, and the word Fire was a part of his name because of his zest for life as a Kiowa.

"Late Fire would be proud to be chief but he says he is no younger than I," White Shadow said. "He, himself, agrees that Black Beak will be a great chief."

"But Late Fire has sons who would be so happy to have the honor of being named chief," Zoe murmured.

"Late Fire still feels that Black Beak deserves it," White Shadow said, placing a gentle hand on Zoe's cheek. He gazed intently into her eyes. "You do not approve of Black Beak being chief after me?"

"I do. It is just that I would honor Late Fire, too," Zoe said, and then twined her arms around her husband's neck. "But what is this talk about someone else being chief? You will be chief for many more moons. You are still young and vital. Lord, White Shadow, you are only thirty-eight winters old."

"Thirty-eight winters *young*," White Shadow said, chuckling.

"*Ho*, thirty-eight winters young," Zoe said, sighing with joy as he lifted her into his arms and carried her to their bed.

"No more talk of age or who will be chief after White Shadow," he said huskily, standing beside the bed and pulling his fringed shirt over his head. "The children are playing now. We parents must have our own play time."

"*Ho*, our very own play time," Zoe said, yanking her dress over her head, and tossing it onto a chair.

When they were both undressed and on the bed, White Shadow blanketing Zoe with his lithe copper body, Zoe forgot everything but the moment.

Their bodies straining together hungrily, Zoe trembled with pleasure as White Shadow lowered his mouth to her lips and gave her a fierce kiss. She wriggled and her skin quivered with awareness when his fingers began a slow descent down the soft flesh of her body, arousing . . . caressing . . . titillating.

His hand moved lower, across the supple broadening of her hips, then lower still, to the brown hair at the juncture of her thighs. There his fingers sought and found her mound of pleasure.

Zoe sucked in a wild breath of ecstasy when he began stroking her. And when he kissed his way down to one of her breasts and flicked his tongue around the nipple, Zoe drew in her breath sharply and let out a cry of sweet agony.

Wanting him, Zoe swept her hands down the full length of his body and found him ready and hot.

Knowing the art of pleasuring him, she twined her fingers around his manhood and moved her hand slowly on him until she could tell by his breathlessness that he was almost at that point of no return.

Her fingers cool against his heat, she led him to her soft wet place and moaned as he slid into her heat and began his eager thrusts.

Her head rolled as the pleasure spread in warm bursts throughout her. She sighed when his lips brushed the smooth skin of her breasts. Then he covered her lips with his mouth and kissed her hard, long, and deep.

Soon their bodies jolted and quivered, their pleasure sought and found again in one another's arms.

Afterward, stretched out beside each other as they enjoyed a moment of quiet bliss away from the duties of the day, Zoe reached over and took White Shadow's hand.

"I could never love you more than now," she

murmured, turning to gaze into his deep, dark eyes.

"Each time we make love you say that," White Shadow said, chuckling. He turned toward her and drew her body against his, her breasts crushed against his chest. "But I never tire of hearing you say it."

Just as their lips met in a soft, sweet kiss, the sound of something hitting the pane of their window drew them quickly apart.

Zoe clutched a blanket around her nudity.

White Shadow jumped from the bed and yanked on his fringed breeches.

"What was that?" Zoe asked as White Shadow went and looked from the window.

"A turkey," White Shadow said, laughing. "A wild turkey being chased by Red Wolf and our daughter Moon Shadow."

Zoe sighed. "They are so much alike," she murmured. "If they weren't cousins, I would say they were meant for one another."

White Shadow went back to the bed and took Zoe's hands and drew her gently to her feet.

He then wrapped his arms around her. "But they *are* cousins and what they share is just a bond of mischief," he said, chuckling. "I believe our daughter gets some of her willful ways from her mother. I will never forget that first time I saw you. You were dressed in man's clothes and wore boots and a Stetson hat. I even recall you wearing holstered Colts."

"*Ho*, I was a bit wild in my younger days," Zoe said, laughing softly. Her smile faded. "I hope

Moon Shadow grows out of her tomboyish ways before *I* did."

"If not for White Shadow, you might even now be sheriff of Gracemont," he said, his eyes dancing.

"*Now* you can tease about it," Zoe said, smiling up at him. "But back then, it was a great bone of contention between us. When I left the badge on the desk I knew how relieved you were."

"*Ho*, because I knew then that you had chosen me over the badge," White Shadow said. He twined his fingers through her long hair and brought her lips to his. He brushed her lips with butterfly kisses. "Are you glad you made such a choice?"

"I had made it the moment I saw you," Zoe murmured. "I loved you even before you knew me. I would have done anything to have you."

"Yet that one day you told me you could not marry me," White Shadow said, leaning away from her so that their eyes could meet. "Do you remember telling me that?"

"Even when I said that to you I knew that I could not live without you," Zoe said softly. "I just had to sort things out in my life and make it right for us."

"Namely your father," White Shadow said, his voice harsh.

"*Ho*, namely my father," Zoe murmured. "And he died before I could tell him that I had chosen you . . . over . . . him."

"And now we have so much together," White Shadow said. He took her by the hand and led her from the bedroom to their front door.

Together they stood and looked at their children as they joined the others in various games and laughter.

"Our family," Zoe said, leaning into White Shadow's embrace. "We have such a beautiful family."

"No true regrets, Zoe?" White Shadow asked, drawing her eyes quickly up to his.

"None," Zoe said. Then she stepped back into the shadows with him.

She moved into his arms and lost herself, heart and soul, in his arms and lips. It was hard for her to remember a life without him, for he was such a wonderful, gentle husband.

Whenever she thought of how some people still called White Shadow "savage" because of the color of his skin, she was tempted to take out her Colts to defend her husband. But then she quickly reminded herself that her husband needed no one to speak or act in his behalf.

Especially not a wife who no longer lived on the wild side!

Dear Reader:

I hope you enjoyed reading *Savage Heat*. The next book in my *Savage* Series, which I am writing exclusively for Leisure Books, is *Savage Wonder*. *Savage Wonder* will be in the stores six months from the release date of *Savage Heat*.

Savage Wonder, written about the Oglala Sioux, is, I believe, my most emotional, heart-wrenching story to date about our Native Americans. I hope you will read it and enjoy it.

For those of you who are collecting my *Savage* Series books and want to read about my backlist and my future books, please send a legal-sized, self-addressed, stamped envelope for my latest newsletter and bookmark to:

CASSIE EDWARDS
6709 N. Country Club Road
Mattoon, IL 61938

Thanks for your support of my books. It is truly appreciated!

Always,

CASSIE EDWARDS

Savage Honor — Cassie Edwards

Shawndee Sibley longs for satin ribbons, fancy dresses, and a man who will take her away from her miserable life in Silver Creek. But the only men she ever encounters are the drunks who frequent her mother's tavern. And even then, Shawndee's mother makes her disguise herself as a boy for her own protection.

Shadow Hawk bitterly resents the Sibleys for corrupting his warriors with their whiskey. Capturing their "son" is a surefire way to force them to listen to him. But he quickly becomes the captive—of Shawndee's shy smile, iron will, and her shimmering golden hair.

___4889-2 $5.99 US/$6.99 CAN